DEADLY SOMMER

NORA SOMMER CARIBBEAN SUSPENSE - BOOK ONE

NICHOLAS HARVEY

HarveyBooks LLC

Printed in the United States of America

First Printing, 2021

ISBN: 979-8466029055 (Amazon only)
ISBN: 978-1-959627-13-5 (IngramSparks)

Cover design: Covered by Melinda

Cover photograph of model: Drew McArthur

Cover model: Lucinda Gray

Editor: Andrew Chapman at Prepare to Publish

Author photograph: Lift Your Eyes Photography

DEDICATION

If you look up 'moral compass' in the dictionary, there'll be a picture of Woody Smith. Well, there should be.
When I first arrived in America as a 21-year-old, with two suitcases and a dream of furthering my career as a race car driver, Woody and his lovely wife, Terry, took me in like a stray dog. From that day on, I've received far more from the man than I could ever return.
His relentless example of kindness and morality is the benchmark we should all strive to achieve.
Thank you, my friend.

FOREWORD

Why would an Englishman, living in the Florida Keys and basing his stories in the Cayman Islands, choose a 19-year-old Norwegian woman as his protagonist? I didn't. Nora chose me.

Her character first appeared in book four of my AJ Bailey series, *Ghost Mountain*, which deals with the difficult subject of human trafficking. The story features several girls from islands in the Caribbean, and to expand the international flavour, I added one from Europe. One of my best friends is from Finland; we share a similar sense of humour, and I always intended to introduce a Finnish character into my series. But the role in *Ghost Mountain* was a smaller part, so I decided to save my Finnish character, and went with Norwegian.

I built a backstory for young Nora with a normal and happy childhood that turned tragically sideways. She now had a dark secret in her past that propelled her into a life on the run, where she fell victim to the bad guys. Her determination and strength at the end of the story played a key role in the book, so much so that my bit-part character left with a perfect breadcrumb to pick up in a later book.

Nora became so much more than I'd envisaged. She returned in *Queen of the Island Skies*, where she and AJ formed a close bond, and then again in *Spanish Bay Reef*, where she had a major role. I loved writing Nora. Her dry and forthright manner, brilliant humour and willingness to run straight into a fight was captivating. We authors often talk of our characters writing themselves. It may sound pretentious, but it's absolutely true. I hear AJ, Reg and Nora in my head. Their actions are obvious to me, like a close friend or team-mate would be. I provide a situation, and they react. Often, the storyline I planned changes as I realise Nora or AJ wouldn't handle it that way.

When I decided to start a second series, I wanted to pull a character from AJ Bailey's world; someone my readers already knew. To maximise the biggest marketplace, my best move would be to pick a male character and place them in the US. I wrestled with the decision for some time until I finally succumbed to the irrepressible draw of Nora. I knew she was the one in my heart, but how could I build complete novels around someone who doesn't like to talk? Dialogue is the backbone of most stories.

The answer came from a joint project with three other fine authors and friends. All part of the Tropical Authors group, we decided to write a fun novella, taking a new protagonist on an adventure to the locations, and with the characters, we all wrote about. The best way was to write in the first person, giving the protagonist's perspective. When I finished my part of *Graceless*, lightbulbs went off in my head. I should write Nora in the first person.

She's intelligent, thoughtful, with a slightly dark view of the world, so writing from her perspective would open up endless possibilities. And it has. *Finding Sommer* is the novella I penned to explain how the rule-breaking Norwegian finds her way from AJ's stories into her new role in the Royal Cayman Islands Police Service. Another favourite character, Detective Whittaker, takes on the challenge of mentoring Nora. He sees her potential, as I did.

The series has an edgier vibe, and leans more into suspense than AJ's books, which are mystery adventures. I hope you enjoy reading Nora Sommer's tales as much as I love writing them.

MAPS

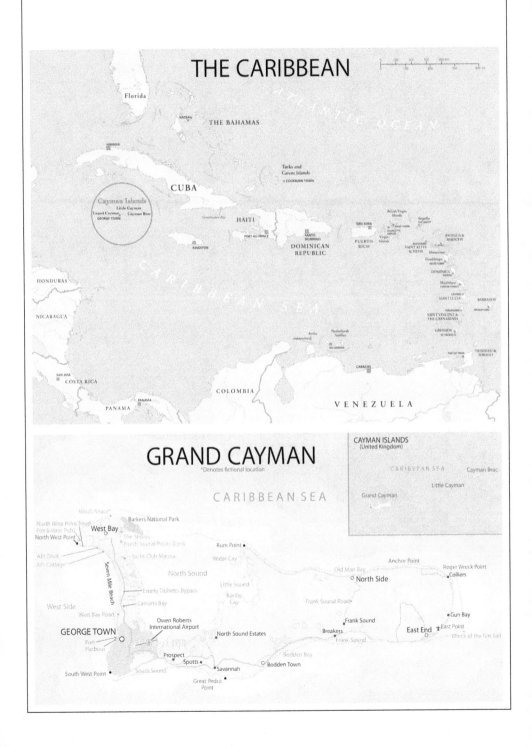

THE CARIBBEAN

Florida

THE BAHAMAS

NASSAU

ATLANTIC OCEAN

HAVANA

CUBA

Turks and
Caicos Islands
COCKBURN TOWN

Cayman Islands
Little Cayman
Grand Cayman   Cayman Brac
GEORGE TOWN

Guantanamo Bay

HAITI

PORT-AU-PRINCE

KINGSTON

SANTO
DOMINGO

DOMINICAN
REPUBLIC

SAN JUAN

British Virgin
Islands

PUERTO
RICO

Virgin
Islands

CHARLOTTE
AMALIE

ROAD TOWN

Anguilla
THE VALLEY

ANTIGUA &
BARBUDA

BASSETERRE
SAINT KITTS
& NEVIS

Montserrat

Guadeloupe
BASSE-TERRE

DOMINICA
ROSEAU

Martinique
FORT-DE-FRANCE

CASTRIES
SAINT LUCIA

BARBADOS

BRIDGETOWN

KINGSTOWN
SAINT VINCENT &
THE GRENADINES

GRENADA
ST. GEORGE'S

HONDURAS

NICARAGUA

CARIBBEAN SEA

Aruba

ORANJESTAD

Netherlands
Antilles

WILLEMSTAD

PORT OF SPAIN

TRINIDAD &
TOBAGO

SAN JOSÉ

COSTA RICA

CARACAS

PANAMA

PANAMA

COLOMBIA

VENEZUELA

GRAND CAYMAN

*Denotes fictional location

CARIBBEAN SEA

CAYMAN ISLANDS
(United Kingdom)

CARIBBEAN SEA   Cayman Brac

Little Cayman

Grand Cayman

Nina's Space*

Barkers National Park

North West Point Road
Fort & Horse Pub*
North West Point

West Bay

The Shores
North Sound Public Dock

Al's Dock*
Al's Cottage*

Yacht Club Marina

North Sound

Rum Point

Water Cay

Anchor Point

Roger Wreck Point
Colliers

Old Man Bay

North Side

Little Sound

Seven Mile Beach

Esterly Tibbetts Bypass

Booby
Cay

Camana Bay

Frank Sound Road

West Side

West Bay Road

GEORGE TOWN

Port
Harbour

Owen Roberts
International Airport

North Sound Estates

Frank Sound

Breakers

Frank Sound

Gun Bay

East End   East Point

Wreck of the Ten Sail

Prospect

South West Point

South Sound

Spotts

Savannah

Great Pedro
Point

Bodden Bay

Bodden Town

1

A TRUTH BEST UNKNOWN

Olivia watched the young woman leave with the disheartening feeling they'd never meet again. She had no way of knowing how true that would be.

Seeing any student drop out was heart-breaking. There was always a story. A reason. Something insurmountable in the young person's life. Or seemingly insurmountable.

They had talked for an hour, and while she understood and sympathised with the girl's plight, she hated the unravelling circumstances that had brought them to this point. A catch-22, a no-win situation. For either of them.

Returning to her desk, Olivia shifted her focus back to the task she could now attack with new information. Usually, she loved problem-solving. Delving into the details, analysing data, and finding solutions. But tonight's problem held no joy. No satisfaction.

It didn't take her long to see the discrepancies. A pang of fear raked through the professor's body like a chill wind. It was one thing suspecting a study had been compromised, but staring at cold, rock-hard proof sent a shockwave through her.

Olivia sat back in her chair and nervously chewed the temple tip of her eyeglasses. There was no way of unknowing the facts before her, leaving only two choices: ignore them, or do something about it. Ignoring them was unimaginable, unethical, and a myriad of other terms she couldn't live with. Acting meant challenging a senior, tenured professor, and the study he had personally over-seen. That could be career suicide. But this was bigger than her career.

Olivia checked her watch. It was 10:55pm. She had long since been the only one left in the science wing of the university. A school she had put her heart and soul into for the past twelve years. The University of St Petersburg was a small, private university nestled on the peninsula in western Florida that formed the city of St Pete. She loved living here. She loved working at the school. Now, having stumbled across these irregularities, all that would change. She sighed and wished 'irregularity' was the right word. But it wasn't. This was no innocent oversight. She had no idea how far up the food chain this went, but she suspected the top.

Plugging a USB memory stick into the computer, Olivia began copying files. She figured later, at home, she would highlight the areas of interest and contradictions, but for now the pertinent files would do. Rubbing her temple, waiting on another file to save, she realised how dog tired she felt. She closed her eyes and drew in a long, even breath. Tonight had been a long run night. She opened her eyes and looked at her gym bag on the floor, untouched. Her strict marathon training had taken a back seat to a bigger problem.

A sound resonated from behind her, and she quickly turned, startled. The air conditioning had kicked on again, and the ducting groaned as cool air once more surged through the vents. The time between cycles had been getting longer and longer since the sun went down, and Olivia chastised herself for being so jumpy. Outside her office, the hallway was dark; the lights having auto-matically turned off after five minutes without movement.

Turning back, Olivia right clicked the next file, selected copy, then dropped it onto her memory stick and watched the two-tone green bar work its way across the window on the screen. She looked towards the dim hallway again. Something was different. Getting up from her chair, she walked over to her doorway and checked both ways. The lights flicked on as the motion sensor picked up her movement. The hallway to her office fed a series of similar offices used by various professors and assistants. They all had windows facing the car park, as she did. On the opposite side were the doors into several laboratories. Olivia looked down the hall to her right. At the end, another hallway ran perpendicular, giving access to the exterior door, and in the opposite direction, more labs deeper in the building. That hallway light was on. Someone else must be in the building.

Gathering up her shoulder bag, Olivia hastily copied one more file before shutting down her desktop computer. She stuffed a handful of papers from her desk into the bag and grabbed her keys. She tried to convince herself it was probably a student who'd left something behind, but her heart still pounded in her chest. There'd been no sound of a door opening and closing, yet someone had tripped the motion sensor in the entry corridor. Maybe they came in quietly? The thought did not calm her nerves. Remembering her gym bag, she stepped back across the room and scooped it up by the strap. As she locked her office door and walked down the hall, Olivia's legs were shaking. Reaching the end of her hallway, she tentatively peeked around the corner, then whipped her head in the other direction. She realised the last time she'd taken a breath was in her office, and she gasped, mocking herself for being so ridiculously paranoid.

The night air was warm and dry, the mild winter a far cry from the Florida summer. Sounds from the city gave her comfort as she strode across the well-lit car park to her BMW. The thought occurred to her, as she opened the car door, that perhaps someone had been leaving the building, rather than entering. She looked all around. There were only two other cars, and neither were occupied. Probably students who were carpooling or sleeping over. Regardless, she decided, getting in the car and locking the doors, she was on her way home where a glass of wine and a good night's sleep awaited.

From the car park, Olivia took Roosevelt Boulevard a short distance to Interstate 275 and headed south. It was 16 miles to her house on Treasure Island, but the cross-city commute still took 30 minutes, even late in the evening. She drummed her fingers on the steering wheel, still consumed by the new knowledge she'd uncovered. She looked at the time; it was 11:26pm. Tapping the phone controls on the steering wheel, she hesitated before selecting the speed dial number. He'll be asleep, she thought, and cursed herself for not calling earlier to set his mind at ease. She hit the button and the sound of the phone ringing came from the BMW's speakers.

"Hey," came a man's sleepy voice after six rings.

"I'm sorry it's so late, hon," she apologised. "I'm on my way now."

"Okay," he replied, and she heard him yawn. "Find anything?"

"Pour me a glass of wine," she said. "I'll give you the brief when I get there."

"Yeah, okay," he mumbled.

"You won't believe it," she couldn't help adding.

"Really?" he said, with a mixture of surprise and disappointment in his voice.

"Really," she replied. "I'll be there in twenty. I'm halfway down 275. Love you."

"Okay, see you in a while," he muttered, and the line went dead.

Olivia smiled and pictured her husband asleep on the couch, oblivious to the last three innings of the baseball game on the television. Wine, husband, and sleep, she thought, feeling slightly guilty for missing the most important one from her earlier list of upcoming necessities.

Exiting 275, she drove down 5th Avenue until it narrowed, then turned south on 58th to Central, where she turned right. Central Avenue would become Treasure Island Causeway, a series of bridges island hopping across the bay towards Gulf Boulevard, the coastal road serving the island communities and beaches on the gulf. Olivia always felt like she was home the moment she left the mainland across the first short bridge to the South Causeway Isles. She crossed over Park Street, where the road narrowed down to one lane each way, and could see the streetlights illuminating the pale concrete pavement of the bridge ahead. What she didn't see was the box truck approaching from Sunset Drive, a narrow bay-front street on her right.

The impact was sudden, loud, and devastating. All the air was pressed from Olivia's lungs as the truck shovelled the BMW across the road into the central dividing wall. The considerable mass of the truck buckled and crushed the passenger door deep into the driver's compartment as the car was bashed across the lane. Olivia's body whipped to the right, then viciously snapped back when the car was pinned against the wall. Her head smashed the driver's side window, and the dislodged passenger seat shoved her midriff hard against the driver's side door.

The ear-splitting sound of crumpled metal, engine revs and glass shattering disappeared as quickly and suddenly as it had begun. Olivia wafted in and out of lucidity and fought to stay awake. Her face hurt and felt wet, but she didn't remember having a drink with her. Where did the water come from? Maybe it wasn't water. There was pain, but it seemed far away, almost disconnected. She knew something was terribly wrong with her right arm, but dare not look. Maybe it wouldn't be so bad if she didn't see the injury. Her legs felt numb and heavy, and something rested on her lap. She tried moving and a sharp pain shot through her ribs, causing her to wheeze. White balloons hung limply all around and somewhere in her hazy mind she realised they were deflated air-bags. The more she came around, the worse the pain ascended from every corner of her body. Her ears were ringing and her head throbbed.

She heard a distant car door with a surge of relief and hope. Help was already here. It was likely a passer-by, but at least an ambulance would be called, and even in her dazed state, she knew an ambulance was needed. She couldn't move her head, but from the corner of her eye she could see the buckled front of the truck embedded in the side of her lovely car. Hopefully the driver was okay, she thought, her concern quickly turning to anger. It was his stupid fault. Something annoyingly hissed from the twisted metal. Damn it, she thought, I just paid off the loan. And my insurance rates will go through the roof.

She heard someone scrambling along the wall on her left, and she looked over as best she could. They must have been using the roof for balance as she heard several thumps above. A shadow blocked the streetlight.

"Thank you," she attempted to say, but all that emanated was a raspy wheeze.

Whoever it was didn't say a word, but she sensed his presence and picked up a slight scent of his cologne. Olivia felt a prick in her left arm amongst the building pain from every limb, and her heart began to race. One moment she had been uncomfortable, yet calmly accessing the damage, and the next, her heart was beating out of control as though she were terrified. The person leaned across her and his shoulder knocked her face, causing a sharp pain in her broken nose. Her heart rate continued to escalate, seemingly out of control, and an overwhelming feeling of panic consumed her. Olivia felt the man pushing and moving things around her, and wondered how any of that was helping to get her out of the wreckage. The weight lifted from her lap and the man withdrew from the broken side window, dragging her shoulder bag with him. Her heart pounded, ready to explode as her head spun and nausea suddenly consumed her. She felt herself passing out and desperately fought to stay conscious, but she couldn't hang on. Then everything stopped, and her heart wasn't racing anymore.

2

ONE FOOT IN FRONT OF THE OTHER

The colours of the shallow reef dazzled like a spring flower garden in the early morning light. I swept my long fins in gentle strokes, heading deeper beside the coral finger amongst a school of blue tangs. A hawksbill turtle ignored my passing, engrossed in her breakfast feast of a yellow sponge. Small chunks splintered into the water under the crush of her powerful beak, much to the delight of two grey angelfish who eagerly swept in for the free meal.

Freediving for several minutes on a single breath requires calm and relaxation, which focused and centred my busy mind. A meditative exercise that flushed the demons and allowed me to function in a world where I no longer cared whether I was a part of it or not. Since the death of my boyfriend, Ridley, I'd been hanging on by a thread. Left unabated, my pain and anger mired me under a melancholic funk I couldn't find the strength to thwart. Each morning, when my work schedule and weather allowed, I would dive and escape the world I'd come to detest, by visiting a world oblivious to my grief.

Gliding towards the surface, I expelled the stale air from my lungs as I ascended. Above the water, I replenished my lungs with long inhales and full exhales. I floated on my back and stared up at the pale blue sky, peppered with scattered clouds. The morning sun warmed my face as I traced the outlines of the clouds, choosing the imaginary creatures they formed. A dragon above me, one of those odd little sausage dogs over to the east, and a one-winged bird to the west. The cloud to the north looked rather phallic, and I almost smiled.

My friends and a new job have held me precariously balanced on the edge of a cliff, without which I surely would have plummeted to the depths of who knows where. Four months ago, if anyone had told me I'd be putting on a police uniform one day, I would have laughed and told them they didn't know me at all. Of course, four months ago I was capable of laughing. But a uniform of the Royal Cayman Islands Police Service waited for me, and glancing at my watch I realised I needed to hurry home to make my shift on time.

With a long, smooth inhale, I dived under and began my underwater return to shore. I surfaced twice more to make the 200 metres back to the small inlet in the ironshore coastline, which used to be a boat dock for the Spanish Bay Reef Resort. Long since demolished and cleared, the land of the old resort remains undeveloped, and my tiny shack occupies a lot of land east of the inlet. A piece of land the developer who owns the surrounding resort property went to great, and devious, lengths attempting to obtain. The shack had been owned for many years by the former maintenance man at the resort, Archie Winters, who gifted the property to me. He'd decided it was time to hurriedly leave the island — a circumstance I pretend not to know anything about. Especially with my new employers. He may return someday, and if he does, I'll gladly relinquish his shack back to him. I miss my friend Archie.

Grabbing the flip-flops I'd left by the steps to the inlet, I made my way along the dusty dirt footpath atop the rough limestone shore. The shack is raised a metre off the ground and nestled into the woods that surround the property, secluded from any other homes. My nearest neighbour is a large house several hundred metres to the east, and legal access to the shack is from the sandy beach, west of the inlet, where a footpath leads from the beach to the road.

I stripped off my swimsuit and stood under the outdoor shower head, pulling the chain and bracing myself for the shock of the cool water following the balmy ocean temperature. After rinsing the salt water from my hair and body, I slipped on my flip-flops and dashed for the deck, making sure I couldn't see any boats. They'd need binoculars to see I was naked, but I preferred not to invite any voyeurs. Drying myself with the towel I'd left on the deck, I checked my watch again. I had twenty minutes until I needed to be at the station.

I call my home a shack, because Archie called it a shack. My friend AJ says it sounds much nicer to say cottage, which she calls the tiny guest house she lives in, but I'm with Archie. Shack reflects the simple way I choose to live. The dwelling may rest on a piece of land worth half a fortune, but to me it has a quiet isolation that mirrors my life. Inside, the open-plan layout has a living area, which is nothing more than a sofa and coffee table, a kitchen on the right, then a small dining table and the bedroom area beyond. The only separate room is the bathroom in the far-right corner.

I quickly dressed, tied my hair back in a ponytail, and grabbed my keys, cap, and belt with all the police junk attached. For someone who'd skirted rules and more than a few laws in the past three years, I found myself in a job consisting of nothing but rules and laws. Wearing a uniform, for example. In Norway, we didn't even wear uniforms in school like most other European countries did. The only thing I liked about the standard police clothing was the fact I never had to decide what to wear to work. But I did have to remember the laundry. I sniffed my shirt as I locked the front door. This one was probably due for the hamper, but it was the last one on the hanger, so it would have to do.

The legal access to the road might be down the beach, but the fastest way was the direct path through the woods. This meant crossing the developer's land – who would throw a fit if he knew. But he didn't know, and I'd trampled a narrow path leading to the fence along the east side of the lot, where I'd clipped the fence to duck through. From there it's a short walk to the road where I leave my Jeep. It's only my Jeep because Ridley is dead. It was his project vehicle, purchased from a man who'd left it in storage for years. The paint is sun-faded blue, and the 1986 CJ-7 has no top or doors. Ridley spent days working on the engine to get it running, fitted new tyres and brakes, and fiddled and tuned until it was reliable transport. The last thing he worked on was replacing the starter motor. That was the day he was murdered. Every time I turn the key and his beloved Jeep starts flawlessly, the engine warms up as my heart grows another step colder.

The drive to the station in West Bay takes four minutes. I rode my bicycle for the first few days until I realised I was arriving dripping in sweat from the tropical heat. Since then, I'd enjoyed the brief trip with the wind blowing all around me and the opportunity to think about the day ahead. They crammed a lot into three months of training, but the real lessons had begun once I'd hit the streets. Most of our day was more like community service and guidance counselling than police work. I'd previously been studying online for a psychology degree, which seemed to be more useful than the extendable baton or pepper spray I carried. I planned on finishing my degree in my spare time, but I was itching to use the pepper spray.

3

OPEN DOOR

One thing I'd discovered during my nineteen years on this planet: the average human is an idiot. Take the gentleman in the back seat of our police car wearing handcuffs, for example. Powered by tequila, and egged on by his equally inebriated friend, he'd decided to drive his hire car on the right-hand side of the road. 'Like we do back home.' Grand Cayman is a British Overseas Territory, so understandably adopts the UK system of driving on the left. In my native Norway, like most of the world, we drive on the right. I don't know the whys and wherefores of how these differences came about, but I'm smart enough not to challenge the validity of the choice at 40mph.

Thankfully, none of the idiots were hurt, as that creates far too much paperwork. I assumed the tourists in the other car were idiots too, who just happened to be driving on the correct side of the road on their way to do something else stupid. They'd need a new hire car to do that now, so perhaps the moron in our back seat, who I prayed wouldn't throw up, saved the tourists from themselves.

The Sunday daytime shift was usually quiet, at least until after lunch, but today had started with a bang. Literally. But that was good. I don't mean it was good that people drive cars into other people, but good that my day was busy. My unlikely job was the distraction I needed, and slow days, with too much time to think, were not my friend. I needed the distraction, which helped the days pass by, and days passing by was the goal. My psychology training, and my friends, assured me time would be the healer. I doubted time would heal anything, but if it built space between the moments I was consumed by the loss, it might help.

My partner, Jacob Tibbetts, slid into the driver's seat and started the car. He won't let me drive. Jacob's a good guy, but he's thirty-something, a career policeman, and I'm three weeks out of the training program. He won't let me do anything. Good guy or not, I may punch him if he doesn't let me arrest someone soon. Not that we do much arresting. Speeding tickets, drunk and disorderlies — who we usually direct to their hotels, or homes if they're locals — and the occasional noise complaint. The guy in the back seat is the first recipient of handcuffs since I've been on active patrol.

It's a five-minute drive from West Bay Road, the busy street behind the hotels and condos of Seven Mile Beach, back to the police station. Jacob hummed as he drove and I watched the tourists wandering along the pavement, enjoying their Sunday morning activities. The central station is in the capital, George Town, a whopping 12 kilometres to the south, but after training, I was assigned to the smaller satellite station. Jacob's previous partner had recently retired, so he was lucky enough to get me. I didn't mind the humming. It was better than the endless questions he was constantly asking about where I was from, how did I get here, blah, blah, blah. People talk far too much. I have limited him to a maximum of two questions per day, and he'd already used one this morning. I guessed he was saving the other for this afternoon.

We arrived at the station, vomit free, and I had the honour of opening all the doors while Jacob steered the idiot into the small building. Next came the paperwork, which Jacob was happy to let me do. There was one other person in the reception area, a tourist claiming his wallet had been stolen from his car. The middle-aged man looked me up and down and forgot whatever he'd been saying to Clara, the constable behind the desk. I get that a lot. I'm tall and slender, with long blonde hair. My Scandinavian features stand out amongst my local dark-skinned co-workers, who are still getting used to me themselves. The man kept staring.

"Don't look at me," I informed him. "Clara's the one who's helping you."

The man turned red with embarrassment, anger, or both. I didn't care either way, I just wanted him to hurry up. We had several neighbourhoods to patrol before lunch and my stomach was already growling. Jacob sat our idiot down on one of the waiting area chairs, where he swayed and groaned and complained about things in general. I stood well clear in case his Sunday brunch made a return. Clara finished up with Staring Man, who gave me a frown as he left.

"Dat one looks a little under da weather," Clara said, leaning over the desk, checking out our man in handcuffs. "He da one crash da car on West Bay Road?"

"Yup. Blew point 2-6 on the breathalyser."

"Oh my," Clara replied, waving a hand in the air. "I can smell da man's breath from here."

The sergeant came out of his office, laughing and joking with another police officer. It was Williams, one of the senior members of the Firearms Response Unit. Another name for the good ol' boys with guns club. No female officers were in the unit, and if Williams had his way, none would ever be. They both noticed me as they walked across the reception area. Williams looked me over and nodded with a sneer. I gave him my best disinterested stare, which I must say is usually pretty effective. He scoffed and returned to his banter with the sergeant. Screw him.

Twenty minutes later, with paperwork completed and drunk guy in a holding cell, Jacob and I were back on the beat. The township of West Bay is actually the northern part of the island's western land mass. To the south is the famed Seven Mile Beach, where the majority of hotels and high-end condominiums could be found, and to the east, a large sound separated the heavily populated west from the larger, less inhabited part of the island. There existed a surprising number of regions and small towns for a 22-mile-long peak of an underwater mountain that barely broke the surface of the Caribbean Sea.

We spent the next hour driving the coastal roads from West Bay dock at the top of Seven Mile Beach to Barker's National Park, the nature reserve on the north-west tip of the peninsula. As usual, nothing of much interest to the police was happening. Most of the locals were either working, or in church. Jacob drove us south to an expensive development known as 'The Shores', where we usually made a lap of the neighbourhood before lunch. Luxury homes lined a series of canals leading to the north sound, the largest properties fronting the sound itself.

Our task was simple. Drive, look around, then leave. Every home in The Shores had an alarm system. Many were holiday homes for wealthy Americans and Europeans who visited occasionally, and very few of them were rented to short stay visitors. In my three weeks on patrol, we'd only stopped twice in the neighbourhood. Once for a wandering dog whose owner appeared and apologised for not using a lead, and the second for a chat with a worker whom Jacob knew. Today seemed to be no different. Until the second to last street, Shorescape Lane. Two huge houses shared the end of the cul-de-sac and something about the one on the left was out of place.

Jacob pulled up to the driveway, and we both stared at the sprawling home. I had no idea who owned the place, but it certainly had enough room for the entire family tree. Two things caught our attention. The first was a large sign made from black stick-on letters adhered to a piece of white foam core, fixed to the fancy wrought-iron gate. Beyond the open gate and the large courtyard were curved steps, bordered by perfectly manicured shrubs, leading to the tall double doors, which were both open. That was the second. Electricity was very expensive on the island, so no one in their right mind would leave their front doors open for the air conditioning to cool the whole of the Caribbean. We both got out of the car and looked at the sign. 'Welcome Police Patrol.'

"D'ya think dat means a cold beer and pulled pork sandwiches waiting inside?" Jacob asked, more in bemusement than humour.

I walked over to the sign. It was zip-tied to the gate, and the letters were neatly applied with perfect spacing in straight lines. Whoever made the notice had taken their time. I heard Jacob call in our location over the radio as I walked towards the house.

"Nora," he called out, "wait up."

This was likely a prank, or maybe something as easily explained as a police fund raiser later in the day, but regardless, I was going to enter this house first. I was tired of sitting on the sidelines and filling out bullshit paperwork. I heard Jacob jogging up behind me.

"Wait up now," he said again. "I'll take a look. You stay outside and keep an eye out."

I trotted up the steps. "You keep an eye out. I'm going in."

"Damn it," I heard him mutter, but I'd beaten him to the doorway.

The entrance to the house was a huge foyer with marble tiled floor and a chandelier hanging from beyond my view above. Two curved stairwells flanked the entry, leading to the second level, and below the light fixture sat a round antique wooden table with a beautiful floral arrangement in the centre. Resting against the flower vase was another sign. This one read 'Congratulations'. Propped on a stand in front of the sign was an electronic tablet.

"Hello?" I shouted loudly as I stepped inside. "Is anybody home?"

My voice echoed around the cavernous space, and I looked up to see the domed ceiling high above decorated with a Baroque style mural of angels and mermaids. Nobody answered. I walked to the table and was startled as the tablet began playing a video of some kind.

"Hello and congratulations," came an American male voice in an even tone. "As the first to arrive, you have been chosen."

I stepped back and looked all around the entranceway. I wasn't sure what I'd been chosen for, but I had a bad feeling it wasn't a free ski trip.

"What the hell is dat?" I heard Jacob say as he joined me.

The video showed a young woman restrained and struggling in what appeared to be the back of a van. Muffled groans emanated from behind her duct-taped mouth, and her eyes were full of fear.

"This is Skylar Briggs, and she has volunteered to be the prize in today's show," the voice announced, and the man turned the camera towards himself. He made no attempt to hide his identity, and I could see the house in which we stood in the background. He pointed to the camera.

"And you are the lucky contestant."

He closed the back doors to the white panel van and walked back towards the house, talking as he went.

"The world will be watching, so tune in and follow along everyone."

"He musta recorded dis no more than an hour ago," Jacob noted. "Look at da shadows."

He was right. The shadows from the trees in the courtyard were not a great deal longer than they were in the video as I compared them, looking outside the open doors. I looked back at the table and noticed a blinking red light from amongst the flowers. I moved the leaves back to reveal a wireless camera and another small electronic device with an aerial protruding from the top.

"Damn," Jacob muttered. "What da hell's that?"

"A camera and transmitter," I replied. "He's watching us."

"Chosen one, I see who you are, and now the world has seen who you are. You, and you alone must play the game. If you win today's contest, Skylar will be returned, and I will hand myself over to the authorities," the kidnapper continued, staring into the camera as though he were addressing me directly. "You will face four challenges. Fail any of the first three challenges, and Skylar starts losing those pretty little manicured fingers." He paused, leaning in closer to the camera. "Fail the final challenge," he said, looking away for a moment before returning his gaze to the lens, "and Skylar dies."

4

NO IS NOT AN OPTION

Detective Whittaker is the man who persuaded me to join the Royal Cayman Islands Police Service. A decision I was regretting at the moment, but nonetheless he was a man I greatly respected and trusted. That was saying something, as I rarely trusted anyone in authority. He's a tall, slender man, with closely cropped grey hair and glasses. A local Caymanian with milk chocolate-coloured skin. He has a calm air about his ways and a pleasant, yet forthright manner.

"I want no part of this bullshit," I said, looking up at him from where I sat on the steps to the house. "I didn't join the police to be broadcast over the Internet. Sir," I remembered to throw in at the end.

The detective's mobile hadn't stopped dinging, ringing, and buzzing since he'd arrived a few minutes before, and he glanced away from me to see what the latest text was about. He frowned at his phone and tapped a few times before sitting down next to me and holding his mobile out in front of us both. It was a web stream. Apparently, the kidnapper had sent the web address to every news agency, paper, and TV station on the planet. Our little island was being inundated with requests to verify the reports of the kidnapping.

"Thanks for tuning in everyone," the dull, almost matter-of-fact voice of the man said. "The show will really start at noon, when our police constable, Miss Nora Sommer, will begin her first challenge to save Skylar Briggs."

"*Fy faen,*" I groaned and watched the video showing the abducted young woman tied to a chair in a dimly lit room. "How does he know who I am?"

"My guess," Whittaker spoke quietly, "is he selected you."

"Why me?" I complained. "All I want is to be left alone. I want anonymity, not a freak show on the world wide web." Leaning in closer, I studied the video stream. "That's a strange room. No windows, or carpet."

"Looks like concrete," Whittaker murmured.

"Like a basement," I added. "But no one has a basement on the island."

Grand Cayman is as flat as a pancake, the highest point being the landfill known as Mount Trashmore. A basement would be below the water table, becoming a swimming pool instead of storage space.

"For now, I'm afraid we don't have a choice, Nora," the detective said. "Until we know more, we need to play along."

"Who's this girl?" I asked, pointing at the terrified young woman on the screen. "Apart from the daughter of someone with a lot of money."

"Donovan Briggs owns this place," Whittaker replied, gesticulating to the huge house behind us. "He's an American businessman. I would have expected a ransom demand, but this fellow hasn't breathed a word about money. All he keeps talking about are these challenges."

"I don't like the sound of those," I moaned.

"Don't worry," he said, "I won't put you in obvious harm's way. We'll try to buy time and figure out where he is."

"Sir, the news crew is here," Jacob announced as he strode over to us. "We have them out front on the street."

Whittaker stood. "Thank you, Constable Tibbetts. Do you have the details of the van?"

Jacob tore a page from his notebook and handed the sheet to Whittaker. "Do we have patrols looking for the vehicle, sir?"

The detective shook his head. "No. I'm about to have the good citizens do that for us." He glanced down at me. "Where do you think the van is?"

I'd noticed he enjoyed doing that to me. He had committed to mentor me if I joined the force, but apparently mentoring meant testing me. Or having me do his job for him. I wasn't a hundred per cent sure which.

"He's already ditched the van and switched to another vehicle," I answered, figuring I'd play along. "The van will be close by in a secluded area, but not well hidden."

"I get da switch," Jacob commented. "But why not hide da van?"

Whittaker grinned and nodded at me to continue.

"Because he wants us to find it," I obliged.

Jacob hesitated, and I guessed he was trying to figure it out for himself rather than seem like he didn't know in front of the boss. His curiosity quickly got the better of him. "So why is dat den?"

Jacob was a smart guy, but he was also a really nice, trusting, family man. He didn't think like a criminal, which, according to Whittaker when he first approached me about joining up, I did.

"He's overloaded us with clues and things to follow up on, so we have to choose which to pursue," I explained. "He knows we're a small island with limited personnel and resources. Every copper busy chasing their tail is one more that's not looking for where he's got the girl."

The detective nodded again as he left, walking towards the news crew waiting anxiously outside the gates.

"Dis is crazy," Jacob said, shaking his head. "Stuff like dis don't happen here on Cayman."

It was typical of my luck. Why couldn't the nutjob have pulled this crap three weeks ago? And why did I choose today to be the first through the door? I looked up at Jacob and saw the concern on his face.

"It shoulda been me, Nora," he said quietly. "It should be me in dis mess about challenges and all dis rubbish. I'm sorry I let you go in first."

I stood up and stared out at the cul-de-sac where Whittaker was giving an interview with the TV news crew. "You didn't let me. And besides, it's better this way," I replied. "You've got a family to worry about."

I walked down the steps without finishing the statement. The obvious part about my not having shit worth living for didn't need to be said. Whittaker was right. We had to play along, and if someone needed to be put at risk, I couldn't come up with a good excuse why it shouldn't be me.

A fancy, expensive looking vehicle that couldn't decide if it was a car or an SUV screeched to a halt in the road where the police had cordoned off access to the house. Whittaker stepped away from his interview and intercepted the man who leapt from the driver's seat. He was middle-aged, dressed like he'd just left the golf course, and very worked up. I presumed he was Mr Briggs. A woman dripping in jewellery and designer clothes emerged from the passenger seat. She was either ageing at a snail's pace, or she wasn't Skylar's mother.

Whittaker looked to be trying to calm down the father as he led him and the arm candy towards the house. Towards me.

"You can hit a fucking baseball and reach every corner of the island," the man was shouting. "How the fuck can you not find this son-of-a-bitch?"

Shit. I've had the misfortune of meeting more than my fair share of these *drittsekker*. Upset is understandable, but screaming and yelling at the people trying to help didn't inspire me to stick my neck out. I could only hope his daughter was worth the effort.

"I assure you we are, and will be, pursuing all avenues available to us, sir," Whittaker said calmly as they approached.

"I've already called the FBI," Briggs claimed, waving a dismissive hand in the air. "I'm not leaving this to you guys."

He stopped at the base of the steps and looked up at me. "Is this kid the constable who's the 'chosen one'?"

Apparently he didn't want an answer from me as he turned to the detective. "Is this a fucking joke?"

I walked down the steps and past Briggs, who swung around. The wife, girlfriend, hooker, or whatever she was, eyed me with disdain. A look I gladly returned as I continued across the courtyard.

"Where the hell are you going?" Briggs shouted after me. "I want to talk to you."

Jacob walked with me, which made me smile, and I managed unusual restraint in not flipping off the obnoxious father. That was for Whittaker's sake. He had enough to deal with. But I ignored Briggs's shouts and kept going.

"What do we do now?" Jacob asked as we reached the gates.

"Avoid this camera for starters," I muttered as the news crew attempted to intercept us.

Jacob leapt in front of the reporter and held out his arms. "No film of da constable, please. We got enough trouble already."

I was surprised the reporter lady and her cameraman both backed off as I ducked around their van and got in the passenger side of our police car. Jacob jogged over and joined me, getting in the driver's seat.

"Where to?" he asked, starting the engine. "Are you sure the detective is okay wid us leaving?"

"Home," I replied. "I need to change."

Jacob hesitated.

"Get going before that news lady changes her mind," I urged, "and don't worry, I'm texting Whittaker."

As Jacob backed down the road and turned around in the driveway of another waterfront mansion, I sent the detective a short text saying I'd meet him at whatever location the kidnapper directed us to. I then searched for the website online. It was easy to find. 'Cayman kidnap' brought up a plethora of news hits, each one listing the kidnapper's web address. The camera was still on the girl, but the sound was muted. In the bottom corner resided a counter which read 8,800 and something. Within a few seconds of watching, it read over 9,000, the last two digits a constant blur as they were changing so fast. I wasn't sure about the world, but a bunch of people were indeed tuning in.

My phone dinged with Whittaker's reply, which asked me to monitor the web feed. I was having a hard time not watching, as apparently my fate lay in the hands of this madman. I directed Jacob towards Conch Point Beach Resort, which was east of my shack where the footpath led from the road to the beach. Where I lived was a closely guarded secret and although I trusted my partner, I saw no reason to change that policy with all the craziness going on.

"What do you think these challenges are gonna be?" Jacob asked as we drove through West Bay.

I shrugged my shoulders and continued watching the video feed on my mobile, looking for any clues.

"I hope it's not puzzles," I replied absent-mindedly. "I hate puzzles."

"Maybe it'll be like those shows where dey drop da people off on da island, den make 'em do those funky courses," Jacob offered. "You know the ones? If dey make it through first, den dey can't be voted out."

"No," I replied.

"No, you hope it ain't that?"

"No, I don't know the shows," I said impatiently. "I don't watch TV."

"Oh, well, you see dey take dees people and dey…"

"Jacob," I snapped. "Stop talking."

He went quiet, and I felt bad for barking at him. But, shit, why does everyone want to yammer on about things all the time? At least Jacob didn't treat me with disdain, like Williams and his shoot-'em-up-club of he-man woman-haters.

"Nora, are you listening in?" came the kidnapper's voice as he stepped in front of the camera. "Hello everyone, and thank you all for joining the show. The action will be starting soon and we have plenty of entertainment for you all afternoon."

That didn't sound good at all. I was hoping for something quick and easy. All afternoon didn't promise to be quick, or easy.

"For the first challenge, Miss Sommer, be at the public dock by Calypso Grill on North Sound by noon. You'll be getting wet, so dress appropriately." He paused and leaned in to the camera. "And no tracking devices, no tools, no weapons, or Skylar will start losing body parts."

He stepped back from the camera to reveal the girl, who was manically panting behind the tape over her mouth. She appeared on the verge of a full panic attack. I felt sorry for her, despite the shitty genes she would have inherited from her father.

"Dat man is so normal looking," Jacob said quietly. "It don't make no sense."

"That's what they say about all the weirdo psycho killers," I pointed out. "Their neighbours always say they seemed so normal. Meanwhile, they chopped up a dozen people and shoved them down the waste disposal."

"Oh, dat's disgusting, Nora, don't even say dat," Jacob said, frowning at me. "I don't need to be thinking about dat girl, or you, being... you know... what you just said and all."

"That makes two of us," I admitted. "Now hurry up, we don't have much time," I added, looking at my watch. It was nearly 11:30.

As we drove on, I wondered who the hell the kidnapper was. Jacob was right, he seemed like a normal bloke. He was making no effort to hide his identity, so I doubted it would take long to ID him. His lines were from a game show, but his delivery was deadpan, like a shy man unused to a camera. I guessed he was fiftyish, slightly overweight and non-threatening in appearance. But I also guessed Skylar Briggs didn't feel unthreatened in her current situation. I was certainly uneasy about what lay ahead.

5

ALMOST A DAY OFF

A skinny nine-year-old boy walked from the dugout to the plate accompanied by a handful of claps from parents in the stands. On the back of his jersey was the number four and his name, Kowalczyk. The kid turned and picked out his father, who gave him an enthusiastic thumbs-up. Number Four returned a nod and a determined expression. Digging his cleats into the dirt, young Kowalczyk carefully adjusted his stance and stared down the pitcher. He whiffed the first pitch.

"That's alright son, eyes on the ball. You got this," bellowed his father amongst a smattering of other, less keen encouragement. He fluttered his golf shirt a few times, fanning some air over his sweaty chest in the South Florida heat.

The kid glanced up at the scoreboard for the umpteenth time, although he knew nothing had changed except the pitch count. They were still down by three in the bottom of the seventh. With two on, he was their best chance at clawing their way back into the game. He dug in again, rolled his bony shoulders, and twitched the bat in his grasp. The pitch was in the bottom corner of the strike zone and little Kowalczyk swung with all his might as he watched the ball hurtle towards him. The sweet sound of a solid hit on aluminium echoed around the park, and the kid took off running.

The crowd rushed to their feet, with everyone screaming a cacophony of instructions, warnings and cheers, varying based on which team their kid was playing for. Yelling loudest was one proud father as he watched his kid clear second and sprint for all he was worth to third. The two other runners crossed home plate, and the coach checked Kowalczyk up at third. The kid looked up at the bleachers and beamed. His father, who at six foot two could be picked out easily, applauded and smiled. He rolled his eyes when he felt his mobile phone vibrate in his trouser pocket. He reluctantly retrieved it.

"Motherfuc..." he mumbled before catching himself. The call ID read 'Office'.

"Kowalczyk," he said unenthusiastically with the phone to his ear.

"You're up, Dan," a man said without emotion. "Kidnapping of a US citizen in the Caribbean. How soon can you be at the FBO?"

"I'm at my kid's baseball game, man. Is there no one else?" he whispered, not as quietly as he intended.

"You're up. How long?" came the unsympathetic reply.

Kowalczyk shook his head and sighed. "Twenty minutes, thirty tops. Where exactly am I going?"

"Cayman Islands. Make it twenty, Dan, this might unfold quickly," his boss replied.

"The fucking Cayman Islands?" Dan responded.

A series of murmurs and groans came from all around, and a woman just below him turned and gave him a stern frown.

Dan covered the phone. "I'm sorry, Jill, I apologise. It's my damn work."

Jill remained unimpressed and turned away, still frowning. Dan gave up and returned to the call.

"I have to tell my wife I'm bailing on our kid's baseball game to fly to the Cayman fuc..." he stopped himself just in time. "To the

Cayman Islands? You're killing me. This better not be another bull-shit hoax."

"Nineteen minutes now, Dan."

"Fine," he snorted. "Hey, one more thing. Who's my partner on this one?"

When he heard a soft sigh and a hesitation before the answer, he knew he wouldn't like what he was about to hear.

"Ricci."

"Motherfucker," he groaned and ended the call to face an evil eye stare from Jill.

Dan ignored her this time and nudged the man standing behind him. "Bob, hey man, could you drop my kid at the house? I got a work thing come up."

The man nodded. "Sure, no problem, Dan." Then he grinned. "Your missus is going to kill you for this."

Dan shook his head. "Don't I know it."

He gave the action on the field one more look, then shuffled towards the end of the bleachers, excusing himself as he went.

"Hey, Dan," his friend called out.

Dan turned.

"I get your golf clubs when she beats you to death," his friend shouted with a big grin.

Dan flipped him the bird and stomped across the car park to his Buick.

Elizabeth Ricci berated herself one more time for having too many drinks the night before. Her whole Sunday, the one day off she would have that week, was now several hours shorter than it should have been. She had slept in until 10am, crammed a few ibuprofen down her throat and chased them with half a gallon of coffee. At least she'd kept enough wits about her to fend off the guy who had spent the evening buying her drinks at the bar. He had nearly got lucky. It had been a while since she'd invited anyone to stay over, and settling for mediocrity seemed like an acceptable plan when she was inebriated. Fortunately, he had ogled a younger woman at the bar, and Beth had regained enough sense to leave him to her clutches. Still, it dented her ego a little; but waking up next to him that morning would have been far worse.

By three miles into her six-mile run at Amelia Earhart Park, she had sweated out the remaining alcohol, along with any cares about the guy at the bar. Beth paused at her turnaround point and cursed the Florida heat. This would have been over with hours ago if she hadn't been talked into a 'girls' night out'. The mobile phone strapped to her arm rang, and she tilted her arm to see the caller ID. It was work. Shit, she thought, here goes the rest of the day off.

"Hey," she answered through the mic attached to the Bluetooth ear pieces.

"You're up. How soon can you be at the FBO?"

Why does this always happen when I'm as far away from my house as possible? she thought. She set off running as there was no point wasting time. She could talk as she ran. Sort of.

"It'll take me twenty-one minutes to get home," she huffed. "Another fifteen to the FBO if I leave without a shower."

"Leave without a shower, and pick up the pace, agent," the man said flatly. "Plane will be waiting on you."

Beth was confident she didn't have sub seven-minute-mile pace in her today, but she kicked it up a notch anyway. It might mean a puke stop, negating any time gained, but she wasn't one to shy away from a challenge. Her boss might have been in good shape back in his day, but he'd let it slide. Too many years behind a desk instead of in the field had put a sizable paunch around his middle. If she could make the run faster than quoted, she would enjoy giving him a shitty look the next time he stuffed his face with a morning doughnut.

"Where?" she gasped. "Where am I going?"

"Grand Cayman," he replied, "There'll be more details when you get to the plane, but it's a kidnapped girl. Daughter of a prominent Florida businessman, so the Governor's already up our ass over it."

Great, she thought, another rich kid putting the scare on Daddy by running off. But there again, she had nothing against a trip to the Cayman Islands. Would have been nice to get a little more time to prepare though. Her 'go bag' didn't contain a swimsuit.

"Get a move on. I'll see you at the FBO," her boss finished.

"Sir, who's my partner?" she asked quickly before he ended the call.

He paused a moment before replying, which told her all she needed to know.

"Kowalczyk," he said firmly. "Now run faster."

The line went dead as she punched the air in frustration and sped up her pace even more. She now had little incentive to reach the plane any faster, but regardless, the adrenaline and anger made her legs pump harder.

"Shit on a stick," she yelled at the seagulls.

Still wearing her sweat-soaked leggings and racerback tank top, Beth jogged from the FBO terminal building across the tarmac to the waiting Learjet 60, her duffel thrown over a shoulder. She trotted up the steps and hunched over to enter the cabin. She was five feet four inches tall, but the doorway to the sleek FBI plane wasn't. Kowalczyk looked up from the file he was reading and leaned out of his seat. "She's finally here, guys, we can leave."

One of the pilots stepped from the cockpit and hit the button to close the door as Beth sat in the seat across the aisle from her partner. If she'd harboured any hope that Dan would be civil to her, those hopes were quickly dashed. Juvenile prick, she thought, tossing her bag on the floor in front of her. Her clothing immediately stuck to the plush leather seats. She reached up and directed every air vent she could touch in her direction.

"Boss leave already?" she asked.

Dan didn't look up. "Yup."

The engines fired up and Beth looked around for her copy of the file. It was sitting on the rear-facing seat in front of Kowalczyk. He clearly wasn't going to offer it to her, and she sure as hell wasn't asking him to hand it over, so she got up and picked up the file. Sitting back down, she hoped her sweat was dripping on his fancy grey suit. Beth buckled in and opened the paperwork, which consisted of a meagre few pages. In the hour and fifteen minutes the flight would take, she expected more details to be forthcoming, but for now she settled in to read what little they had.

As the plane taxied and the co-pilot talked back and forth with Ground Control, arranging their priority take-off, Beth raised an eyebrow. For a twenty-year-old daughter of a wealthy family, Skylar Briggs had already accumulated more than a few scrapes with the law. Interestingly, charges against her had a habit of being dismissed or withdrawn. Daddy must indeed have friends in high places, she pondered.

"Fucking rich kids," Kowalczyk mumbled just loud enough for her to hear. He tossed the file on the seat in front of him and pulled earbuds from his go bag.

For once, Beth agreed with him.

6

A HEAVY WEIGHT

Jacob picked his way around too many vehicles at the end of Batabano Road, leading to the public dock. Several news teams filmed us passing by and people shouted a myriad of questions or statements. Maybe it was encouragement. I couldn't tell, and I kept my head down. After years of hiding from public attention, I would rather have a root canal, mammogram, and pelvic exam all at once than face cameras and interviews. Near the end of the road, by Calypso Grill, a police barrier stopped anyone going any further, and I was relieved when they dragged it aside for us to come straight through.

The small car park for Calypso Grill and Tukka West, another waterfront restaurant by the dock, was full of police vehicles. The dock was nothing more than a single boat ramp with piers extending into the North Sound on either side. When I got out of the car, the first person I saw was my friend, AJ Bailey. She's more like a big sister and best friend, all rolled into a petite tattooed English woman with purple streaks in her blonde hair. If there was one person I could be in this world instead of me, it would be AJ. Except I'd talk less. She walked over and hugged me and I wished we could stay like that all day and let the world continue its madness around us.

"Got yourself in a bit of a pickle here," she said, letting me go and stepping back.

I shrugged my shoulders, reluctantly returning to the real world. "I'm lucky that way."

I could tell she wanted to tell me I didn't have to do this, but we both knew I did. AJ would trade places with me in a heartbeat, but that wasn't possible either, and I wouldn't let her anyway. Her soulmate is still alive and well. She went to speak, but I interrupted her.

"I know," I said firmly. "It's okay, let's just get on with it."

AJ nodded as Whittaker approached us.

"You probably saw, a little earlier he told us to have scuba gear for you," he said. "So I had AJ bring your gear, and she and Reg are on standby in case they need to go in the water."

Reg was AJ's friend and mentor who also ran a dive boat operation, as she did. They both assisted the police when divers were needed. I was a certified divemaster, thanks to AJ training me, which apparently was key in at least the first challenge.

"You're right," I said to the detective. "He chose me."

"Jensen Massey," Whittaker replied. "That's his name. We were able to match facial recognition to entry records at immigration. And yes, all evidence so far points towards him selecting you in particular."

We walked towards the boat ramp where my scuba gear was set up and Reg was waiting.

"How could he know I would walk into the house first?" I wondered aloud. "I didn't know until we arrived there. If Jacob hadn't called in on the radio, he probably would have beaten me to the door."

"We have limited resources when it comes to technology forensics, but the head of our Crime Scene Investigation Unit is pretty handy with computers," Whittaker replied. "She's taken a look at the tablet, camera and other electronics he'd set up at the house. It looks like he had another version he could have played if you weren't the first in the room, which still selected you."

Knowing I'd been hand picked by a kidnapper gave me the creeps from my hair follicles down to my toenails. "So all he had to know was it would be Jacob and me patrolling The Shores this morning."

"Exactly," Whittaker affirmed as we reached the dive gear.

"Morning, Nora," Reg greeted me in his gruff London accent. "I've put a second, smaller dive knife in your left side BCD pocket in case he makes you ditch the one on your cummerbund."

"Thanks." I looked down at what I was now wearing and wished I'd thought more about concealing weapons. I had a snug-fitting Lycra shirt over a one-piece swimsuit and water shoes on my feet. I had no idea what to expect after whatever was about to take place in the water, but at some point I'd be back on land and would need shoes. Hopefully.

"He's back on the feed," Jacob shouted, holding up his mobile.

We huddled around to watch as the man I now knew as Jensen Massey stood before the camera, blocking our view of his captive. The counter in the corner of the screen read 28,000 and something. Then 29,000 and something. Even the hundreds digit had almost become a blur. I needed to stop looking at the number and picturing half the population of the island watching the feed. It was freaking me out.

"It's time to get started, ladies and gentlemen," Massey began. "Our contestant, Nora, will enter the water and face her first challenge." He took a step to the side and waved a hand towards Skylar Briggs as though presenting the grand prize on a TV game show. "And here is the reward for the challenge. If Nora successfully negotiates the challenge, and nobody breaks the rules or interferes, this young lady will remain intact."

I noticed her wrists were now strapped tightly to the arms of the chair.

"If you fail the challenge, fail to follow the instructions precisely, or your friends break my rules," he said, stepping back and tapping on the young woman's hand, "then fingers will be lost."

Skylar quickly curled her fingers under, balling them into fists, and squealed behind the duct tape over her mouth. She fidgeted in the chair, which appeared to be fixed in place. Massey stepped back towards the camera.

"Nora, you have five minutes to get ready before you'll enter the water down the boat ramp, using scuba gear. Follow the channel and you'll find your next instruction waiting for you."

"Detective, sir!" came a voice shouting from the roof of Calypso Grill. "I think I've found one!"

We all looked over at a policeman from the tactical unit atop the roof. He was pointing to something in front of him.

Whittaker yelled back. "Cover it with your hand."

I turned back to the video feed and realised Massey had stopped talking. He was staring off to the side of the camera. He looked back at the lens.

"Rules. Here's the first rule, Detective Whittaker. Yes, I know who you are. Do not interfere with my cameras." He looked to the side of the camera filming him again where he presumably had some kind of display with his camera feeds. I wondered how many he'd set up and how long that must have taken.

Whittaker waved to the policeman on the roof. "Leave it be, constable."

"Thank you, detective," Massey said. "A few more rules. Nothing in the air, no helicopters, planes or drones," he continued, pacing back and forth in front of the camera. "Nobody accompanies Nora, nobody follows Nora, and nobody enters the water. You may position a single patrol boat, one half mile from shore to keep all other boats away. Is that understood, detective?"

A picture-in-picture smaller window popped up in the top right corner of the feed. It was from the camera on the roof aimed at the boat ramp. And all of us. We watched on the mobile as Whittaker turned to the camera on the roof and gave a thumbs-up.

"Good. Four minutes, Nora. You'd better get ready," Massey said calmly.

I tore myself away from the small phone screen, but couldn't help catching a last look at the counter. It was over 30,000. That was a crazy number of people already following the drama. I felt the tingling nerves I used to get before swim competitions in school and sailboat races. My legs seemed to lose all their strength and stability and I instantly felt out of breath, standing still. As unreal as all this seemed, it was actually happening, and happening right now. Someone's hand was on my arm.

"Come on, let's get you geared up," AJ said softly.

Reg picked up the dive tank with my buoyancy control device, or BCD, already fitted. I slipped my arms through the straps and he let the hefty weight hang on my shoulders. I pulled the cummerbund around and fastened the clasp. My gear felt much heavier than normal and I turned to AJ, who I presumed had set it up.

"I think there's…"

"Shush," she whispered back. "I loaded you with six one-pound weights, three each side. Use them as markers if you can."

I nodded and fastened the chest strap.

Whittaker stepped in front of me and put his hands on my shoulders. "Do not put yourself at risk, Nora. Understand? If this challenge is life threatening, turn around and come back. We'll negotiate our way through this."

I nodded, but it seemed like I'd be guaranteeing another human's death if I gave up. I didn't know shit about Skylar Briggs, and it was probably better that I didn't, as her life appeared to be in my hands. If she was a chip off the old block, I doubted I would bother getting in the water at all.

"Buy us as much time as possible, okay?" Whittaker continued. "Delay whenever possible. Every clue he leaves gives us a better chance to find him. He can't be far from where we're standing right now. FBI agents are on their way to help and time buys us options, okay? He's not allowed me to speak directly with him yet, but that's my highest priority. If we can speak with him, we can find out what he wants from all this nonsense. Opening communication is key." He smiled warmly. "Good luck and we'll see you when you come out."

I nodded again, but his words made me think. The kidnapper had talked about four challenges. Would my instructions bring me back out to the boat ramp where we'd set off for another location? That didn't seem right in my mind, and I was about to say something when Jacob spoke, holding up his mobile.

"Hey, he's back on, I think it's time."

"Grab a beer and some popcorn everybody," Massey said, managing a slightly more dramatic tone. "The first challenge begins now."

AJ handed me my fins and mask. "Good luck, Nora, be careful. Don't do anything too… Viking-like, okay?"

"Okay," I said, as there wasn't much else to say. I walked down the boat ramp towards the North Sound, relieved my legs were cooperating and moving my body along, but I felt a desperate need to pee from the nerves. When I reached chest-deep water, I picked up one foot and slipped a fin on. I repeated the process for the other foot, then turned for a last look at the crowd watching me from dry land.

"AJ, my mobile is in the car," I shouted. "I hope my parents aren't watching this shit-show, but if they are…"

If they are, what? I had no clue what to say. Hi Mum and Dad, hope you're having a good day, I'm off underwater on the whim of a lunatic, call you later. Maybe.

"I'll let them know," AJ shouted back. "Don't worry, just be careful."

I guessed that would have to do.

The sound of someone shouting came from across the car park at the police barrier, and I saw Briggs waving his arms and realised it was him yelling at the policemen. The camera crews didn't know whether to film him or film me. It was a good incentive for me to leave. I turned to the clear blue water, pulled my mask in place, put the regulator in my mouth, and slipped under the surface. The nerves immediately evaporated in the quiet of the undersea world, replaced by an overwhelming sense of loneliness. I had no one to talk to, no one to listen to, and no one to help me. If I screwed this up, a young woman would be mutilated. The magnitude of the consequences weighed far more than the extra ballast AJ had given me.

7

I KNOW HIM

Detective Whittaker watched Nora disappear into the North Sound and told himself his police officer was doing the job she had signed up for, as any constable would do. But Nora wasn't just any officer fulfilling her duties. She was the young woman he had persuaded to join the force under his tutelage. Only three weeks into active duty, she was being thrown to the wolves.

Donovan Briggs's bellowing pulled him from his concerns, and he turned to face the man marching across the car park.

"What the hell are you doing, Whittaker? The FBI should be handling this."

The detective let the angry man approach without responding, allowing him to blow off steam, hoping he'd calm down after a good rant.

"Well?" Briggs shouted as he stomped up uncomfortably close to Whittaker.

"I'm in touch with the FBI, Mr Briggs. They're on their way, but won't be here until this afternoon. I could wait until they land if you'd prefer, but if this fellow, Massey, is to be believed, your daughter will be at least one finger short of the number she currently possesses," he said calmly. "While we figure out where he may have taken her, I've chosen to put my constable at risk in an effort to buy time and keep Skylar intact."

Whittaker walked towards a RCIPS-marked pop-up tent that had been erected in the car park, indicating for Briggs to follow him. "I'm sure the FBI will provide us with helpful insight, as they deal with these situations more often than we do. But this is still our jurisdiction, Mr Briggs, and as such, I must handle the case using my best judgement."

They arrived at the tent where folding tables had been set up and the Internet video feed was streaming to a large computer monitor. Several other police personnel were busy at computers.

"Do you know the kidnapper, Mr Briggs?" Whittaker asked, as they looked at the live picture of Skylar Briggs tied to the chair. "His name is Jensen Massey."

Briggs shook his head. "How would I know him?" he blasted back.

"Our information tells us he's from the Tampa Bay, St Petersburg area," Whittaker said in a pleasant tone. "Isn't that where you live and your business is located?"

Briggs threw his hands in the air. "So I'm supposed to know everybody who lives there? That's millions of people for Christ's sake."

"Sir," Jacob interrupted politely, holding out his mobile phone. "This is the station for you. They say it's urgent."

Whittaker looked at Briggs, who was pacing around the tent. The man hadn't actually answered his question, although he'd given the impression of not knowing Massey. He took the mobile from Jacob.

"Sorry, sir," Jacob said quietly. "They said they'd been trying your phone."

The detective's phone had been ringing and buzzing with texts non-stop and he'd chosen action over talking for the past thirty minutes or so. He knew he could be missing vital information, but there was only so much he could do at one time.

"This is Whittaker."

"Dis is Pam in communications, Roy," came a woman's voice with a slight island lilt. "I'm putting a call through to you I think you should take."

Before he could accept or protest, Pam was gone, and the line clicked.

"Hello?" Whittaker said impatiently.

"Hello?" came another female voice, this time with a South Asian tint to an American accent.

"This is Detective Whittaker. How can I help you?"

"Oh, good. Hello, detective, I'm Myra Shah with the *Tampa Bay Gazette*."

"Ma'am, I need to direct you back to our communications group for the Royal Cayman Islands Police Service. I'm in the middle of a time-sensitive case and I cannot reveal any details to the press," Whittaker interrupted and was about to hang up.

"I'm not calling for the paper, detective," Myra said urgently. "I know this man. I know Jensen Massey. Please don't hang up, it's taken me hours to get through to your communications group, and finally you."

Whittaker took a deep breath and stepped from under the tent, away from anyone else. Briggs in particular.

"I'm sorry about that, Miss Shah, but our communications group is actually just Pam, so you can understand we're all stretched rather thin today. What's your connection with Massey?"

"I've been working on a story with him for over six months, detective, until a month ago," Myra explained. "I'm stunned he's kidnapped Briggs's daughter – that's not at all like the man I was dealing with."

"You say you were working on a story, Miss Shah. Why did it stop a month ago?"

"I'm still working on it, but Jensen stopped talking to me about a month ago," she replied. "How much do you know about Skylar Briggs?"

Whittaker didn't have time to dance around. If this woman had information that could help, he needed it now, so he'd have to trust her.

"We've seen her police record, if that's what you mean, Miss Shah."

"Please, call me Myra," she replied. "And that's exactly what I'm referring to. Jensen went off the radar and stopped returning my calls the day Skylar Briggs was most recently arrested. I haven't spoken to him, or seen him since. Until today that is."

"Why does Massey have a beef with a twenty-year-old rich kid going off the rails?" Whittaker asked and prayed it wasn't a sordid affair gone wrong.

"He doesn't, detective," Myra replied. "His problem is with her father."

"Sir, sir, he's back on the feed," Jacob shouted from the tent.

Whittaker looked at Donovan Briggs, who was anxiously watching the monitor. He knew the man was lying, but why, when his daughter's life was on the line, was still a mystery.

"Miss Shah, I mean Myra, would you mind staying on the line? I need to see what Massey's up to now. I have a diver in the water and we're trying to figure out where he's hiding the girl."

"No problem, detective, I'm watching it here too," she said, and he put the call on hold.

He handed Jacob his mobile as he returned to the tent. "Don't disconnect that call."

Massey was back in front of the camera, "...while Nora, our Royal Cayman Islands Police Service constable, makes her way to her initial challenge, here's the first in a series of videos I've put together to entertain and educate you on today's events and the people involved." He took a step back so Skylar was in view. "So let's sit back and enjoy a few fun facts from history."

Massey clicked a controller in his hand, and the feed switched to a video presentation. An illustration of three well-known monkeys filled the screen, the first with hands over its eyes, the second with hands over its ears, and the third with hands over its mouth.

Jensen Massey's calm voice began the narration, "Everyone has heard the 'see no evil; hear no evil; speak no evil' proverb. They often tie the origins to a 17th-century carving over a door of the famous Tōshō-gū shrine in Nikkō, Japan. Using monkeys to depict the proverb was nothing more than a play on words in the Japanese language, and the term 'evil' was only added in western use."

The presentation moved to a depiction of ancient-looking scrolls.

"But the philosophy originated centuries earlier in China, and brought to Japan in the form of a Tendai-Buddhist legend. The famous Chinese philosopher, Confucius, created a book 2,000 years earlier composed of a large collection of sayings and ideas, known as the Analects. Amongst them was the phrase 'look not at what is contrary to propriety; listen not to what is contrary to propriety; speak not what is contrary to propriety; make no movement which is contrary to propriety'."

A fourth monkey was added to the earlier group of three, its hands clasped together in front of its body.

"Our modern-day version of the philosopher's narrative has become 'see no evil; hear no evil; speak no evil'; and the fourth, the very important, although often overlooked, 'do no evil'.

"So let us start today with 'see no evil'. While Nora makes her way to her first challenge of four, which will reflect the 'seeing' element, I've prepared a brief glimpse into the world of the Briggs family, so you can see exactly who we're trying to save."

The video switched to footage recorded on a mobile phone of Skylar Briggs at a series of parties and dance clubs. In each clip, which Whittaker presumed had been gleaned from social media sites, the young woman was clearly inebriated.

"Shut this fucker down!" Briggs screamed, turning to Whittaker. "He's gotta be here on the island. Turn the Internet feed off!"

"That's not possible, Mr Briggs," Whittaker replied, remaining as calm as he could, "for a multitude of reasons."

"I don't give a shit about reasons," the man continued yelling, "shut down the Internet!"

"Mr Briggs," the detective replied, holding up a hand and catching Jacob's eye, "please settle down. I neither have the authority, nor the means, to turn off the World Wide Web on the Cayman Islands. I also lack the desire to do so."

Jacob quickly stepped between the two men as Briggs moved towards the detective.

"You son-of-a-bitch, if I tell you to shut it down, you'd better shut it down," Briggs seethed. "You'll go from banana republic detective to shining shoes at the fucking airport over this!"

Whittaker finally raised his voice. "We're using the Internet to try and find the man, you fool," he blurted, then quickly regained his composure. "We're attempting to trace the feed," he said, pointing to the officers trying not to look up at the spectacle in the small tent. "That's what these people are doing. Besides, if we take his outlet away, what use does he have for your daughter, Mr Briggs?"

The feed had switched to footage of Skylar being arrested and shoved in the back of a police car.

"Then hurry up and damn well find my daughter," Briggs blurted, with less fire in his voice. "This piece of shit is making Skylar out to be the bad guy."

"And you're still sure you don't know this man, Jensen Massey?" Whittaker asked, looking at Briggs standing before him, sweat running down his face, his own fury adding to the midday heat.

Briggs shook his head, but didn't speak.

"Jacob, take Mr Briggs to your car where he can rest in the air conditioning please."

Briggs gave the detective a stinging look, but didn't resist, and Jacob pointed towards his police car.

"Jacob," Whittaker said, and his constable turned. "Mobile."

Jacob tossed Whittaker his phone before leading Briggs across the car park. The video feed was now showing a series of newspaper headlines describing Skylar's falls from grace. Cocaine was a word which kept cropping up.

"He's not having to try too hard to make her look bad," he mumbled to himself as he took the mobile off hold. "Myra? I'm sorry about that, are you still there?"

"I am," the journalist replied. "Quite the show Jensen's putting on."

Whittaker kept an eye on the screen as he talked. The counter had surpassed 75,000 viewers, and he pondered if that could be real. "I think we know what he's been up to since you last spoke. This took some time to figure out and prepare."

"He's a very intelligent man, detective. I'm guessing you're having a hard time tracing the website and where his cameras are sending their signal?"

"We've had no luck so far," Whittaker admitted. "My people tell me he's bouncing everything around through moving IP addresses and a bunch of other things I certainly don't understand."

"I know you have to keep trying," Myra replied, "but I wouldn't hang too many hopes on finding Jensen that way. He's not your standard, sharper than the rest of us, IT guy. He's next-level clever when it comes to computers, and especially networks."

"Good to know, thank you," Whittaker replied, glancing towards the water and wondering how far Nora had made it. "If you could make this as quick as possible, Myra, without leaving out anything crucial. Please tell me everything you know about this fellow, Jensen Massey."

As the detective listened carefully, he turned back to the video feed where a shot of a large, sprawling factory with several huge chimney stacks filled the screen. The sign out front read Briggs Paper & Packaging International.

8

COUNTING ON BOTH HANDS

The North Sound is five miles across and six miles from the outer reef to the southern shore, but only 15 feet deep. If you took a shovel, there might be a few spots you could get to 20, but most of it is 10-12 feet of crystal-clear water and a sandy bottom with occasional patches of eel and turtle grass. I understood why Massey didn't want anything airborne over the sound, as they would easily spot and track me.

A wide channel led away from the boat ramp, dredged slightly deeper than the surrounding shallows, which I followed for what felt like 500 metres or more. I had no idea what I was looking for, but water clarity and visibility were excellent, so I had to believe I wouldn't miss any clues. Surely he would have made them obvious? The unknown has a devious way of making you second guess yourself. But if I kept going down the middle of the channel as he'd demanded, I convinced myself I'd find something.

My nerves had settled and gentle breaths through the regulator provided a steady rhythm to my fin strokes. I'd pumped extra air into my BCD to compensate for the additional weight AJ had given me, staying half a metre off the bottom. I took my time, trying not to expend too much energy, with no idea how much strength or air I would need for what lay ahead.

Finally, in the distance, the channel appeared to melt into the rest of the sound, its edges becoming indistinct. Dead centre of my path was an object of some kind. I had passed by a few rocks and pieces of rubbish lost over the sides of boats, but this was something more substantial. As I neared, I realised it was an underwater scooter, or DPV – diver propulsion vehicle – to use its official term. I'd never used one before, but they were becoming popular with divers and freedivers.

I finned my way to the DPV, which looked like a stubby torpedo with a handle around its midriff. The propeller was protected in a plastic cage, a compass mounted on top of the handle, and laminated instructions were clipped to the body. I read the directions.

'Head due east for approximately 14 minutes at full speed. You'll find your first challenge with a buoy line to the surface. At no time go to the surface. Further instructions await.'

The needle on the compass was pointing exactly east, so the DPV had been set down on the sea floor in the correct direction. I checked my dive computer; I'd already been underwater for 16 minutes. I didn't know how fast this thing would go, but my guess was he was taking me a long way from shore, or at least from the dock I'd just left. The boat ramp was in the north-west corner of the sound, so due east was heading across the open water towards the outer reef, which angled slightly south as it stretched between the peninsula of Barkers National Park and Rum Point.

I took hold of the handles on either side of the DPV and found the throttle triggers under both thumbs. I bumped the throttle and the prop quickly spun up, stirring a cloud of sand into the water behind me. Shit, I needed to get off the bottom or I'd make a mess of the sea floor. That thought made me wonder if I could mark my trail for Whittaker to see, but without the option of elevation, I figured they'd never spot the sand swirls in the water. I remembered the weights.

Taking one from each pocket, I set a weight in the sand, then using the compass on the DPV as a guide, I moved forward a few metres directly east and placed another weight. Hopefully, they'd figure out my crude directional pointer.

I picked up the DPV again, this time lifting it well clear of the sea floor, and pressed the throttle with my thumb. The electric motor whirred and the prop spun, thrusting a stream of water underneath me and pulling the DPV forward until my arms extended. My body weight slowed its progress, but not for long. The powerful little motor soon picked up speed and dragged me along with it. The instructions said at full speed, so I pressed the trigger all the way down and hung on tightly.

My mask fluttered and for the first minute or so I was biting on my regulator mouthpiece, making sure it wasn't pulled from my clenched teeth. I wasn't sure how fast I was going, but it was certainly quicker than I could swim, and it took some strength to keep my body pulled up over the top of the little torpedo so I could watch the compass.

After a while, I relaxed and felt comfortable letting the DPV do the work. I focused on staying streamlined in the water and keeping the machine tucked up against my chest. The jet stream of water tingled down my legs and the slightest movement in my fins immediately steered the DPV. I maintained an eye on the compass needle and resisted the urge to check my dive time too often. A few degrees off could easily put me out of visual range of the buoy line over the distance I was covering.

I began wondering what this challenge would consist of and felt the butterflies returning in my stomach. Did Massey want me to succeed or fail? I kept asking myself that question. I presumed he wanted me to carry on past each challenge, as that continued his weird online show. But I had no idea if he was excited to cut off some fingers, or hoped he didn't have to. He certainly craved the world's attention, and I tried not to think about that damn counter and all the people watching this very real 'reality TV'.

It felt like I'd been travelling forever across the bottom of the sound, scattering the occasional schools of fish and scaring several stingrays who shot from the sea floor in a cloud of churned-up sand. The farther I went, the farther I felt from the people who could help me, and the closer I felt to the clutches of a madman. Droning on through the clear water, a sense of isolation and exposure gradually built, reminding me of the loneliness I felt each night at home.

My new job had distracted me five days a week and AJ did her best to fill in the other days for me. But each night, I faced my empty house, where Ridley and I had just begun to make our home. I knew I'd be better off living somewhere else, away from the memories of us together in the shack. Our laughter and our contented silence filled every space in our home, touched every surface, and hid behind each cupboard door. I could picture him drinking from the coffee cup with the chip on the handle. Drying himself with the threadbare blue towel. Lying next to me on the left side of the bed. His side of the bed. The empty side of the bed.

Leaving the shack felt like I would be leaving him. He was stolen from me, but I could never abandon my soulmate. I couldn't bear to move his clothes; how on earth could I walk away from the home we shared? Maybe when all his shirts had lost the scent of him. The shirts I curled up with every night. Or maybe not then either.

I realised I'd been lost in the bullshit my stupid mind conjures up and hadn't checked the dive time. I looked at my computer; 32 minutes. *Faen*. It had been at 16 minutes when I'd found the DPV; I'd messed around and set the weights before leaving so probably 17, and the instructions said 14 minutes, which added up to 31. I released the throttle trigger and slowed to a stop. What an idiot. I'd probably overshot. I hadn't noticed anything in my field of vision, but there again I'd lost focus and allowed my brain to wander. If I didn't think this through and find the dumb challenge, I would be responsible for someone having a piece of their body severed. It would be one thing if I failed whatever the challenge was, but getting lost on the way was completely on me, and inexcusable. My fellow officers, like Williams, who already didn't think I belonged in uniform, would love that.

Carefully scanning as far as I could see, I made a 360-degree sweep. Nothing. Okay, I needed to run a search pattern. Most likely, I'd shifted a few degrees off due east, which could easily put me out of visual range after the several kilometres I guessed I'd travelled. Any slight current could have pushed me off course, but I couldn't feel a lick of pull in the water and the eel grass was sitting upright, not even swaying. Every time I'd checked the time, I'd rotated my right wrist to see my computer. I wondered if I'd accidentally tilted the DPV each time, veering it slightly left. I would have corrected again when I checked the compass, but perhaps it was enough deviation to alter my course.

A decision had to be made, and there was only one person around to make it. I gambled on left of my trajectory, so now I needed to backtrack. If I screwed up again, I'd be completely lost in the middle of the sound without a hope of finding Massey's buoy line. I aimed the DPV precisely zero degrees, due north, and pressed the throttle, counting 20 seconds off in my head before stopping again. Turning another 90 degrees left, I pointed the compass west and took off again. If I was right and I'd crept off course to the north, my parallel return should get me within visibility of the buoy. If I was wrong, Skylar Briggs would only be able to count to nine.

Relieved didn't come close to describing the feeling when, after less than 100 metres, I saw something directly ahead on the sea floor. As I approached, I made out the line and could see a buoy bobbing on the surface above. If anyone had been with me, I would have hugged them. But there wasn't anyone with me and the realisation I now faced whatever this maniac had concocted for a 'challenge' hit home.

Letting off the trigger, I glided up to a wire cage held down with a bunch of lead weights inside. The top of the cage was a metal plate forming a small table sitting on the sea floor. A post rose up from the centre, extending a metre above the deck, and the buoy line was tied to an eyelet at the top. I dropped the DPV to the sand and swam over for a closer look. Also attached to the top of the post, aimed down at the tabletop, was a small underwater camera. A wire ran from the camera to the buoy line, wrapping around in a spiral as it made its way to the surface. I noticed a blinking red light on the camera. It was recording. Or more accurately, it was broadcasting via an aerial at the end of the wire on the surface.

It took a lot of self-control, but I resisted flipping off the camera. Then I noticed what was on the tabletop. To one side were instructions clipped in place. Before me was a hexagonal frame about the size of a dinner plate, and to the other side were eleven odd-shaped wooden pieces.

It was a fucking puzzle. I yelled Norwegian obscenities into my regulator and couldn't stop myself from flipping off the camera.

9

NO MORE MISSING WOMEN

Detective Whittaker resisted his first reaction of grinning at the monitor as he watched Nora giving the middle finger to the camera.

"How is he doing that?" Whittaker asked, glancing at his IT personnel under the pop-up tent. "You can't broadcast a signal from underwater, right?"

"No sir, that's correct," one of the officers replied. "Has to be a hard wire connection or an aerial above the water."

Whittaker looked out of the tent towards the water. "AJ, Reg!" he called, and the two turned from where they were keeping an eye on the North Sound. He beckoned them over to the tent.

"How far could Nora have swum underwater since she went in?" he asked as they walked up.

AJ looked at Reg, who shrugged his shoulders. "You like doing math, not me."

She turned to Whittaker. "She's been in the water about 40 minutes or so. She's a really fast swimmer and has fins, but the scuba gear would slow her down as it's bulky and not very stream-lined." AJ paused and thought it over. "I'd say 2 mph average would be the absolute best she could do. More realistic would be 1.5 mph over 40 minutes."

"What does that mean in terms of range?" Whittaker asked, starting the math in his head.

"One mile exactly, sir," the IT officer replied.

"But that's assuming she swam at full speed from the moment she left," AJ added, nodding her admiration to the officer for her rapid math skills. "I doubt she went all out until after she found the instructions and we don't know where that was exactly."

"It was farther out than we could see her bubbles on the surface," Reg said, "and we could see them for a quarter mile at least. I bet she's less than a mile from us."

Whittaker turned to the officer. "Bring up a map of the sound and give me a one-mile radius and let's see what we have. Make sure it's a nautical map, please."

He pointed to the monitor where Nora was looking down at what appeared to be a flat, man-made surface with some kind of puzzle laid out. The camera was above, pointing down, and showed part of the table, Nora, and the sandy sea floor immediately around them.

"Is there anything in this view that gives us a clue as to where it might be?" he directed to AJ and Reg.

"Not really," AJ replied. "We were looking on our mobile and wondering the same thing. It's relatively shallow, because of the colours showing up." She stepped closer to the monitor and pointed to a whistle attached to Nora's inflation hose. "That whistle is orange as you can see, which means she's in less than 30 feet, otherwise the water would have absorbed that colour spectrum," she continued, pointing to a button on the inflation hose. "In fact, that button is red, which means she's shallower than 12 feet otherwise the red spectrum would be lost."

"Okay, that's helpful, thank you," Whittaker said.

"Not really," AJ replied. "That narrows it down to pretty much anywhere as far as you can see across the North Sound. It's only the middle and south-east parts that are generally deeper than 12 feet."

"It still may help us," Whittaker countered. "He's able to broadcast, which means he has a connection to the surface in some manner. We'll start with inlets or marinas within a one-mile radius, with a depth of less than 12 feet. Some are dredged deeper, so we may be able to rule them out. What we're looking for is a line running into the water from the shore."

"Here's a nautical map, sir," the officer said, and Whittaker, AJ and Reg all huddled around to look. A red line with a 1.0 mile radius circled the dock where they stood.

"That's a big area," Reg pointed out. "There's a few dredged canals that could be the spot."

"Looks like Governors Creek is too far," Whittaker thought aloud. "Salt Creek is barely possible, and then we have two small inlets to our north, followed by the canals running through The Shores."

"From the height of the camera above her, we know it has to be at least six feet deep as she's kneeling in the sand and the view is several feet above her head, yet still submerged," AJ noted.

"That rules out everything to our north other than the canals," the IT officer said. "This end of the sound is really shallow."

"We know she went straight out from the boat ramp as we watched her bubbles," Reg added, "so no way she could have made Salt Creek. It must be the canals to the north."

Whittaker took his handheld VHF off his belt and then paused, staring at the device. "He's bound to be listening in," he mumbled and switched to his mobile phone. While he typed out a long message to the sergeant in charge of coordinating the police patrols, AJ continued studying the map. When Whittaker finished, she pointed to the map again.

"Could the broadcast be sent from a wireless signal rather than a hard line?"

"Yes," Whittaker replied, "we believe so."

"We shouldn't rule out the area directly east of us," she said, tapping a finger on the open water of the sound. "I know the chart shows 3 to 6 foot, but there are pockets of slightly deeper sections in the sandy areas."

"We can't fly anything over and he's watching the single boat we have keeping traffic away," Whittaker replied, "but I've instructed one of my guys to get up as high as he can somewhere close by and search the sound with field glasses for anything floating that could contain an aerial."

"That'll be tough to spot at this distance," Reg pointed out. "Even three storeys up is still a relatively flat view."

Whittaker nodded. "Agreed, but worth the effort. I have all available constables on their way to walk the canals to the north, looking for any kind of electrical line running into the water."

"What about going in the water for a look around?" AJ asked. "I might be able to find whatever was left for instructions."

Whittaker nodded towards the camera on the roof of Calypso's. "He'll see from here and who knows where else he has cameras. It would be risky."

They all thought for a moment while they watched Nora on the monitor, alone in the water.

"Dolphin Cove!" AJ blurted. "Have someone official call over there to get permission and I'll go in through their pens. I could be back to the channel here in no time."

"That might work," Whittaker replied thoughtfully, looking south along the coastline towards the buildings and outdoor pools, where tourists could swim with dolphins. "Do you have more gear? I think you should leave your kit you already have on the boat ramp. If he sees you taking that he'll get suspicious."

"Yeah, I've got rental gear for customers in my van," AJ said, "and plenty of tanks. But call over and tell them I'm on police business or they won't let me in."

Whittaker looked at her with a puzzled expression.

"I'm against keeping the dolphins cooped up in small pens for human entertainment," she said, rolling her eyes, "and I've been a bit outspoken about it, so they know who I am. When they see my van roll up, they'll probably be calling the police station to have me removed."

"Okay, I'll call them," Whittaker nodded, with a slight grin.

"This'll go down like a fart in a spacesuit when I show up on official police business," AJ laughed. "I can't wait to see their faces."

Whittaker shook his head. "I'll prepare them as best I can. And you'll have to return to the Dolphin Cove centre as well, you can't exit the water here."

"No problem," she said, and started to leave.

"AJ, how long can Nora stay under on one tank?"

"At this depth, literally hours," she replied. "Nora's part fish anyway, she's really good on air consumption, so the only thing that would have caused her to use more is a long, hard swim. Even then I'd guess she could stay down for well over an hour."

Whittaker glanced at his watch. It was 12:48pm. Their blind hunt could go on for a while, and he considered whether they could expect her to return to the boat ramp, or be sent somewhere else. The instructions she received in the water could be crucial.

"Okay, be as quick as you can, AJ," he said, "and for goodness' sake, don't you go missing too. I've got all the lost young ladies I can handle."

AJ smiled. "I'll be back before you know it."

10

SEE NO EVIL

I calmed myself as best I could and stared at the puzzle pieces.
There were too many to picture them in an organised form and I
knew he'd rotated each one in the wrong direction and scattered
the order. I looked at the laminated sheet and began reading the
instructions.

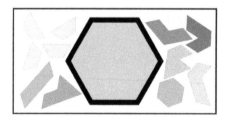

This is a Hexagon Tangram Puzzle.
Fit the eleven pieces into the frame to complete the puzzle.
Start when the green light turns on.

Take all the time you need to solve the puzzle abiding by these two rules:

1) Do not surface or make signals to the camera, except a thumbs-up when you're ready to begin.
2) Take your regulator out when the green light comes on and do not put it back in your mouth until it's solved.

Turn this card over when done with the challenge.

I'd already broken rule one. Hopefully, he was more concerned with signals giving away my position and less bothered by my insult. It was unlikely Whittaker would have figured out a sea scooter was used, so I couldn't imagine their search area would extend as far offshore as I was sitting. I checked my dive computer. I still had half of the 3,000 psi of compressed air I'd started with remaining. With no idea what was coming next, I still needed to conserve air, although unless I could solve the stupid puzzle on a single breath hold, it wouldn't matter much.

I stared at each of the puzzle pieces in turn, memorising their shape while taking long, slow inhalations. I would need my lungs fully oxygenated with all the spent carbon dioxide which lingers when we breathe normally expelled. My freediving experience would be key, and reminded me once again that Massey had undoubtedly chosen me for his show.

The average person can hold their breath in a calm environment at the surface for up to a minute. A Navy SEAL must be able to hold their breath for over two minutes. The world record for a single breath hold is almost 25 minutes, which would render almost anybody else dead. A freediver holds the record. I was only six feet underwater, but even at that shallow depth, the surrounding water pressure made it more difficult. I couldn't hold my breath anywhere close to 25 minutes, but I was better than average.

Trying not to think too much about the time aspect, I focused on my breathing exercises and learning the puzzle pieces. But I could only manage one pass around each shape before my mind would drift again. I wondered how many people were now watching through Massey's annoying camera, and then I'd return to concerns over how long I could hold my breath. I was routinely freediving for two to three minutes on the reef at 30 feet, swimming and expending energy the whole time. In theory, my mind would be the only thing taxed for the puzzle while my limbs would simply be moving pieces around. It was possible I could extend my time to 4 or 5 minutes.

My anxiety built as I faced the challenge, completely at odds with my breathing preparation, and I forced my focus back to my lungs. This had to be super boring if it was indeed broadcasting live across the Internet feed. I was sitting in the sand staring at the table, taking long breaths through my regulator. Riveting stuff. I hoped it was shitty entertainment and people were switching to videos of cats or porn sites. I realised I wasn't making any progress on my breathing – my stupid mind was too scattered – but I had visualised all the wooden blocks. There didn't seem much point delaying any longer, and before I could second guess myself again, I looked up and gave the camera a thumbs-up.

A bright green light I hadn't noticed before at the base of the pole lit up, and my heart skipped a few beats. I closed my eyes and took a few final breaths through the regulator before letting it slip from my lips and dangle on its hose by my side.

Two of the pieces had an edge that appeared to be the exact length of one side of the hexagon, so I picked them first. The wooden pieces were surprisingly difficult to pull from the table and I realised they were magnetic. I flipped the first one over in my hand and saw a circular magnet imbedded in the underside. That made sense; wood floats. I placed the first piece along the top side of the frame and it matched the length perfectly. A good start, now ten to go. I put the second one aside.

Another piece was a hexagon, a smaller version of the frame itself, but its angles naturally matched. I recalled from geometry class in school that the corners were known as vertices, and I placed the piece in the next vertex around. This left a gap between the hexagonal piece and the full-side block I'd first placed. There were four identical pieces in the shape of a trapezoid, and the long edge of those matched the gap. Isosceles trapezoid, I recalled, was the correct term, as they were symmetrical. I now had three outer blocks placed, and my confidence was building. Maybe I like puzzles after all, and hadn't known it until now.

Another trapezoid piece nestled against the hexagon and begged for the second of the long blocks. I now had four odd shapes and two trapezoids left. Each of the odd shapes had at least one side that was two-thirds the length of a hexagon section. None of them seemed to fit, so I threw another trapezoid in next. Now I tried all the odd blocks until one appeared to complete the outside of the puzzle. I only had four pieces to place, and I stole a quick look at my dive computer. Which told me nothing, as I'd forgotten to check it when I'd taken my reg out. Shit. Well, it didn't matter because I was kicking the puzzle's arse.

I had one more trapezoid block and three odd-shaped ones. The space they needed to fill was also irregular, with an assortment of zigs and zags. Surely it would be obvious where the shapes went? One of them had a vee cut-out which matched the first piece I'd placed perfectly, so now I had three to go. An elbow-shaped piece nestled perfectly and left me with two pieces still to fit. But the remaining two pieces didn't match the open space that was left. All of a sudden, nothing fitted and I feared my perfect outer grouping must be wrong. My lungs began to burn, and I wondered how long it had been. Two minutes? Four minutes? I had no idea, but I knew I needed to figure this out in a hurry. I felt a nagging pang of encroaching panic, which I knew would be the death of me. Well, I could put the regulator back in my mouth, so I guess it wouldn't be my death. But it would certainly be the demise of Skylar's pinkie. Or whatever finger was sentenced to be chopped. The pinkie seemed the obvious choice for ease of access.

None of these thoughts were helping me solve the stupid puzzle, and I pulled my mind back into focus. I took the last two pieces back out and studied the remaining blocks again. The trapezoid fitted there, but it too left a weird shape the remaining pieces wouldn't fit. As my tension grew, so did the aching in my lungs for a fresh breath of air. I was in deep shit if I didn't figure this out, and the panic lurked, ready to pounce at any moment. I closed my eyes and cleared my mind, relaxing my whole body.

When I slowly opened my eyes again, I was sure the outer pieces were either correct, or all wrong. There were two odd shapes with vee cuts and I had started the inside blocks with one of them. I chose the second one and nestled it around the final outer block I'd placed. It fitted and filled the area across to the small hexagon. Maybe it was right. But now I had two vees in the remaining area and only one odd block with a V-shaped cut-out. It didn't look right after all. I could chase my tail around this stupid puzzle in a perpetual state of three pieces left over.

My throat was tightening; my thoughts were beginning to get hazy and it was difficult to maintain clarity. My body, and especially my brain, was begging for oxygen. It didn't matter how long I'd been holding my breath. Maybe it was a personal best, maybe I'd done a shitty job of it. Either way, I only had a short time before I needed to breathe. At that point, if the regulator wasn't back in my mouth, my body would trigger the breathing reflex and attempt to gulp air, whether it was available or not. I would drown with a half-full tank of air strapped to my back and the surface six feet above me. Williams would have a field day over my stupidity.

One by one, I picked up each remaining piece and tried them in the open area. The trapezoid block fitted everywhere, which didn't help me. The two odd pieces were an elbow shape and a goofy piece with the vee cut-out. I blinked several times and fought to stay lucid. Banging and turning the two pieces around, I manically tried forcing them into the space but they wouldn't all fit. My lungs screamed and my head was thumping, but I desperately needed a few more seconds of clear thought.

Closing my eyes again, I focused on an imaginary spot before me, and a white light appeared. My whole body relaxed, and the panic receded. I felt a calm and peace wash over me. Whatever happened next would be okay. If I slipped away, I'd join Ridley on the other side, whatever, whenever, or wherever that might be. The draw to be with him again was almost overwhelming, but a nagging obligation to save a woman I didn't even know pulled me back.

I opened my eyes and dropped the elbow into the frame. The goofy one nestled perfectly into the remaining vee, leaving a trapezoid-shaped hole for the final piece. Slapping it home, I wheezed the remaining air from my lungs and swept the regulator up to my mouth. Pressing the outer face of the reg, I purged the water from the mouthpiece and gasped in the precious gas. As my head cleared and I stared down at the table, I reminded myself of how much I still hated fucking puzzles.

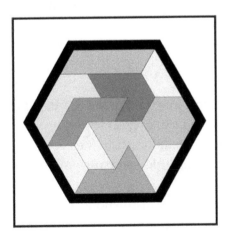

11

A SIGN

Jacob, Reg and the two IT officers applauded, and cheers could be heard from the crowd gathered behind the barricade. Whittaker was bent over with his hands on his knees, panting as if he'd run a marathon. He hadn't intended to, but he'd held his breath along with Nora for the last minute or so. She, however, had held a single breath for 7 minutes and 6 seconds according to the dramatic time counter Massey had run across the top of the screen. The kidnapper was now congratulating her over the video feed, still running live from underwater where Nora sat back and looked up at the camera.

"Bloody good job, Nora," Whittaker muttered at the screen.

Muffled shouts and banging came from Jacob's police car where Briggs was beside himself, locked in the back seat, watching on his mobile. Whittaker had little sympathy for the man and ignored him.

Nora reached for the instructions clipped to the table and appeared to take a quick glance before tucking them under her arm. She then put her hands together as though in prayer, and Whittaker felt a surge of relief mixed with guilt for getting her into this mess. Finally, a sense of fear returned as he wondered what would come next. Nora lowered her left hand, then slid her right hand deliberately upwards and reset her mask. She took the laminated sheet from under her arm and the feed abruptly switched to Skylar Briggs strapped to the chair in the concrete room.

Whittaker assumed the directions to the next location were on the back of the laminated sheet, which Massey didn't want them seeing. The IT guys had already taken a still image of the challenge notes and zoomed in to see if there was anything to be gleaned. It gave them nothing new. The detective thought for a moment, and wondered where those directions would be sending his young constable next. He checked his watch. It was a little after 1pm. AJ wouldn't be back from her search for another 30 or 40 minutes and he glanced out over the North Sound. AJ was probably less than a few hundred yards from where he stood, but with Massey's well-placed camera watching them, plus the possibility of more they didn't know about, she couldn't risk surfacing nearby.

Whittaker pondered the last shot he'd seen of Nora with her praying hands. He didn't know her religious beliefs, but he guessed she wasn't a regular churchgoer. Spiritual maybe, but he couldn't imagine the young Norwegian with her troubled past following an organised religion. He considered whether his spotty attendance at his own church might have played into the day's proceedings. His wife would think so. Making a silent promise to return to regular attendance, he thought back to Nora. He took out his mobile and texted a question to a cousin who lived with her husband and daughter on the north side of the island. She might have the answer to an odd thought that had crossed his mind.

As he hit send, the mobile buzzed in his hand. He'd been ignoring the constant stream of calls and messages, but he noticed this was Pam, the police communications lady who had to be having the worst day of her professional career.

"Whittaker," he answered.

"Roy, I'm sorry to bother you," she started, sounding as overwhelmed as he'd imagined, "but I'm not sure what to do with the arriving press, sir."

"I'm sorry, Pam," he replied, "What do you mean by arriving press?"

He heard Pam sigh. "Roy, every seat on every commercial plane, plus multiple charters and private planes are coming in this afternoon," she explained. "The worldwide press are arriving. Many of them don't have a place to stay or hire cars. Everything is sold out."

"Oh," Whittaker mumbled, unsure why this was his concern, as much as he was sympathetic to her plight.

"What am I supposed to do with all these people?"

"Keep them away from me and where we're working would be my first answer, Pam," he said, as kindly as he could. "Beyond that, I'm not sure I mind what you do with them."

He thought he heard a sniffle, and felt equal parts guilty and irritated. "I'm sorry, Pam, I'm sure it's a problem, but surely the Chief should be handling this with you?"

"You didn't hear?" she said in surprise.

"Hear what?" he said and knew amongst the voicemails and texts on his mobile was probably the answer he was about to hear.

"The Chief is having emergency gall bladder surgery," Pam said. "You're the acting Chief."

"Oh," he said again, surprise turning into disbelief. "That's perfect."

An uncomfortable silence fell across the phone line and he looked over at the monitor where the viewership now read 290,000. He had no idea what constituted a large audience for an Internet live-stream, but he guessed that had to rank pretty high and was showing no sign of slowing.

"Set up a media ops centre somewhere, Pam, and direct everyone there to receive their official press passes."

"Press passes?" she echoed. "We don't usually have press passes, Roy. I have nothing made up."

"Cut them out of cereal boxes or print them off your computer, my dear. I don't care which," he said softly. "But make sure they all have to come and see you before going anywhere else on the island."

"Okay, I suppose," Pam replied hesitantly. "But where can I get a room big enough to handle all these people on a Sunday afternoon? For sporting events we've used one of the hotels before, but this will be far bigger than we've ever seen."

Whittaker walked around in ever-increasing circles as he spoke. "The Hamlin Stephenson Market at the cricket grounds. Tell them we need to commandeer the building for the afternoon," he said, desperately hoping it would only be necessary for the afternoon.

"But that's an open-air building miles from here, Roy," Pam replied. "Wouldn't somewhere on the way over to where you are be better?"

"Not at all, Pam," he said, spelling it out more clearly. "The best thing would be if they weren't coming at all. The next best thing is to delay them with bureaucratic BS over press passes, and hopefully this will be over before they get in my way. I'm trying to catch a madman, save a young woman's life, while not getting my constables harmed, Pam. The world's press will not be assisting me in doing any of that."

"Oh," Pam said, mirroring the policeman's surprise from earlier. "Of course, sir. I'll see what I can do."

"Thank you, Pam," Whittaker said politely and ended the call, wondering what more could go wrong.

"While our valiant Royal Cayman Islands Police Service constable, Nora, moves to our second location, let's talk about the subject of the second challenge," Massey announced, standing before the camera on his video feed.

Whittaker guessed whatever the kidnapper had up his sleeve next would not be the improvement he was hoping for.

"Hear no evil," Massey continued. "Our ears are constantly bombarded with information these days, from entertainment to news and advertising. But is there a difference between any of those things? Does the television and print media bring us a balanced, non-biased version of the news we all need to know?

How do they choose what to show you and what to sweep under the rug and ignore? Why does a court hearing about a Florida politician's embezzlement case take precedence over an earthquake in Sulawesi killing over a hundred people?

"Why? Because most Americans, and many people around the world, have no idea where Sulawesi is. So, they're more interested in a juicy story about a sham charity set up by an elected official. Let's step back and ask a bigger question."

Massey paced back and forth before the camera, gesticulating to emphasise his points. "Why do news channels exist? To bring the general public information about the world and their local area, right? Wrong. They exist to make money. They are purely and simply profit centres, concerned solely about their ratings and beating their competition. Ratings mean value in the eye of the advertiser, and the advertiser's dollars are what fund the show and drive the profit. So how do they choose what to show you? They show you whatever will make you tune in and watch. Not you as concerned citizens hoping to keep up with the world around you, but you as moths drawn to the flame.

"Danger on the streets of your town! Tune in at 11 and we'll tell you how to stay safe."

He threw his hands in the air then leaned in closer to the camera, theatrically looking at his watch, "If it's going to save my life why do I have to wait until 11? Because that's when they'll serve you a bunch of ads to buy shiny cars, sudsy washing powder, pills to make things soft, and pills to make things hard. Then, at 11:27, they'll get to the story about some bullshit they've blown out of proportion to scare you into watching in the first place.

"So, the news is entertainment, TV news, print news, Internet news, it's all the entertainment industry. A news webpage is almost impossible to even read as the article flies off the screen, shoved aside by pop-up ads, videos, and links suckering you into clicking by pretending to be part of the story. What about the ads them-selves? Do you really think the airline's main concern is helping you see your family like they show in their ad? How about the insurance company that pledges to be right there if something happens? The fast-food company that shows the laughing happy children eating fat-filled chemically laced burgers with free gifts when you buy the combo meal?

"Lies. They're all pumping you full of lies to sell their products to make money. Our ears are constantly barraged with bullshit. You all choose your news station based not on them telling the truth, but the truth as you want to hear it. It's still bullshit, or at best a truth spun into a form they think you want to hear. So why would we be surprised when corporations follow suit? Charity donations carefully guided by accountants keeping the tax dollars from going back to the communities. The same communities their workforce resides in, desperately trying to claw out a living.

"So gather round folks, invite your friends and families to tune in, because shortly we'll listen to some of the lies your ears have been subjected to by none other..." Massey stepped back, once again gesturing towards Skylar whose terrified eyes followed his movement, "than our very own Briggs family."

He moved out of camera shot and soft music played as the viewers were left with the young woman's pleading stare at the camera.

Whittaker wondered what on earth the international press would do with that little segment. Probably run some ads and keep looping it. His mobile buzzed again, and he checked the text. It was from his cousin, and she'd sent a short video. The detective watched and smiled.

"Clever girl," he muttered under his breath, and looked around outside the tent.

"Reg!" he called over to the Englishman, who stood on the pier by the boat ramp.

They walked towards each other and met by the boat ramp, facing the water away from Massey's camera.

"When do you expect AJ back?" Whittaker asked.

"I could see her bubbles, until she headed farther out the channel," he said, keeping his hands in his pockets so he didn't point as he talked. "Depends on what she finds I suppose, but my guess would be another 30 minutes."

"Okay," Whittaker replied nonchalantly. "The second she's out of the water I need her to run to Governor's Creek and I'll have her picked up by a Marine Unit boat."

"Okay, I'll text her and tell her to call me as soon as she's out," Reg said. "You figure something out?"

Whittaker smiled. "Our clever Norwegian gave us a clue."

12

APATHY

It took me a few minutes to gather myself and truly clear my head. Looking at my dive computer, I'd tried to figure out roughly how long the reg had been out of my mouth. There was no way to be sure, and the effort added to the headache that raged from the oxygen deprivation. Besides, my day was far from over. The directions on the back of the laminated card were simple.

Bring this with you.
Take a heading of 354 degrees to inlet.
Go ashore and stay out of sight.
Leave transport hidden in mangroves.
Follow signs.

I clipped the directions to the DPV and used the compass to point the scooter on the provided heading. Taking a weight from each side of my BCD, I lined them up in the sand, also at 354 degrees. That left me with one pound in each BCD pocket, which was fine for my body mass without a wetsuit, and well over 1,000psi left in the tank. I was lean enough not to need any ballast until the aluminium tank became slightly buoyant as the gas pressure and density lowered. After setting the weights, I carefully accelerated away to the north.

My relief at solving the stupid puzzle quickly wore off, and I wondered what would come next. I felt numb. My brain had certainly been fuzzy near the end of my breath hold, but the feeling of indifference remained clear in my mind. Since Ridley's death, I'd often wished for the pain to stop and there seemed only one way for that to happen. I couldn't actively take that step. I wouldn't do that to the people who loved me, but if an external force took my life, I'd have been fine with it. In theory. In psychology it's referred to as passive suicide ideation. I'd read about it before experiencing the phenomenon.

Up until the challenge, it was nothing but a sense, a theory. But I'd been face to face with a life-threatening situation and my apathy was no longer hypothetical. That should have depressed me, but it didn't. I just felt numb. Further proof.

The North Sound quickly became shallower, and I was having a hard time keeping from breaking the surface or brushing the sandy bottom. Parts were only a metre deep, but when a darkness appeared up ahead of me, it deepened to twice that, and the sea floor became littered with small twigs and decaying foliage. I slowed as I approached the shoreline with twisted mangrove roots forming a barrier before me.

The mangroves appeared to surround me and, presuming I was in the small inlet, I had no choice but to surface. Next to the roots it was only a metre or less deep again, so I kneeled in the sand and lifted my head clear of the water. It took me a second to orientate myself. Only 4 or 5 metres wide, the inlet was about the same long. Mangroves partially blocked my view of the western shore of the sound, especially the northern end where I'd left from. Massey had cleverly chosen the spot to hide me from sight.

I turned to the shore. The mangrove roots had been cut back to reveal an exit point onto dry land. It didn't look like anything that had been done recently, so at some point in time this must have been access for someone. I stood and shuffled over that way, dragging the sea scooter with me. It was heavy out of the water, but I lifted it onto the bank and pulled myself out of the water to sit on the firm ground. Unbuckling my BCD, I slipped it and the heavy tank aside and took off my fins. I wondered if I'd ever see my gear again. Dive equipment was expensive. That *drittsekk* Briggs would be buying me new stuff if my gear went missing. And I was still around to care.

Shoving everything into the brush, I noticed a set of stones forming an arrow, pointing into the thick foliage. Whoever had originally used this trail had obviously long since abandoned it – the flora had grown over any path. I kicked myself again for not sharing my thought about not coming back to the boat ramp. Hopefully Whittaker had come to the same conclusion and if not, I'd now been gone an hour and a half. Surely he'd figured it out?

I looked down at my BCD and remembered the knives. I was wearing a swimsuit and a snug-fitting Lycra shirt. Where the hell could I hide a knife? Digging my water shoes from the BCD pocket where I'd shoved them, I was glad I'd thought to bring them. I brushed the dirt and sand away from the soles of my feet and wriggled them on. I was about to check out the second knife when I noticed something strapped to one of the trees. Another damn camera. Sure enough, the little red LED light was blinking. So much for the knife. He was watching me once again, and could see I knew it.

I looked over the water one more time, pushing my luck on the staying hidden part of the instructions, but I needed to know where I was. To the east I could see a change in water colour on the horizon and recognised the outer reef. I had to be somewhere in Barkers National Park. There was very little in the park beyond a grid of marl roadways lined with narrow canals promoting the growth of mangroves and housing several species of protected birds. On the northern shore was a kite surfing school, and a horseback tour over there somewhere, but I didn't think the stables were in the park. The place was deserted most of the time.

Following the stones, I pushed through the undergrowth and was surprised to find a pathway open up almost immediately. A screen of foliage had been left, but a narrow trail had been cleared beyond that, and going by the fresh cuts, the work had been done recently. The woods were dense and without the trail there was no way I would have been able to penetrate the thickets without a machete. I followed the path, with sharp branches scraping at my arms and legs. I hadn't gone more than 20 metres when I came to a T-junction. The trail ahead was more overgrown and hadn't been fully cleared, but a turn to the left had been.

I tried to see what lay in front as I turned the corner, but all I could make out was the trail curving away and either side a mass of dense woods. Continuing down the path, I soon spotted something darker, and my nerves tingled. I was completely alone, in an isolated part of the island, where no one knew to find me. Civilisation, people and gorgeous beaches were less than a mile or two away, yet I could die here and be reduced to dust before anyone stumbled across my remains.

Forcing one foot in front of the other, I continued, and when the path met another tee, a building appeared on my left. It was an old single-storey concrete structure with a tin roof. Brush and trees had overgrown all around, claiming the unused building as part of the coastal woods. The area in front of the structure had been recently cleared, revealing a rusty metal door. To the right of the tee, the trail had been knocked back just enough for passage. I looked at the ground and noticed an array of footprints in the damp soil. Few were distinct, as someone had obviously walked back and forth many times. What I could make out appeared to be from the same shoe.

I was not in the least bit excited to enter the building, but I figured it was the next step in this madman's silly game. Another tiny, blinking red light caught my eye, and I spotted the camera mounted to the roof, aimed my way. I wondered how many people around the world were caught up watching this bullshit by now. I was tempted to provide the viewers with another rude sign, but provoking the loony probably wasn't in my best interests, so I walked up to the door instead.

The metal was painted dark green to match the walls, long since faded and flaking to reveal patches of brown rust. I guessed the building had once been some kind of maintenance or storage facility for the park, but clearly abandoned for years. Taped to the door was another laminated sheet.

Come inside.
Put on the helmet and do not remove it.
You will not be able to see.
You will receive verbal instructions from there.
Enter the next door only when told to do so.

I should have let myself drown on the last challenge. He expected me to step inside this creepy old building, effectively blindfold myself, and then do whatever I'm told next? I'd heard about one of those gory horror movies where people were trapped in a room and every way they tried to escape was booby trapped with disgusting ways of maiming them. Why would anyone want to watch something like that? Why would anyone want to make a movie like that in the first place? Because some people were indeed willing to pay to watch it, I supposed. If we still held Colosseum-style gladiatorial combat to the death, I was sure they'd fill the stadiums. And yet we call ourselves civilised.

I had a personal rule: I refused to pay for anything that scared the shit out of me. Rollercoasters, horror movies and dentists were all on that list.

Why my brain was serving up these thoughts was beyond me, and certainly not helpful, but I tried to calm myself. There would be no challenge three if he chopped me up on number two, and I was sure he wanted me to make it through his tests. At least until the final challenge, when the show could come to an end. That one might be a little more unpredictable and harmful. Of course, I'd almost drowned on challenge one, but that was more due to my ineptness at puzzles and reluctance to admit defeat. I had always been a regulator breath away from safety. Skylar Briggs's pinkie couldn't say the same. But even if I'd failed the challenge, the games could have continued.

Before I could conjure up more visions of vicious traps, I pulled on the door handle and dragged the heavy old door open.

13

INDIAN CREEK

The heat and humidity hit the two FBI agents as they descended the stairs of the Learjet to be greeted by a Caymanian immigration official. Beth had finally stopped sweating and wrestled herself into a pant suit in the tiny airplane lavatory. As she stepped to the apron at the base of the stairs, she could already feel a trickle of sweat returning, running down her back. They were both used to the tropical climate in Florida, but it was still a shock after the chilly air-conditioned cabin.

Within three minutes, their passports had been stamped and they found themselves in a Caymanian government vehicle pulling out of the FBO of Owen Roberts International Airport. Their satellite uplink on the Learjet had been spotty, but they'd followed most of Jensen Massey's Internet broadcast. They had also received more background information on the kidnapper and the Briggs family. So far, there was no obvious connection beyond residing in the same part of the country.

"Did you see how small this place is?" Kowalczyk said, staring out of the back window of the SUV. "You could see the entire island end to end on approach. How the hell can this guy hide in a place this small?"

"Twenty-two miles, sir," the driver commented in accented English.

"What's that?" Kowalczyk asked.

"Da island, sir, it's 22 miles long," the man repeated.

"Most of it looked like swamp," Kowalczyk muttered back.

"Mangroves and woods, sir," the man said, and Beth noticed his frown in the rear-view mirror, "not swamp."

Massey continued to rant about the lies the world was being told, and Kowalczyk rolled his eyes. "Fucking radical bullshit," he mumbled. "No wonder we can't tell these idiots the truth."

Beth started to say something, but thought better of it. The less interaction they had, the better as far as she was concerned. Fixing her partner's shortcomings wasn't her problem, and she wondered for the umpteenth time what his wife had seen in him. Someone for everyone, she thought. The woman must be a saint, or a complete sap.

"Definitely looks like a basement," Kowalczyk commented, and angled his mobile towards Beth.

"Not a basement, sir," the driver said, glancing in the rear-view.

"Really?" Dan replied. "Well, it sure looks like a good old-fashioned basement to me. Concrete walls, no windows, poor lighting."

"Do you see any water in der, sir?" the driver asked, and Beth sensed he was grinning.

"Of course not," Kowalczyk snapped back.

"Well, if it be a basement underground, you'd be seeing water, sir," the driver answered, and Beth guessed he was enjoying this. "Do ya see all da hills and such around here, sir?"

Kowalczyk looked out the window. "I can't see past all the buildings, but the island looked pretty flat flying in."

"As a pancake, sir. You dig down six feet and you'd be standin' in two feet o' water."

Kowalczyk grunted. Beth suppressed a grin of her own.

"If it's not a basement," Kowalczyk challenged, "what kind of building is it?"

"Just about any house on da island, sir," the driver replied.

"'Bout every home built wit concrete block that way. Locals' homes dat is, sir. All da fancy rich people homes, dey like da windows everywhere 'cos dey got da money to pay da big electric bill. Local home have da smaller windows, house stay cooler dat way you see."

"The wall behind the girl appears to be painted concrete block," Beth noted. "Do the local homes not use drywall on the inside?"

"Most do," the driver conceded, "but da poor folks don't. Could be a garage or outbuilding or some sort too. But only rich folks have da garages, and dey like to paint dem brighter colours."

They were on a dual carriageway and passed under a long bridge, causing the feed on the mobile phone to drop out for a few moments. Beth pulled a computer tablet from her bag and woke it up, clicking to a map of the island she'd already studied on the plane. They came back out into the bright sunlight and the cellular modem on the tablet connected. A small dot moved on the map, showing their location.

"This is the tourist area of the island, correct?" she asked the driver.

"It's da visitors' area, yes," he replied.

"How do you mean, visitors?" she questioned politely.

The driver negotiated a roundabout in what seemed like an endless series of them. "The tourists are mainly on Seven Mile Beach, over to da left of us," he explained, and Beth saw the long, curved beach labelled on the map. It was only a few hundred yards west of them but blocked by hotel buildings and businesses.

"Dis strip behind da Seven Mile Beach dey decided to call Seven Mile Corridor, and it's where most of da foreign residents stay and people have der holiday homes and such. So more like visitors dan tourists, if you get my meaning."

"I do," Beth agreed, and Kowalczyk sat silently brooding over the pleasant conversation being had without his involvement.

Beth stared at the narrow strip of land they travelled along, with the broad North Sound to their right and a larger extent of land ahead to the north, forming a shape similar to the head of a hammer.

"And north of here, that's called West Bay?"

"Yes, ma'am," the driver replied. "Dat's where we're heading."

"Is that visitors, tourists, or locals?" Beth asked.

The driver laughed. "Dat's a mixture, is best way to say it," he replied. "On da water, you find condos and some hotels for da tourists, and den homes and condos for da visitors. Den, in da town itself, it's all da local folk."

Beth studied the map as they continued north. "So, our kidnapper takes this young lady from her home in West Bay," she tapped her finger on a mark she'd made on the map in The Shores. "He has the policewoman enter the water from a dock in West Bay," she traced her finger over to the boat ramp which was only a third of a mile away, "and he has all this coordinated and the kidnapped girl on screen within an hour of her being taken."

She looked up at the rear-view mirror and caught the driver looking back at her. "Doesn't seem like enough time to get clear of all the expensive property you're describing along this stretch of the island."

"If he hurried, he could reach da airport area or da back o' George Town," the driver replied. "Plenty o' building look like dat around der. But he'd be rushing some."

"Where does Seven Mile Corridor end?" Beth asked.

"You lookin' at da map?"

"Yup, and I see where we are on Esterly Tibbets Highway."

"Okay, dat last roundabout back der," he replied, "dat's da end o' da corridor, next buildings and such you see in a mile or so, we be in West Bay."

Beth drew a line across the map using the stylus for her tablet. She showed Kowalczyk.

"We're looking for a dwelling or building Massey has a connection to above this line. Maybe he rented some place, or found an abandoned structure."

Kowalczyk grunted. "Maybe. Or maybe he took off by boat."

"That look like a boat to you?" Beth asked, pointing to the feed on the mobile.

"No," he snapped back. "Just saying he could have got a lot farther away than you're saying if he left by boat."

They had come to the end of the dual carriageway and turned right. They were now approaching a sea of vehicles and Beth could just make out water beyond them between several buildings. Beth powered down her tablet and shoved it in her bag.

"I think he's close by," she said firmly.

"Well, that's the assumption bullshit that got you in trouble on the Indian Creek case," Kowalczyk curtly replied. "You're not dragging me aboard your sinking ship. We're here to observe, help where possible, and only when asked."

The SUV pulled to a stop as there was no way through the mess of vehicles parked at odd angles everywhere. A policeman was trying his best to get cars moved to keep an open lane but wasn't having much luck. Beth got out, then leaned back in. "Thanks for your help, sir, much appreciated," she said to the driver.

Kowalczyk snorted.

"Fuck you," she directed at her partner and slammed the door.

14

TALKING UNDERWATER

Whittaker spread a map of the North Sound out across the table under the pop-up tent. Taking a pencil, he used the edge of an A4 notepad as a ruler and drew a line across the map, leading away from the boat ramp.

"Sir?" Jacob called, jogging across the car park towards the tent. Whittaker looked.

"We found the van, sir," Jacob announced.

"Where?" Whittaker asked.

"Behind some homes, back of Glade Drive, sir."

"Just over here?" Whittaker asked, pointing to the north-west.

"Yes, sir," Jacob confirmed. "Not more dan half a mile from da Briggs's house."

"The van?" AJ asked, surprising them both.

"Where did you sneak in from?" Whittaker asked, turning around.

"I came in through the back of Tukka West – figured it was better he didn't see me on the camera," AJ replied, her hair dripping water. "I had to park back on Garvin Road, it's a mess out here," she added, nodding towards the road.

A man and a woman dressed in suits walked towards them, and Whittaker groaned.

"Feds are here," he said quietly.

"They're FBI?" AJ asked.

"I don't know if they always had that look, and the movies mimicked it, or the other way around," he said with a smirk, "but they all look the same."

"Detective Whittaker?" the man asked as he walked up, holding out his badge.

Whittaker nodded.

"Special Agents Kowalczyk and Ricci, FBI," he announced, and extended a hand.

Whittaker quickly shook the man's hand, then repeated the procedure with his partner.

"Beth," she said, and smiled.

"This is Constable Tibbetts," Whittaker said, holding a hand out towards his officer. "Jacob was first on scene along with Constable Sommers, who you've no doubt seen on the feed." He held out a hand towards AJ. "And this is AJ Bailey. She and Reg Moore, the gentleman down the boat ramp over there, handle much of the diving for us."

"She left us a sign, Roy," AJ blurted, ready to be over with the formalities.

"Let me guess," Whittaker replied. "East."

"Exactly," AJ said in surprise. "Wasn't much down there, just two of the extra dive weights I gave her, but she'd lined them up facing east."

"How do you know she left them?" Kowalczyk asked, his face stern behind his aviator sunglasses.

"Because they're one-pounders which most people don't use and they're marked 'MM' for Mermaid Divers," AJ quickly retorted.

"Look at this." Whittaker led AJ over to the computer in front of one of the officers. "Roll that video please."

The footage began with Nora kneeling on the sea floor in front of the table where she had completed the puzzle.

"She did it, huh?" AJ asked. "She was working on the puzzle when I got in the water."

"She did, just in time too," Whittaker confirmed.

Nora looked up at the camera and put her hands together.

"That's weird. Nora is not religious at all," AJ commented.

"Wait, watch this," Whittaker said, pointing at the screen.

Nora dropped her left hand and slid two fingers of her right hand vertically before adjusting her mask.

"North," AJ confirmed. "That's sign language for north. It's how we talk to each other underwater."

"That's not exactly the sign for north," Beth said, bending her hand at 90 degrees before making a similar sliding motion. "That's the sign for north."

"American sign language," AJ and Whittaker replied at the same time.

"She did the UK sign for north," AJ clarified.

Beth grinned. "Cool, so she's telling you she went north?"

Whittaker returned to the map and pointed out the line he'd drawn across the sound. "That's straight east from the dock here."

"It just heads out into this big lagoon," Kowalczyk pointed out.

"Sound. It's the North Sound," Whittaker corrected. "It's where she did the first challenge. But she gave us the signal on the feed after the challenge, and the only spots deep enough for the challenge are farther offshore than we anticipated."

He drew a second line at 90 degrees to the first, heading north to the coast of Barkers.

"That's how you knew the sign I found was east," AJ said. "It was the only direction that made sense if she's now gone north."

Whittaker tapped a finger on the peninsula of land forming the north-west corner of the sound. "I have a relative with a daughter who's deaf. I asked her about the sign. So my money's on Barkers here. If she went east to one of these spots in the sound, that's deep enough for the challenge. North would then take her to Barkers. She's leaving us a trail."

"This kid's a rookie cop?" Beth asked.

Whittaker and AJ both smiled. "She is," Whittaker replied. "Just nineteen years old, but smarter and more resourceful than your average teenager."

"As we arrived, did I overhear you saying you've found Massey's vehicle?" Kowalczyk asked.

"We have, yes," Whittaker said, taking his mobile from his pocket. He pointed to a spot on the map not far from where they stood. "He switched vehicles here."

"Switched?" Kowalczyk asked. "You know the vehicle he's in now?"

"We don't," Whittaker answered.

"Then he could be near where the van was found," Kowalczyk countered.

Whittaker sighed and turned to his constable. "Jacob, check with our man watching the sound. Find out if he's seen anything. Tell him to keep an eye on the shoreline at Barkers."

"Yes, sir," Jacob replied and stepped from the tent.

"Do you have men searching the surrounding area where the van was found?" Kowalczyk persisted.

Whittaker took another deep breath. "Agent, if you were a kidnapper, would you ditch the van in a relatively easy place to find, close to where you were hiding?"

"I'm not a kidnapper, detective," the agent retorted.

"Nothing yet, sir," Jacob said, coming back under the tent, and Whittaker welcomed the interruption.

"Okay," he replied, "thank you." He turned to AJ. "Did you speak with Reg? He left a message for you."

"Shit, did he?" she said apologetically. "I left my mobile in the van and didn't check it when I came out of the water. I rushed back here."

"No problem," the detective explained. "Get to the Yacht Club fuel dock. You remember Ben with the Marine Unit?"

AJ nodded. "Of course."

"He'll pick you up there. Massey allowed us one boat making sweeps to keep traffic clear of this end of the sound. Ben will covertly drop you near these coordinates I'm about to send him," Whittaker explained, tapping the map at his intersection between his east and north lines. "There must be a buoy on the surface for the aerial to transmit, so get close to the coordinates and find the buoy, then dive. Make a search pattern around the challenge site and see if there's any more clues. Don't touch anything that's not immediately useful, and stay away from that camera if you can, in case it's still on. He aimed it down at the puzzle on the table. Okay?"

"Got it. On my wa…" AJ started.

"So, you don't need anything from us, it seems," Kowalczyk interrupted sarcastically.

Whittaker stared at the tall man. "Can you get me a drone or a satellite with heat trace capability?"

Kowalczyk laughed. "That's funny."

Whittaker shrugged. "Then it appears you can't do much to help at the moment, agent."

"Wait a minute here," Kowalczyk snapped back. "You're serious? You expect the US government to redirect a satellite over your little island here?"

"I'm not expecting much at all, agent, but you asked about helping, and that would be helpful."

AJ knew she needed to leave, but this was too good to walk away from.

"You've got yourself a big mess going on, detective. I don't know what you have planned to deal with your man Massey here, but the FBI is on site, offering to help. You might want to take that seriously."

Whittaker took a half step towards Kowalczyk. "Just so we're clear, agent, this is *your* guy, *your* girl, and *your* mess. Why your citizens had to bring it to our peaceful island is beyond me, yet here we are. So far, apart from wasting our time second guessing what we're doing, you haven't brought much to the table. If you have something constructive, I'm all ears. Until then, my plan is to rely on my constable successfully navigating this fellow's party tricks and buying us enough time to figure out where he has the Briggs girl holed up. Then, we'll arrest him or put a bullet between his eyes, whichever seems appropriate in the moment. If you have the means to get me heat trace capability, it would be of great use. If not, I suggest you gather as much information as you can on Donovan Briggs and find his connection to Jensen Massey, because I guarantee this is about the father, not the daughter. He's in the back of Jacob's police car if you'd like to speak with him." Whittaker glared at the FBI agent. "Anything else you feel needs to be discussed before I get on with finding *your* kidnapper?"

Kowalczyk shook his head. "We'll talk to Briggs."

Whittaker turned to AJ.

"Sorry, leaving," she said quickly, and scurried away.

The detective pulled up a contact on his mobile and dialled the number.

"Casey? It's Detective Whittaker. Are you following this madness?"

"I am. What can I do to help?" the woman replied.

"Can you join me at the boat ramp by Calypso's five minutes ago?"

Casey laughed. "I can be there in three minutes. Will that do?"

"I'll take it," he replied and ended the call, glancing at the video monitor.

"Hear no evil," Massey announced into the camera on his Internet feed. "So I'll warn you in advance, you will hear untruths in this next segment."

The video feed switched to a prepared segment with Donovan Briggs standing on a podium addressing a crowd of people. He keenly announced the many contributions to the environment his company was making with clean energy policies and procedures. A series of speeches were edited together, saying much of the same thing. The counter in the corner had rolled past the 750,000 mark.

The two agents walked towards the police car, with Jacob following to unlock the doors.

"Still think he's on a boat?" Beth couldn't resist asking.

"Shut up," Kowalczyk growled.

15

TERMINATOR IN A BATHING SUIT

The old building didn't appear very big from the outside, so I'd expected a single room inside. I guess I should have known from the instructions talking about a second door, but it still surprised me to walk into a small area only two metres deep. It was the width of the structure, with no windows and one dim light glowing from above. There had to be power running to the place from somewhere. The floor was swept free of dirt and debris, but the concrete was stained and grubby looking from years of storm floods and neglect. The second door was located in the centre of the partition wall, and next to it a small table. On the table was a helmet. Two blinking red lights flickered from the dark recesses of the ceiling at either end of the narrow entry room, reminding me once again my every move was being watched.

The helmet wasn't a crash helmet like the one I wore on the back of AJ's Ducati motorcycle. It was more futuristic or military looking, with sharp angles. It was flat black, and the visor was dark tinted and presumably opaque. Around the base of the helmet was a black fabric skirt. I didn't know what or who was waiting for me through the next door, but if they weren't expecting me, I guessed the helmet I'd be wearing would freak them out. It looked intimidating. Of course, my skinny swimsuit-clad wet body sticking out from underneath might offset the Terminator vibe.

I really didn't want to put the helmet on. Whittaker told me to buy him as much time as possible, and I understood why. On the other hand, my goals in all of this were probably out of alignment with everyone else's. Currently, my main objective was to wring Massey's neck as soon as I could lay hands on him. He'd ruined my Sunday. Kicking Donovan Briggs in the balls held a strong appeal as well. As for the girl, having the unfortunate fate of being Briggs's offspring didn't bode well for her being someone I'd care to meet. With a bit of luck she'd be carted off to be pampered and mobbed by the press, and I could go home.

I slipped the helmet over my head and fell into complete darkness. Even looking down inside the helmet, I couldn't see a speck of light. The fabric skirt efficiently sealed the underside to my body, and the visor was black, as I'd predicted. Thinking about being unable to see was starkly different from being unable to see. A moment before, I knew my surroundings. Now, I felt disorientated and unsure whether I was about to walk into the table, or the wall, or something else that had silently encroached on my space.

"Hello Nora."

The voice scared the shit out of me. The helmet had speakers by my ears, so Massey's voice sounded like he was inside my head and I jumped, swinging my arms around.

"It's okay," his voice said in a soothing tone. "This is how we'll guide you through the next challenge."

"*Fy faen,*" I muttered and took a few deep breaths.

He laughed. "Try not to swear, Nora, we have many younger viewers watching."

"Shit, you can hear me?" I blurted.

"The world can hear you, Nora," he replied. "So if you could be careful with the swearing, regardless of the language."

"You're threatening to cut a young woman's fingers off and kill her at the end of all this, and you're concerned about offending people?"

The words came out before my filter kicked in. Well, I don't really have a filter, so I could only hope I hadn't pissed him off too badly.

"Fair point," he countered softly. "But Skylar and everyone watching are hoping you'll prevent any of that nastiness."

For the first time he struck me as someone who didn't sound like a monster. Or a madman. His voice, speaking to me so intimately inside the helmet, sounded placid and almost hopeful that things wouldn't become violent. Maybe he hid his angry, serial killer personality well, or had a split personality and was ready to snap into Looney Tunes at any time. But in that moment, he seemed like a reasonable human. I wondered if Whittaker had established communication with him yet. My heart skipped as I realised I might be the first contact with him since this shitstorm had begun. Talking directly to the man was Whittaker's top priority, but I was about the worst person to conduct any kind of hostage negotiation. I was far too honest for that. Blunt was the word AJ used to describe me, but I think she was being kind.

"Okay, let's get on with it," I said, scared I'd screw something up before we started.

"Find the door handle, Nora; it'll open towards you," he instructed, and I fumbled around until I felt the handle.

I opened the door straight into my foot. "*Føkk!*" came out before I could stop it, and I hoped my mother missed that part. "Sorry."

I moved my foot and opened the door, then felt for the door jamb to make sure I went through the opening.

"Close the door behind you."

I reached back, found the handle on the inside, and pulled the door closed. I could tell by how easily the door swung it was a lightweight interior door, and felt good about breaking it down if needed. The partition was painted black, but it had appeared cleaner than the concrete walls, and I wondered if Massey had built it himself. If he had gone to that much trouble, what could I expect next?

My breathing echoed around inside the helmet, and I hoped my nervousness wasn't being broadcast to the planet. I pictured that damn counter he had running on the screen and prayed it had stopped at the 30,000 I'd last seen. After my fumbling attempt at the puzzle, they'd probably all switched off by now. Fingers crossed.

"Nora, meet Skylar," Massey said. "And Skylar, meet your new best friend, Nora."

I stood still and wasn't sure whether the kidnapped woman was standing before me or this was a theoretical introduction.

"Hello," came the weak and shaky voice of a female American through the helmet speakers.

"Skylar?" I asked. "Are you okay?"

"No, I'm not okay," she replied, sounding feistier. "This asshole kidnapped me and I've been tied up for days. My father won't stand for this."

I rolled my eyes. Now she sounded like an entitled little spoilt brat. I didn't blame her for being pissed off and scared, but whining and pulling the daddy card was pathetic. And days? It had been about three hours.

Massey sounded slightly amused. "With that being said, this challenge is about what we hear, and what Nora will hear is Skylar," he explained. "Skylar will direct you around the room, where you'll collect a set of throwing rings. Once you have all four, your goal is to land the rings on a target across the room."

Great, now we were going to play fairground games, like some TV reality show. I never watched them, but I'd heard enough babbling about them over the years. It reinforced my feeling that Massey wasn't interested in hurting anyone. He was doing this for the attention. Whether that attention was simply his day of infamy, or if he had a bigger message, was hard for me to know, as I wasn't watching the broadcast. I was starring in the show. My worst nightmare. I quickly corrected myself; my second worst nightmare. The vision of Ridley's bloodied corpse laying on the deck refused to leave me alone at night, and I suspected it never would.

16

HEAR NO EVIL

"You'll have five minutes to complete the challenge, and you'll want to stay away from the railings," Massey said. "Good luck, and the clock starts now."

I waited for my first instruction but heard nothing.

"Well?" I said impatiently. "Are you going to give me directions?"

There was a brief pause before Skylar spoke.

"This is stupid."

I didn't know whether to laugh or shout at her.

"It's your body parts on the line," I replied. "I can find the door, no problem. I'm more than happy to go home."

"This isn't fair," she squealed.

"What are you, a five-year-old?" I'd said it before I could think about it. "Start directing me, or hold out your finger and let him lop it off and we'll move on to the next challenge. Shit, have him take two and we'll go straight to the end."

Skylar made a sound halfway between a cry and a groan. I waited.

"Move forward," she finally mumbled, and I took two steps ahead in the way I was facing.

"Go right," she said, and I turned to my right.

"Right!" she shouted, and I turned more to my right.

My hip touched something solid and a jolt of pain shot through my body, sending every nerve twitching. "*Fy faen!*" I yelled and jumped back. My tongue felt fuzzy and weird.

"I said right!" Skylar barked at me.

"I went right, you idiot," I moaned. "Damn that hurt. Was that a railing?"

"Yes, that's why I was telling you to go right," Skylar continued to argue.

"Listen, you, fu…" I stopped myself and thought for a moment. "What are you looking at?"

"I'm looking at you," she answered, as though it were the dumbest questions ever asked.

"Obviously, but are you looking straight at, or from behind me?"

"I'm looking at you," she replied more calmly.

"So your right is my left."

"Oh, I suppose," she muttered after a short silence.

"And the railings are electrified, so I'd appreciate you pointing them out to me."

"I can't do this," Skylar said quietly, and I could hear she was crying.

"We don't have a choice and we're wasting time," I replied, proud of myself for using 'we' when 'you' was the correct term. "Just remember to reverse the direction left or right when I'm coming towards you. Come on, let's go."

"Fine. Turn around," she said, sniffing the tears away.

I turned all the way around.

"Take two steps."

I took one step, moving slowly, and was about to take the second when Skylar shouted. "Stop! Turn a little to your right."

I hesitated before turning my best guess at 45 degrees to my right. Without a visual reference, I couldn't even tell the extent of my movements.

"Okay, now take two steps."

I did and was relieved when I wasn't met by another shock.

"Go one more step and reach out."

I nervously took another pace and stretched both hands out before me, above waist height, in case another railing resided close by. My left hand touched a wall.

"Move your hand down and left," Skylar instructed. "Shit, I mean right, down and right."

I took a deep breath and corrected the direction of my hand along the wall. It bumped into something solid and I winced, expecting another shock. But nothing came. I felt something moving around against my hand.

"That's two of the rings!" Skylar shouted excitedly. "They're on a hook, take them off and we'll get the other two. They're on the opposite wall."

I fumbled around until I had hold of the rings and lifted them from the hook. They felt like they were made of metal, about the diameter of a football, and heavier than I would have guessed. I turned what I hoped was 180 degrees and waited for my next direction.

"Okay, take one step, then turn right."

I took the step, then halted. "I'm going away from you now, so are you sure it's my right?" I wasn't keen on another zap. My tongue was just feeling normal again.

"Um, yeah, it's your right, turn right."

I turned to my right.

"Too much!" she shouted.

"Can you give me degrees? Or numbers of a clock?" I asked, "Give me some idea how much to angle each turn."

"What?" she replied.

"Okay, watch," I said, and put my hands out in front of me. I turned what I hoped was 90 degrees. It felt like it was.

"I just turned 90 degrees, a right angle, got it?"

"Okay," she replied, not sounding like she got it.

I turned halfway back. "So that's 45 degrees."

"You're confusing me," Skylar complained.

How anyone could reach the age of whatever she was, having grown up in a first world country, and not know the degrees of a circle was beyond my comprehension. I took a few breaths and imagined the clock winding steadily down.

"Look," I said, turning back to where I started. "This," I rotated my best version of 90 degrees, "is hard right. This," I continued, turning back half the amount, "is turn left." I rotated half again, which should have been 22.5 degrees. "And this is slight left. How's that?"

"Okay," she replied, with only slightly more confidence. "Take a step now."

"Am I facing the right way?"

"Yes, take a step already."

Maybe she'd taken a look at the timer as her voice held more urgency. I took the step.

"Two more steps."

I did as instructed.

"Now slight right and half a step."

I followed along and held a small hope she might get the hang of this.

"Hard left and take one step, then hard left again."

I moved with growing confidence.

"Shit."

"What's the matter?" I asked. "You were doing good."

"The stupid camera switched. You're coming towards me again. Well, you're actually sideways to me so it's really confusing and harder to see."

"Okay, is there anything in front of me?" I asked.

"I don't think so, but it's hard to tell from this angle. You've got to go past a railing and then turn… um, turn to your right to come to the wall."

"I'll start walking straight ahead and warn me if I'm going to hit a railing."

I took a tentative step and waved my hand in an arc ahead of me. I brushed something and a quick shock made my finger feel like it had exploded.

"*Faen!*" I groaned. "It's okay, I know where it is now, I need to stay left a bit."

I took another small step, veering slightly away from the railing, and when I wasn't zapped again, I took one more step.

"Stop there," Skyler said. "Take a hard right."

I rotated 90 degrees and paused. "That look okay?"

"That's good. Should be two or three steps and you'll feel the wall."

After two long paces, my outstretched hand touched the wall, and I made a quick sweep at the same height I'd found the other hook. My hand smacked the hook on the return pass and I pulled the two rings free.

"Okay, what now?" I asked.

"You have to go back to the middle of the room," Skylar explained. "So back track the way you came... no wait, there's a faster way. Turn all the way around."

I pivoted 180.

"Take three steps."

I did so and stopped.

"Remember the next part, as you may have to retrace from here, okay?"

Maybe she wasn't as stupid as I'd thought. She was thinking ahead now.

"Two more steps forward, then hard left."

I did as instructed, picturing my movements on a chessboard.

"One good step, another left, then step again."

Once I'd followed those directions, she told me to turn hard left and informed me I was now facing the target.

"Oh," Skylar blurted. "The camera switched again, I'm looking straight at you. I think this camera is right above the target."

"What is the target?" I asked.

"It's a stick on the wall, you have to land the rings on the stick, I think."

I pointed ahead of me. "Am I pointing at the target?"

"No, you're left and high," she answered, so I adjusted.

"Shit, sorry," she said, "I'm backwards again. The height is good, but aim more to your left."

I moved my finger with my arm extended straight, slowly to my left.

"Stop there, down just a little more."

I did so.

"Perfect, you're pointing directly at the target."

"Okay, I'll try throwing one and you need to tell me which way I miss, and then watch for where the ring lands on the floor so we can get it back."

"I will," she replied. "Hurry, we only have a minute left."

I tried to visualise the target where I was pointing, then slowly drew my right arm back and took a ring from my left hand. I realised I had a rough direction but no idea how far away the target was.

"What's the distance?"

"Huh?" Skylar replied.

"How far away from the target am I?" I asked, trying to keep my head still with my blindfolded eyes focused on an imaginary point I had to hit.

"Oh, shit," she mumbled. "I don't know, like eight or ten steps I guess."

I knew I was wasting time asking for more detail. It was time to throw a ring and hope for the best. Maybe she'd be able to guide me from there. I threw the first ring in what I hoped was a smooth arc and heard a muffled clatter as it bounced off the wall and hit the concrete floor. The helmet robbed most of the sound in the room so I couldn't tell what direction the noise came except that it was in front of me.

"That was way high and slightly right," Skylar said. "Shit, no. Your left. Sorry. It almost hit the ceiling and was a few feet to the left."

I rotated my feet and lowered my head a little to adjust the height. Or maybe I needed the throw it the same way with less force. I needed another data point to gauge the scale of my adjustments. I lifted my head back to where I hoped it had been, and sent the next ring sailing across the room.

"You hit it!" Skylar yelled, but I heard the ring hit the floor.

"What do I need to do differently?" I asked quickly.

"Oh, uhh..." she hesitated. "It landed on top of the post thing which is sticking out of the wall, so a bit lower."

I kept reminding myself to keep my feet and head still so I had my base position consistent, but I could feel my body swaying slightly as it does when you close your eyes and try to remain stationary. Taking the third ring, I made two practice movements, then let it go and listened carefully. I heard rattling, but nothing more.

"You got it!" she screamed. "It's on the post!"

I tried to shut out her excitement and breathe softly, staying focused on my point in space in the darkness before my eyes. I threw the fourth ring and this time there was more rattling and clinking, but still no sound afterward.

"You did it again!" Skylar squealed. "Hurry, hurry, you have to get the other two."

Shit, now I had to leave my perfectly calibrated position to retrieve the other rings with very little time left. Standing there wasn't going to get it done, so I began my steps of retracing my movements around the railing I stood behind.

"Okay, where are they?" I asked.

"Turn hard left and take two steps," Skylar hurriedly instructed, and I turned and boldly stepped.

"Reach down to your right, it's a few feet in front of you on that side."

Sweeping my hand around the floor, I knocked the ring once, then quickly gathered it up. I realised in doing so I'd turned my body and was no longer sure exactly which direction I was facing. I stood up.

"Where now?"

"Um, um, turn hard left and take one step," she said.

I did so, moving quickly.

"Stop!"

I came to an immediate halt and tried not to lean forward.

"Okay, careful. You're right next to a railing and they angle towards the target," Skylar explained, breathlessly, "Turn right."

I rotated what I hoped was 45 degrees.

"Okay, now take a step."

I took the step but was more tentative, knowing I was very close to being shocked.

"You need to get down on your hands and knees and reach out to your left, it's the other side of the railing."

I dropped to the floor, which was cool to the touch. I turned a little to the left to allow my arm to sweep farther and reached out, making another arc across the concrete. My fingertips knocked the ring away. I edged my knees forward and stretched out. My shoulder bumped something hard and instantly my body spasmed violently as the electrical charge shot through me. I dropped to the floor and lay there, shaking and rolling my furry tongue around my mouth. I clutched the ring in my fingers.

Shuffling backwards until I hoped I was clear of the railing, I lifted my head. If I didn't move quickly, it wouldn't matter if I banged my head or got electrocuted again. The clock would expire. I stood.

"Guide me back, let's go."

"We have 18 seconds. Shit," Skylar yelped, on the edge of panic.

"Guide me, damn it!"

"Turn, turn to your left," she began, and I rotated. "Step, take two and one small one, now stop!"

My legs still quivered and tingled from the shock and weren't keen on doing anything, but they reluctantly followed my urging.

"Turn hard right and take two more steps," she continued. "Oh shit, we're running out of time!"

I guessed I was back on the target side of the railing that I was supposed to shoot behind. There was no time to walk around. I dived to the floor and crawled under the railing – or where I hoped the railing was – and stood up. I turned 180 degrees and pointed ahead of me.

"Guide my finger again!"

"Oh, lower, lower. Now right... Shit! Your left. More. There, that's it!"

I took the first ring, made two practice swings, hoping my muscles had built enough memory to repeat my last two throws. Being shocked in between couldn't have helped. I hoped the shock hadn't rebooted my brain and erased all memory. I flung the ring and heard it rattle. When no sound followed, I immediately launched the final ring with the same effort, and held my breath. From the isolation of the helmet the clink and clank of the metal rings was softened, but I didn't hear a following thump on the concrete floor. After that, everything was drowned out by Skylar screaming in my ears.

"We did it, we did it!"

"Seriously?" I asked, amazed I could have got that lucky.

"With four seconds left," she enthused. "The last one swung all over the place but stayed on the target."

"Cool," I replied, slightly bewildered. I hoped my mum and dad saw that part.

"You better do something worthwhile with your fingers after all this shit," I said, wondering if Skylar had ever contributed anything worthwhile to the planet to date.

"We'll see after two more challenges," Massey said, his flat tone echoing in my ears, reminding me I was only halfway through this hell.

17

ASSUMPTIONS

Whittaker looked over at the two IT techs who were standing up, cheering. He allowed himself a brief smile.

"This will make us all old before our time."

He took a deep breath and once again studied the room in which Nora had completed the task. It was well lit, and approximately 20 feet square. The walls were concrete block brightly painted pale blue with broad red circles around the ring hooks and the target, where the four metal rings hung. The camera view had switched as Nora had moved around and no single view had shown the complete space, but Whittaker was able to piece together the details. Metal railings fabricated from heavy drainage pipe were strategically placed throughout the room. The whole set had clearly taken some time to assemble and decorate.

"Okay, back to it," Whittaker said, and stood behind one of his constables at the table. She had a satellite map of the island on her screen. Casey from the Department of Environment had arrived while Nora was completing the challenge, and stood next to the detective.

"Where are the buildings in Barkers, Casey?" Whittaker asked. "Any structure at all that's at least the size we just saw."

"There aren't many, Roy," she said, studying the map and thinking. "Zoom into the west side for me, please."

She pointed to a small red-roofed building tucked away at the end of a narrow gravel trail, away from anything else.

"That's storage," she explained. "And it's big enough. But it's stuffed full of equipment and junk. I don't think this guy could have relied on no one showing up there in the time it took him to construct all we saw."

Whittaker let her think it over some more. He scoured the map himself, looking for the tell-tale signs of any kind of man-made object amongst the woods, mangroves, marl roadways, and narrow waterways.

"I do remember an old building on the south side somewhere," Casey said, pointing to the coastline fronting the sound. "I think it was a storage facility and pump house years ago. It may have even been torn down by now. I only know about it as there are some trails to line fishing spots on the sound. Every once in a while, we do spot checks to make sure no one's using nets or traps. Been a year or more since I went by there though."

"Where exactly is this building?" Whittaker asked. "I don't see a roof anywhere."

"The mangroves along the shore turn into thick woods," she replied. "I bet the roof's covered." She shrugged her shoulders. "Or like I said, it might be gone by now."

"Did it have any windows?" Whittaker asked.

"I've no idea, Roy, I only walked by it a few times and it's buried in undergrowth and branches. Let me call someone whose been with the DOE longer than me, they might remember." Casey stepped from the tent to make the call, and Whittaker dialled a number himself.

"Sergeant, are the Firearms Response Unit ready?"

"Yes sir," came a Caymanian man's voice. "We have three vehicles and six men per vehicle, plus the drivers, sir."

"Okay, move them into Barkers," Whittaker ordered. "Assemble by the sea pond and await further orders. I'm getting a location now."

"Yes, sir," the sergeant replied, and they ended the call.

Casey walked back under the tent and pointed to the satellite image on the constable's screen. "It's still there apparently, but it's not been used for anything in years. It flooded so badly in Hurricane Ivan they decided it wasn't worth storing anything in there anymore."

She leaned in closer. "He said it's around the area between the shore and the south road. The trail is probably overgrown, but you should be able to find it."

"The cover might be good, seeing as this guy likes putting cameras all over the place," Whittaker commented thoughtfully. "Hopefully he won't see the lads coming. I'm sure that's where he is. I'd just like to hear from AJ first. She's diving in the sound and if Nora left us another set of direction markers, that'll be good enough for us to go in."

Whittaker walked to the other end of the table and spread out the nautical map he'd marked.

"That puts the building farther west of where we initially estimated, but that was from a basic north direction," he said, showing Casey his lines on the map. "You think the building is left of my mark, correct?"

"Best I can figure from what my co-worker said, yes," Casey replied.

Beth walked under the tent and joined them. "Any progress, detective?" she asked politely.

Whittaker was glad she hadn't brought her partner along with her and returned a pleasant smile. "We have a possible location. Hoping for confirmation soon."

Beth nodded. "That's good. I see what you mean about Donovan Briggs, detective. He's hardly cooperative considering his daughter is being held hostage."

"He swears he doesn't know Massey," Whittaker pointed out,

"and I'm confident he knows something about him, even if he's never met the man."

"We're running more thorough background checks on Mr Briggs and his company, as well as his daughter," Beth said, "He's very well connected politically in Florida, so if there's anything shady, he'll have it buried I'm sure. But we'll see what our analysts come up with."

"Will that be a problem?" Whittaker asked, eyeing the agent with concern. "His political connections."

"Not as far as I'm concerned," Beth replied.

Whittaker nodded. "Good. Let's hope your office feels the same way."

"We also have a team heading to Massey's house in St Petersburg," Beth continued. "I'll let you know if they find anything useful."

The detective paused and thought for a moment. "From our immigration records, we know he's been here on Cayman for three weeks," he said and looked up at the monitor where the Internet feed was back to a static shot of Skylar Briggs tied to the chair. "Jensen Massey put a lot of planning and thought into this. My guess is you'll find a very neat and tidy house of a man who didn't expect to return."

Beth considered the island policeman's words carefully before responding. "I'm sorry for my partner's lack of tact earlier, detective. He can be abrasive sometimes."

Whittaker shrugged his shoulders as he scanned his mobile, searching through the myriad of text messages for anything that might be of use amongst the well wishes and questions from family and friends. "I really don't care about tact, Miss Ricci. What I care about is putting an end to this debacle on our island." He looked up and managed a smile. "I'm very open to constructive help and suggestions, but second guessing and criticism is a waste of time. None of us can change what has already been done. We can only affect what happens next. And right now, I'm hoping what happens next is we catch this guy in the building he's using at Barkers."

Beth nodded. "Do you have an armed team, detective?"

"We do," he replied. "They're well trained, but I'd be lying if I said they were experienced in this sort of thing. We don't take many buildings by force on the Cayman Islands. Our Marine Unit has dealt with a few drug-smuggling boats over the years, but mainly our police work involves knocking on the front door."

"There's always a risk he'll kill the hostage," Beth said carefully. "I don't mean that as a criticism, detective, just a point of fact."

Casey stood back, listening intently to the exchange, stunned along with most people on the island that anything like this was happening in front of their eyes. And she had a front-row seat to the inner workings and decisions from one side of the confrontation.

"Two hostages," Whittaker corrected. "I believe Nora is in that building too."

"Which suggests he may be in the location where he plans to stay for the final two challenges," Beth commented.

"Perhaps," Whittaker replied. "Let me ask you this, Agent Ricci. What do you think Massey's main objective is?"

Beth thought carefully for a moment before replying. "The show," she said firmly. "He has a message to deliver."

"I concur. Which leads me to two important conclusions," he said, then paused a moment. "I suppose assumptions would be a more accurate term than conclusions."

He turned his mobile around and around in his hand as he continued. "Firstly, I don't think he's a killer, and he's hoping this concludes with Nora being successful. I don't see him as a man capable of cutting Skylar's throat when the door gets bashed down."

Whittaker felt his mouth go dry as he verbalised the possibility of such violence on his watch. He swallowed hard to carry on. "Secondly, he wants his whole story told, and he hasn't got to the good part yet. Killing himself or the girls would prematurely stop the story from being told. I'll be gambling those young women's lives on those two assumptions."

"Not sure if it means anything," Beth responded, "but I agree with you."

The detective looked over at the agent. "It helps," he said.

His mobile buzzed in his hand, and he quickly checked the text message. It was from Ben with the Marine Unit. He glanced out across the sound and quietly announced, "Our diver's in the water."

18

NAVY SEAL

AJ Bailey had entered the water in all manner of ways over the years, but none quite like the entry she had just made. The Marine Unit boat slowed to under 10 knots for her to sneak into the water from the corner of the broad swim step, avoiding the thrashing propellers. Even at the slower speed, the water had been akin to a washing machine putting AJ through the spin and rinse cycle.

Her mask was flooded and she was still tumbling, but at least she was submerged and hidden from view. She hoped. It was hard to tell. But once all the motion had stopped, she cleared her mask, made sure her strap was safely in place and kicked the few feet down to the sand. The drone of the motors slowly faded as she used her compass to orientate herself with no other way of knowing which way she was facing.

Ben had dropped her west of the buoy they'd spotted, so she set about her swim in search of the line. She was in shallow water, her computer reading four feet with her staying another foot or so off the sea floor to avoid kicking up the sand. It didn't take long, and she spotted a line ahead, but the depth was lessening as she approached. The rope hung loosely in the water, tied to a cement block lying in the sand and a new-looking white buoy bobbing on the surface. This was not the one they were looking for.

From the boat, they'd only seen two possibilities. Which wasn't surprising, as the only buoys allowed in the North Sound were for DOE dive sites out near the reef, and a handful of resort boat moorings near shore. In season, lobster and crab traps were legal, but couldn't be marked by a buoy. Finding two markers in the open water was a surprise. They'd chosen the shiny white one as they figured Massey would have recently placed it. Now AJ had to make a decision.

The second marker they'd seen didn't even look like a buoy, it appeared to be a piece of floating foam or debris. It was south-west of where she was, and at least 500 yards away. The plan had been for Ben to make an innocent-looking sweep of the western part of the sound under the pretence of keeping boats clear, before returning to a spot a few hundred yards north of her drop point. There he would slow, throw her a dragline, and haul her in like a stunt double in a James Bond movie. Or a Navy SEAL. At least, that was how she envisioned the process. If she took off in search of the second marker, she'd not only have to swim a great distance, but retrace her steps and then make it back to the rendezvous point. Ben would have returned long before she made it there and would wonder what had happened. She couldn't surface and signal, as the kidnapper was likely watching the area.

AJ held her compass in both hands ahead of her body and aimed south-west. She decided Ben was a smart man, he'd figure out to make a second perimeter run if she didn't show up on time. It was that or burn up more time and risk being seen repeating the whole process. She kicked hard, in long sweeping motions with her legs, making the fins do the work. AJ was much shorter than Nora and couldn't make the speed her Norwegian friend could manage. But her legs were strong from carrying heavy dive tanks around each day, and she set into a steady rhythm at a good pace.

South-west was the approximate heading she'd noted from the boat and she knew it could easily be ten or more degrees off either way. AJ wished she'd taken a more accurate reading, but they'd been convinced the white buoy was their target. Now she was swimming somewhat blindly towards a marker she would need to be within 50 or 60 feet of. The water clarity was excellent, but a pale 3/8-inch line was easily lost in the light-infused blue water.

AJ's thighs and calves began to burn as she pushed on, but there was no way she would let up. Her friend had been through more heartache and pain than anyone deserved, and now she was caught up in this latest madness. Just three weeks into a job that everyone had hoped would take her mind off the tragedy of losing her boyfriend to a vindictive Mexican cartel. This wasn't Miami, Chicago or even Jamaica; Cayman was a safe place. Police work here was supposed to be safe. AJ kicked a little harder.

Ahead, to her left, appeared something darker than the surrounding sand and patches of turtle grass. AJ veered that way, but the object seemed to stay to her left. And then it moved more to her right. A young nurse shark weaved its way in a wide circle around the strange bubble-making diver and AJ cursed herself for moving off course. She reset on the south-west heading and continued, making a mental note that her path was now offset by a step south. Too many deviations and she'd be lost in the middle of the sound with no option but to surface and flag Ben down. Or swim west until she hit the shoreline. She knew they didn't have time for that. Whittaker needed answers now.

AJ was more suspicious of the next dark object she saw, far to her right. She stopped swimming and watched carefully to see if it moved, but it appeared to be stationary. She headed towards it, figuring a weave in that direction would counter her earlier deviation. As she approached, the line to the surface came into view, and she recognised the cage and post that Nora had kneeled in front of 45 minutes earlier. AJ made a wide arc to avoid the camera mounted on the post, and once she had come around the back of the makeshift table, she saw the first dive weight in the sand.

The second weight was six feet beyond, and AJ settled into the sand behind the first one she'd spotted, using the second as her sighting. Taking her time and checking several times, she determined the heading was just off due north, at 354 degrees. After a quick look around for any other clues, AJ took a last look at the completed puzzle on the table before kicking away on a reciprocal heading for the white buoy.

By the time the line came into sight, her legs were screaming. She was mighty relieved to see the buoy and know she'd found her marker. Once she reached the line, AJ turned to the north and didn't ease up. The water was down to only three feet deep in spots and she let her fins skim the sand rather than break the surface. If the boat happened to race over her at this depth, she'd be propeller chum. All she could do if she heard the motors approaching was stand up and be seen. By the boat, and anyone else watching. Judging 200 yards while swimming at a wide-open pace was near impossible, and the water was continuing to thin. Much shallower and the boat couldn't reach her anyway.

AJ came to a stop and eased her head above the water. She took the reg from her mouth and sucked in a few deep breaths, panting from the effort. To the south-east she could see a boat and hoped it was Ben. The vessel was half a mile away but appeared to be coming her way. She put her reg back in and stayed low in the water with just her mask peeking above the surface. The boat was going to pass south of her, so once it was a hundred yards away, she risked a quick wave. The grey boat immediately turned towards her and slowed.

Having a 40-foot coastal patrol boat bearing down on her was a little unnerving, but AJ focused on the line she could see trailing in the wake. She took off her fins and stuffed them under the cummerbund of her BCD. As soon as the boat was alongside, shielding her from the mainland, AJ stood and shuffled in the same direction the boat was travelling. She could barely make any speed in the waist-deep water, but at least she was heading the same way as the line that skipped and bounced towards her. As the rope reached her, she lunged and grabbed hold with both hands.

The boat was going no more than five knots, but the pull on the line felt like it would wrench her arms from their sockets as her body, clad in dive gear, was dragged through the water like a sack of potatoes. She hung on with all her strength, but there was no way she could keep hold for long. The water shoved her mask askew, blinding her with salt water like a pressure washer stinging her eyes. She heard the engines drop to idle and the clunk of the boat coming out of gear. AJ could just make out the blurry image of the back of the boat in front of her and she stood and waddled towards the stern. With several strong hands pulling her from the water, she was dragged onto the rear deck where she rolled over with her tank clanking against the metal deck.

"That seemed to go well," she spluttered at the two officers looking down at her. They were both laughing. Shitty way to greet James Bond, she thought.

19

FACE TO FACE

So much for worrying about a quiet Sunday. I'd take the drunken moron over this shit. I'd been told to keep the helmet on, so I stood still in the room and waited, nervous to move anywhere in case I nudged a railing. It was strangely silent without anyone talking to me and I guessed the microphones had been muted as all the background sounds of movement had gone too. I had noticed them when they'd been talking, but I wished I'd paid more attention. Maybe I could have gleaned a clue from the noises.

I'd been caught up in the adrenaline rush of the challenge, but now, standing alone in the building, still blinded, I felt desperately vulnerable. The helmet dulled the sounds around me, but every once in a while I heard a hint of movement, and tensed with each scrape and knock. It was probably the tree branches on the old steel roof, swaying in the ocean breeze, but my mind began to conjure images of figures all around me. I felt the panic rising from within and swept an arm around me to prove I was alone. My hand hit something firm and I jumped, waiting for the surge of electricity. Nothing.

"The rails are no longer charged, Nora." His voice startled me. "Please be patient, you're perfectly safe."

Safe my arse, you prick. Somehow I managed to keep my ranting to a thought and didn't say a word. The speakers had muted again, and I relaxed a little. Although safe was not a word that described anything I was feeling. It occurred to me once more that I was in the unique position of talking to the kidnapper. I wondered if Whittaker had managed to yet. If he was already in communication, the last thing he needed was me interfering. If he wasn't, I was sure he'd want me to try.

Detective Whittaker had a lot more confidence in me doing things I was absolutely sure I shouldn't attempt. He had a calm, assertive manner about him that made me feel settled and centred in his presence. Then I find myself alone, up to my eyeballs in *dritt*, with no idea what to do. His calming bullshit wasn't helping me now.

Dealing with people wasn't my strength. On my list of worse jobs I could ever do, selling anything to anyone would be right at the top. "You don't need this stupid diet pill. You need a treadmill." Everybody has too much stuff and keeps buying more stuff because they think more crap makes them happy. The landfill is over-flowing with temporary joy-supplying junk. If the day ever comes that we're having to buy air to breathe, maybe I could sell that. "Here, buy some air, you actually need this." But then again, I'd get fired for refusing to sell air to the idiots.

Second on the list would be negotiating with unstable people. I figured my current situation fell into that category. What do I say to the guy? That stupid girl isn't worth going to jail over? Well, that's too late. He's already going to jail for kidnapping. I assumed he'd already decided it was worth all that to send out whatever message he seemed hell bent on streaming to the world. "How about you give up now and let's all go home for tea?" I'd almost be disappointed if he said yes.

"Why are you doing all this?" I finally asked. It was the best question I could come up with. Mainly because it was the only question that interested me.

There was silence inside the helmet and after a while I figured my microphone had been muted too. But then he replied.

"It's about the truth."

He spoke softly, but passionately, without anger. His voice was resolute, and with blindness heightening my senses, his words spread themselves across my consciousness. I was certain this man had placed his stake in the ground. He was tied to his position, and would fight until the end, however that may come.

"We live our lives in what we believe is a civilised world, where laws are upheld, and people in authority will do the right thing," he continued. "Until one day, life is turned upside down, and underneath the polished veneer of all we know and trust is a rat's nest of lies and deceit. Orchestrated by those with the purse strings."

I had no idea what he was specifically talking about, but his impassioned speech was impressive.

"Couldn't you have held a press conference instead of kidnapping someone and threatening their life?" I asked, thinking if he spoke that well, surely people would listen.

"Nora, we currently have 1.1 million people watching our Internet stream," he said with a hint of humour in his voice. "How many people do you think would have shown up for an IT engineer's press conference?"

My legs felt weak at the thought of all those people watching. The number was too big to fully comprehend. I always thought 'going viral' was a horrible term – I mean why would a virus be appealing? Now I was certain I hated the phrase. Apparently, I was part of the disease. Ullevaal Stadium was the largest venue in Norway, and if I remembered correctly, it held around 30,000 people for the football matches. I couldn't begin to do the math on how many times that stadium would be filled, emptied, and refilled, to seat all those eyes on me. Too many times. It was terrifying.

"Okay, but you've got the world's attention," I persevered. "Why don't you make your point while you can and let's be done."

"All in good time, Nora," he replied. "The audience continues to grow. People love a good spectacle."

"So this about your ego," I said before my non-existent filter could hold my tongue.

"No, in fact it's not about me at all," he responded, surprisingly calmly. "It's about people far more important than me."

I didn't feel much wiser as to why this man was putting us all through this, but I recognised his passion and believed him when he said it wasn't about him. Presumably, his videos were going out while we were between challenges and the public knew a lot more than I did about his cause. I kept thinking of other questions to ask and then worrying about aggravating the situation, so I stayed silent.

I heard the trees scratching and bumping the roof a few more times and shifted my weight from one foot to the other, trying to keep my leg muscles loose. For the first time, I realised how thirsty I was. Hungry too. I wasn't sure of the time, but I hadn't eaten since breakfast and guessed it to be early afternoon.

"Can I get a drink?" I asked.

"In just a minute," he replied, and I stepped back, bumping against a railing.

His voice didn't come through the speakers. He was standing next to me.

"*Faen*," I muttered and put my hands on the helmet to lift it off.

"Leave the helmet on, Nora," he said firmly, and I paused. "I'm going to pass a tube under the skirt of the helmet. Guide it to your mouth, and drink."

I fumbled for the tube and pushed it under the helmet until it found my lips. I was parched and about to suck on the tube, when I realised I had no idea what I was about to drink.

"Wait, what are you giving me?" I asked.

"It's water, Nora," he assured me. "Take a drink."

"You would tell me that regardless of what it was," I pointed out.

"Nora, if I wanted to harm you, don't you think there's a thou-

sand ways I could have done that without saying a word to you?"
he responded. "You're standing, blindfolded in the middle of a
room."

I shrugged my shoulders. He had a point. I sucked on the tube
and cool liquid that seemed just like water felt great going down
my throat. I didn't get dizzy or feel like throwing up, so I took
another long pull on the tube and quenched my thirst.

"*Takk*," I said and pulled the tube from the helmet. I felt him
take it from me. I had seen him on the video feed, but somehow I
couldn't picture him before me. His voice sounded kind, but his
actions spoke otherwise. I felt on edge and defenceless, yet calm
and curious more than frightened.

"I'm sorry to put you through this, Nora," he said. "I know
you've not had an easy time of things. But I'm afraid you fit the role
I needed."

I don't know how he knew who I was or anything about me,
but it confirmed for certain I'd been chosen. Maybe he thought I'd
be flattered. I wasn't. I hadn't thought about Ridley for a while
until he brought up what I'd been through, but this was a shit way
to be distracted. It was a bit like sticking pins in your finger to take
your mind off a headache.

"Let's just get on with it," I said flatly.

"Fair enough," he replied.

20

NOOKS AND CRANNIES

AJ's report on the heading she'd found, along with the GPS coordinates Ben gave them of the first challenge site, allowed Whittaker to update his map. His new trajectory to the shoreline at Barkers led to a small cove, where not far away amongst the trees was the concrete building Casey had told him about. The FBI agents had finally proven useful with a higher resolution satellite image in which the roof could be seen in the woods.

The Firearms Response Unit communicated over a secure digital radio frequency, and Whittaker listened intently as the armed police manoeuvred into position. A gravel road ran parallel to the shoreline with 200 feet of thick woods between them. Buried amongst the trees, shrubs, and undergrowth, was the cement block building. Alongside the road, narrow canals fed brackish water throughout the National Park, sustaining the mangroves cultivated to preserve the natural habitat. An old wooden plank served as the bridge across the canal to the single trail leading to the old pumping station and storage.

Two of the police vans parked on the road, a hundred yards on either side of the trail, and the constables in full tactical gear brandishing automatic weapons made their way on foot towards the makeshift bridge. The entrance to the park was guarded by several police cars, and the third van waited at the intersection just under half a mile west. With Marine Units watching the coastlines, all exits were blocked or under observation, and everyone was in position. Whittaker gave the order to take the building.

The RCIPS Firearms Response Unit consisted mainly of men in their thirties with ten years or more on the force. For most of them this would mark their first time taking a location by force, and a mixture of nerves and excitement buzzed through the group. They pushed their way through the overgrown foliage of the trail until they reached a tee where the pathway split. Ahead lay the building, and to the left, the North Sound. They moved forward, the narrow cut in the woods keeping them single file until they arrived at the east door. Four men moved to the right of the structure and four more moved left, both groups trying their best to fight through the brush to reach the west end where a second door was rumoured to be. The constables on the right side found a pathway cleared after they broke through a light screen of branches, and soon found the other entrance. The team on the far side made no progress and returned to the east entry. Once in position, both teams flung open the doors and entered the building, announcing their presence.

The east group found the exterior door led into a dimly lit entry hall the width of the building, with another door in the centre next to a small table. They swiftly opened the second door and burst into a brightly painted, well-illuminated room with a series of oddly position metal railings. They announced the room was secure and waited for the other team.

From the west, the men charged through an unlocked door into a room with bare concrete block walls and one interior door. A sturdy chair was bolted to the floor, and a table set up like a command station with three computer monitors, an office chair and a stack of computer equipment. The monitors were on and one showed a split screen of multiple cameras, several of them showing the police inside the rooms. They opened the interior door to meet their fellow officers in the brightly painted challenge room. Four metal rings rested on a pole mounted to the wall by the door.

Whittaker received the radio call reporting the building was definitely the location of the second challenge, but now deserted. It was information he already knew. Massey had shared the raid live-stream across his feed from the cameras mounted inside and outside the old pump station. Up until then, what appeared to be a live shot of Skylar tied to the chair had been on the screen for over 15 minutes. 'Stay tuned, you won't want to miss this,' had scrolled across the bottom. The detective assumed that must have been a looped video playing while Massey escaped with both women. But where?

Whittaker spread the map out across the table and studied the marl roads he'd already stared at too many times. They made up a simple criss-cross of lanes on the National Park peninsula. The name itself made the area sound expansive, but in fact it was less than two miles from the entrance to the tip, and less than half a mile wide. If it were meadows or simple woods, the whole place could be searched in less than an hour with a team of constables. But the dense foliage, mangroves and waterways made for endless hiding spots.

If Massey had seen or sensed the raid coming and was now on the run, that was one thing. But Whittaker guessed he wasn't through with his show, and his scrolling message indicated the same. It was as though he had predicted the location of the first building would only be hidden for a short time, and he'd planned to move all along. If that was the case, he had a second location and was on his way, or already there. But how could he sneak himself, two prisoners and presumably some electronic equipment past the police who had already been staged in Barkers?

The southern shoreline of the Park met the western coastline of the North Sound in the north-west corner where The Shores was located. There were no roads out of the luxury home neighbourhood into Barkers, and the narrow waterways bordered the park, with no bridges across. But spanning the canal at a narrow point wouldn't take major construction. He had assumed Massey had driven Skylar to the building in whatever vehicle he used after the van, but as yet no vehicle had been discovered, so Whittaker began to wonder if the trip had been made partially on foot.

He grabbed the secure digital radio and ordered the third van to the end of the road where the Park met The Shores. He then used his mobile to call the sergeant and sent several police cars to the corresponding border from the residential side. Although he desperately wanted to put the chopper in the air and search from above, he was reluctant to provoke Massey any further while the man held both women. Raiding the building was certainly an aggressive move. As the kidnapper appeared to have predicted the strike, Whittaker hoped to smooth over the aftermath. But if Massey didn't make contact shortly, the detective had already decided an all-out search would begin.

"Sir," one of the IT techs called out and pointed to the monitor.

Shots of the police milling around and searching the concrete building continued, but a new statement scrolled across the bottom of the screen.

'Nice try, RCIPS. Anything overhead and Skylar loses body parts.'

Whittaker breathed a sigh of relief that he hadn't sent the helicopter up, and looked around for the female FBI agent. He'd decided she was useful. She was standing with her partner near Jacob's police car, where Donovan Briggs remained ensconced. The detective preferred to deal with the far more pleasant Ricci, but time was against him. He waved to the two agents, and they walked towards him.

"I take it you saw his latest message?"

The two agents nodded as they entered the tent. Whittaker returned to the map on the table. "Here's the building; here's where we had our men staged; and here are the roads they approached from," he said, pointing to the locations on the map. "I have men searching the border between Barkers and The Shores, as I believe rather than going all the way around to the main entrance of the park, he may have walked Skylar to the building from this point." He tapped on the map. "This area is cleared and waiting for construction, but it's where they store vehicles and heavy equipment. If the vehicle he switched to is there, then he walked in and crossed the canal somewhere. In which case, I wouldn't expect him to return as he would predict we'd find the car."

"But you haven't found anything there yet?" Beth asked.

As if on cue, his mobile rang. It was the sergeant.

"Whittaker."

"We have a car with no plates parked between a front loader and a skip in da corner of Da Shores. Matches the description of a rental dat went missing dis morning from Yacht Club. The couple didn't know until dey came back from der snorkelling trip."

"10-4, have your men look for a way across the waterways into Barkers," Whittaker replied. "Should be a bridge of some kind."

"Yes, sir," the sergeant replied and ended the call.

Whittaker turned to the two FBI agents. "With that verified, unless I'm missing something, he's still in Barkers. I don't see a way he could've got out."

"He's not gone live again over his feed, so he may still be on the move," Kowalczyk said. "Is there anywhere he could have switched to a boat?"

"We've been watching the shoreline since we figured out he was in Barkers, and the Marine Unit have kept all traffic away," Whittaker replied. "I really don't think he's left by air or sea."

"What does he need next?" Beth asked.

"Another location," Kowalczyk responded, and Whittaker was pleased the man seemed to have dismounted from his high horse and decided to contribute.

"He still has two more challenges and now three people in his group to deal with," the agent finished saying.

"We've checked these other storage buildings and they haven't been disturbed," Whittaker explained. "We're out of buildings in

Barkers. His message is clear — nothing overhead — which suggests we could spot him from the air."

AJ walked under the tent and joined the group, her hair still wet and a baggy Mermaid Divers T-shirt covering her damp swimsuit.

Whittaker acknowledged her arrival. "Good job, AJ, thanks for confirming the direction."

She shrugged her shoulders. "No problem, but I hear he bolted."

Whittaker nodded. "We missed him, but we think he's still inside Barkers," he said, scratching his head. "How he's evading our guys I have no idea. We've swept all the roads, and I don't see how he could make it through the mangroves and woods."

AJ leaned over the map. "What about the little canals alongside the roads?"

"Wouldn't the officers see anyone in there from the roadways?" Kowalczyk asked.

"In many places, yes," AJ said, "but there are loads of little nooks and crannies to hide in, and some of the banks are steep. Be hard to see them from the middle of the road if they stayed by the edge of the canal. The road varies its height above the water as they act like levees in the storm floods. In some parts the roads are five or six feet above the canal."

Whittaker took out his mobile once more.

21

VIBRATIONS

I had no idea where we were, except that we were on the water. I was led from the building and guided through the woods, then assisted aboard what I guessed was a canoe. The bottom seemed to be curved, and it was narrow. I could easily touch both sides. He'd made me keep the helmet on and encouraged me to behave by poking a gun barrel in my back. Honestly, for all I knew, he could have been prodding me with a stick or a carrot, but the downside of that gamble didn't seem worth the risk. He'd assured me Skylar would be the first victim if anything went wrong, which I found interesting. He was assuming I'd be more likely to behave with her at risk. In my mind, she hadn't earned that status yet, but I didn't tell Massey.

I could barely hear Skylar grunting and snorting through her nose, so apparently she was gagged again. We were both made to lie down in the canoe while our kidnapper paddled. It seemed like he was taking his time and we stopped on several occasions. I heard what sounded like a vehicle go by at one point and wondered where we could be in the North Sound with a road close by. It was hotter than hell inside the helmet and we were either passing under overhanging trees or there were lots of clouds, as the sun on my skin alternated between scorching and bearable. I couldn't feel a lick of breeze, but I was in the bottom of a canoe, so it wasn't surprising.

It felt like we'd been paddling for 10 or 15 minutes when we finally stopped and bumped against the shore.

"Stay there," Massey ordered, and the canoe rocked as he stepped out.

There was more bumping and jerking, but I couldn't hear well enough to tell what was going on. After a minute, he helped Skylar out and then he addressed me.

"Get to your knees and hold out your hand."

I did as he ordered and felt a firm grip on my hand. The thought occurred to yank him as hard as I could and send him into the water, but being blinded took all my confidence away. I had no clue where we were at all. I couldn't imagine we wouldn't have been spotted if we'd paddled along the edge of the North Sound.

"Take a step out," he said.

I wasn't sure whether to expect a splash into the shallow ocean or the sharp rock of ironshore, so the firm, smooth bank surprised me. Massey pulled and after a bit of slipping underfoot, I was standing on dry land.

"I'm putting your hand on Skylar's shoulder," he told me, and lifted my arm.

It was strange to touch the person I'd heard about, spoken with, but only seen as a character in an online broadcast. I was now connected to the human being known as Skylar Briggs. She was shorter than me, and petite by the feel of her thin shoulder. She tensed as my hand rested upon her, but quickly relaxed and I gave her what I hoped was a comforting squeeze.

I heard the rustling of trees and sensed Massey moving around us.

"Take the trail," he said firmly. "Stop when I tell you."

Skylar walked forward, and I followed, taking tiny steps so I didn't kick her heels. My shoulders brushed through foliage and small branches slapped against the helmet, making me jump. We went about twenty paces into the woods.

"Stop there," he called from behind us.

I heard more rustling and movement, but it was faint, and I guessed he was still down by the water. It sounded like he was dragging something, which had to be the canoe. I moved my hand to the side of Skylar's face and touched the tape across her mouth.

"Are you okay?" I asked. "Nod or shake your head."

She shook her head.

"Are you hurt?"

She shook her head again.

"I didn't ask if you were pissed off. We're both pissed off," I clarified. "But has he hurt you physically?"

She shook her head.

"Are your hands tied?"

She nodded.

"Does he have a gun?"

She nodded again.

"Be quiet Nora, enough chatter," Massey said, sounding more disinterested than angry. "Two more challenges and you can both go home. Just play along and everything will be fine."

I was glad my vision of a cartoon carrot hadn't led me to do something stupid.

"You mean, just win the challenges and everything will be fine," I pointed out.

"Have faith in yourself, Nora. I do," he said. "Walk."

Skylar continued with me in tow.

"Is that why you chose me?" I asked.

"Partly," he replied, "and partly because the public would find you interesting."

"I'm not interesting," I said, my voice echoing strangely inside the sweaty damn helmet. "Dogs like to take a shit facing north or south — that's interesting. I'm just a policewoman on a quiet island three weeks into the job. No one cares what I do."

"They certainly do now," he replied. "Push the door open,

Skylar, and go inside." I felt the prod in my back again, and knowing it was indeed a gun, I flinched. "You're quite the celebrity now, Nora; you'll be able to ride a wave of fame and make a fortune."

"If you knew anything about me at all," I protested, "you would know I have zero interest in attention, or money."

I stumbled over the threshold but regained my balance and felt an even floor underfoot. My steps echoed slightly, and the floor gave a little with each step. I guessed it was a wooden structure of some sort.

"Yes, I do realise that," he replied. "And I share your reluctance for the limelight. But sacrifices are being made for the greater good."

"And we're the lucky sacrifices," I scoffed.

"All three of us, yes," he replied. "I'm going to take your hand and lead you across the room," he continued, and I felt him lift my arm from Skylar's shoulder. "Stay there, Skylar," he ordered, and guided me a few steps before I heard another door open. He put his hands on my arms and steered me from behind, so I took small steps again, unsure of what lay before me. He turned me around.

"There's a chair behind, you," he said. "Please sit down."

I felt the edge of the chair against the back of my legs and lowered myself until my backside touched the seat.

"Keep the helmet on for now, Nora. Stay seated and I'll give you further instructions shortly."

I heard the door close and a lock of some sort slide in place. I was back to feeling alone once again. I was seated in a room that could be empty apart from me and a chair, or full of sharp objects and booby traps. The idea of going through life without sight was unimaginable. To a person with sight. I felt overwhelmingly fortunate, despite my current predicament.

All was quiet. I could feel more than hear their movements in the other room. I noticed this building was very different from the first one, where I had no clue they were present until Massey spoke to me. But this structure vibrated and reacted with each step. It was faint, but I heard a low drone from somewhere distant, and above me, the sound of air moving. I realised I wasn't sweating anymore, and the room was a bearable temperature. It was air-conditioned.

I was completely puzzled as to where we might be. Hopefully, Whittaker had found the directional clues I had left earlier, but I'd been at a loss about how to continue leaving marks since we left the first building. I'd dragged a toe in the dirt as we'd walked each trail, but I figured our footprints would be evidence enough. The problem was the water. We'd been in the canoe for a while, and although we'd moved slowly, I had no way of truly gauging distance. I'd also lost all sense of time.

My patience was wearing thin, and I felt my anger rising. Massey had carefully orchestrated every move to control the situation on his terms. I needed to change that. I could wait it out and continue participating in his stupid challenges, but I'd only scraped by the first two, and I doubted they'd get easier. Since being in Skylar's presence, I felt a greater responsibility to help her. I wasn't sure why. She was still the spoilt rich kid I barely knew, but touching her and sensing her fear through my fingertips had built a sympathy that surprised me. I felt a greater pressure to pass the challenges, along with a dread that I'd fail. It had become more than looking like a fool before the ridiculous number of viewers, or even my critical fellow officers, like Williams.

Escaping sounded far more appealing. Although I was locked in a room, it was time to take some of the control away from Jensen Massey. I began lifting the helmet off my head.

"You can take that off now," came his voice over speakers in the room.

So much for going against his wishes. I lifted the helmet off and looked around me. It was not what I was expecting.

22

ENGAGING SMILE

Beth and Kowalczyk listened intently to a radio feed coming across her computer tablet. It was a live link to the operations van parked down the street from Jensen Massey's home in St Petersburg, Florida.

In St Pete, FBI agent Don Brandt knocked on the door to the house and waited. Neither he, nor his partner Faith Graham, expected a response. He knocked several more times while Faith stepped across the lawn and peered through the front window. No lights were on in the home and the bright afternoon sunshine made it hard to see much inside. But she caught no movement.

"No response," Brandt announced over his collar-mounted microphone. "Send over the guys to bust the door open."

"Hold up," came the reply from operations command in the van. The man's voice clear in their wireless earpieces. "You have a neighbour coming your way."

Faith saw the man approaching from the house next door. He was wearing the ugliest golf trousers she had ever seen and a bright yellow golf shirt with a country club logo embroidered on the left chest.

"Hello there," the man she guessed to be in his sixties called over. "Jensen's not home."

Both agents presented their badges in a well-practised flip of the wrist.

"I was wondering when you'd show up," the man said. "Had some news crews come by earlier, according to my wife. I was playing 18 this morning."

Faith was glad his outfit at least had a purpose beyond scaring away the wildlife.

"I was just getting up to speed on all this nonsense in the Caribbean," the man finished, as he stopped a few yards away from the agents.

"You know Mr Massey well?" Brandt asked.

"Sure," the man said jovially, and then seemed to think about the implications. "Well, as a neighbour you understand. Not like we've gone on vacations together or anything. Backyard barbecues. Hold the ladder while we put up the Christmas lights. Been fishing a few times. He told us he was heading out of town for a few weeks and asked us to collect his mail and keep an eye on the place. I've been inside once a week just to check the AC's still working and what-have-you. Can't say we ever suspected he was off to kidnap someone and all this trouble he's caused. Most unlike the man."

"You have a key to the house?" Faith asked.

"Of course," the man replied, smiling at them.

"Would you mind getting that key?" she added.

"Oh, sure," he said, and finally beetled back towards his house.

Faith found herself transfixed by his generous behind, squeezed into the oddly patterned trousers. Was that plaid, or a patchwork of some description? She wasn't sure when none of the squares matched in colour. She tore herself away and wished she could steal back the storage space in her brain that the hideous garment now occupied.

After a less than a minute, fancy pants waddled back towards them and held out a door key. "Here you go."

Brandt put the key in the door and paused for a moment. Faith smiled at the neighbour. "Please head back to your house and remain inside, sir. Someone will be by to talk with you shortly."

The man looked disappointed but reluctantly dawdled away, glancing over his shoulder as he went.

Brandt unlocked the door and swung it open, confident no surprises lay in store as the neighbour had been in and out over the past few weeks. The house was a three-bedroomed bungalow with a large open-plan living space encompassing the lounge, dining room and kitchen. They could see the canal out the rear windows beyond a short backyard. They both donned gloves before entering and slipped covers over their shoes before leaving the doormat.

The place was spotless. Nothing was out of place. The fridge was almost bare, no cartons of milk to spoil, or left-over meals. Just a handful of jars that would keep forever. A few packets of frozen vegetables and an oven-ready pizza remained in the freezer. The front lawn had been neatly kept and, looking out of the sliding glass doors to the backyard, Faith noticed the weeds were pulled and pathways swept. He'd likely continued his gardener's regular visits.

The two agents moved from room to room, opening closets, cupboards, and drawers, without disturbing anything. In the master suite, Faith examined the walk-in closet and discovered half of the space was occupied with women's clothing. She picked up picture frames from the dresser and saw the now familiar Jensen Massey with a pleasant-looking woman with curly brown hair and an engaging smile. Several of the photographs were from international trips with distinguishing architecture behind the happy couple. One was the woman in a running race of some kind, a number pinned to her singlet.

Faith entered the last bedroom and found her partner already in the room. A futon sat against one wall and a large desk dominated the room, a chair on each side. The desk was clear of clutter with a modern monitor stand supporting two matching monitors back to back. The leads ran through an access hole in the desk and Faith crouched down to look underneath where the wires hung to the floor.

"So what's the only thing missing?" she asked.

"The one thing you'd expect an IT engineer to have an abundance of," Brandt replied.

They both opened desk drawers on either side to find stationary, office supplies, and little else.

"Not a single computer, external drive, thumb drive or even a notebook or diary," Faith commented.

"It's much easier when they have a wall full of pictures and articles all linked with pieces of string," Brandt said, grinning as he stared at the blank, pale green painted walls.

"Yeah, that's handy," Faith agreed. "Have you ever seen that? Even one time?"

"Oh yeah, loads of times," her partner replied. "On TV. Not once in 12 years as part of the Bureau."

They both chuckled. Brandt keyed his mic. "House is clear, there's nothing here of interest we can see. You can have the lab guys do their thing."

The agents walked back to the living room and methodically searched one more time with little expectation. Brandt stood in front of the thermostat on the wall and read off what he saw. "78 degrees."

Faith nodded and carried on opening drawers to the coffee table.

"What do you set your AC to when you go away?" he asked her.

She closed the drawer and sat up on the sofa. "Hmm, I'm trying to remember the last time we went anywhere for more than a day or two. Two Christmases ago, we went to my parents in Colorado, but I couldn't tell you what we did with the thermostat in the condo. My husband may have changed it. I was too busy shepherding the kids."

"This thermostat is one of those fancy ones you can control from a smartphone and has different settings for times of day, days of week, and all that jazz," Brandt said, and then pointed to the front door. "Same network the alarm is on. All controllable remotely."

"But the alarm wasn't set," Faith pointed out.

"Exactly," Brandt replied, taking his mobile from his pocket. He went to settings, then Wi-Fi, and waited for the screen to populate with options. A long list of every Wi-Fi network in range sprang up, varying in name from the standard manufacturer tags and numbers to 'MossWiFi', 'Madhouse', and even 'FBI_Surveillance_-Van'. That one was always a favourite with the agents. He wondered how many curtains were being pulled back and people pointing at the innocuous white van parked down the road, letting their spouses know they'd finally found the mysterious van.

Brandt didn't know what he expected from the list as he wouldn't know Massey's Wi-Fi name if it was on there. But his hunch was it didn't exist anymore. He returned to the thermostat and studied the screen. The small network icon blinked in the corner with a cross through it.

"No Wi-Fi network," he said. "He even disabled or removed the network, which is why the alarm isn't set. He's left us nothing we could use to quickly trace his online or cloud-stored information."

"Hardly surprising," Faith commented. "From everything we've seen so far, the man has meticulously planned every move."

Brandt left the thermostat and paused by a series of photographs arranged in a modular frame on the dining room wall. Faith walked over and joined him.

"I think he planned on never returning," her partner said quietly.

"He had to know he couldn't, however this ends," she replied. "I'm guessing in his mind there's nothing here for him anymore, regardless."

Brandt looked around them. "Well, I don't think anything's been disturbed since he left, and we know that was three weeks ago."

"My guess is nothing has been disturbed much in eight months," Faith replied, staring at the face of Massey's wife, standing on a podium with a medal around her neck. "This guy hasn't moved on since Olivia died."

"You think there's a connection?" Brandt asked, "They haven't found much of a link so far."

Faith tapped a finger on the photograph. "Oh, it's about her all right. I don't know what happened or why, but what he's up to now has something to do with the woman he loved."

23

CONTRARY TO PROPRIETY

Whittaker alternated between text messages on his mobile and listening to the digital radio calls. Police vehicles were systematically searching every road in Barkers National Park. While that added up to a mere five or six miles of marl lanes, they were thoroughly checking the canals on either side, which took a great deal longer. Casey from the DOE had made a series of phone calls, making sure no one knew of any other buildings hidden away in Barkers, regardless of their condition. She'd drawn a blank.

Currently, three humans had disappeared into thin air. Logic told the detective they had to be in the woods of the park somewhere, but without aerial assistance, finding them was going to be tough.

The two FBI agents joined Whittaker under the tent, and he looked their way, hoping for a new lead.

"Massey's house turned up nothing of interest," Kowalczyk reported. "Neat, tidy, clean, and void of all computers and network equipment. He knew we'd be looking there."

"Did he have an office? Storage unit?" Whittaker asked. "Any other location that might be useful?"

"None that we've tracked down," Beth replied. "He worked from home. He freelanced his IT services, but mainly worked remotely for one company in California. No ties we can find to Briggs or his company."

"The agents on site seem to think his wife's death may play into this somehow," Kowalczyk added sceptically. "But we don't have anything to prove that theory."

Whittaker held up his mobile. "There's a reporter who contacted me this morning," he said. "She had been helping Massey research his wife's accident, and what he claimed was potential foul play. He stopped speaking with her a month back, around the time Skylar Briggs made the news for her most recent arrest," the Detective recalled and pulled up a contact on his mobile, hitting the call icon.

"Hi Pam, it's me. Do you have the number for the reporter you put through this morning?"

"I do," she replied, sounding just as frazzled as she had earlier. "Somewhere in this pile of paperwork I'm accumulating."

He heard rustling and a thud over the line followed by Pam swearing and then apologising to whomever was standing nearby.

"Here it is," she said. "It's…"

"Text it to me Pam," Whittaker said, cutting her off. "Right away, please."

"Okay, Roy," she began, "and I've delayed these press folks about as long as I can now, Roy, dey be coming…"

"Yup, yup, thanks Pam," he interrupted again and hit 'end call'.

"I'll have a number in just a moment," he continued, turning to the agents. "Her name is Myra Shah, and she works for one of the newspapers in Tampa. I don't recall which one. When I talked to her this morning, she was sure there would end up being a connection back to his wife's death. In her time working with Massey, they never found hard proof, so the story hasn't run. But they do have a link between Olivia Massey and Briggs Paper & Packaging International. It's tenuous at best, and Myra couldn't remember all the details as she's moved on to several other stories in the past month. She was heading to her house to get her notes. I got the impression she worked old school with paper and pen. Anyway, I asked to speak with her again once she'd refreshed her memory."

Whittaker showed Beth his mobile screen as the text dinged through.

"You'll have to scroll down, detective," Beth said with a grin. "I think your communications lady is going to make her point one way or another."

Whittaker looked at the screen and the long text message, which appeared to explain how the police communications department was not building very good international relations by stalling the world's press. He scrolled down to the number and held the mobile out to Beth again.

"Sorry, here you go," he explained. "It's been a trying day for everyone in our little police department."

Beth noted the number and stepped away, dialling the FBI office in Tampa, who had taken the reins on the investigation.

Massey's online feed switched from what they now knew was a looped shot of Skylar, to what appeared to be a live view. It was Skylar once again, but tied to a different chair in a new room.

"He's back," one of the IT techs shouted, and Whittaker and Kowalczyk immediately rushed to the monitor.

"Are they black curtains?" Kowalczyk asked.

Light shone down from above the Briggs girl, but the background was a dark material.

"Maybe covering the wall," Whittaker replied, "or a divider of some sort."

"Certainly appears to be inside again," the agent noted. "I don't hear wind noise or birds, but I think the mic's on."

They could hear faint movement on the feed, and Massey appeared behind Skylar.

"Welcome back, everyone, and I hope you enjoyed the entertainment courtesy of the Cayman Islands' finest. They seem like a good bunch of people and quite determined to track me down, as you can imagine. A stark contrast to my experience with Florida's police back home, who proved themselves highly unmotivated when it comes to less obvious crimes."

Whittaker noticed the man gritting his teeth and although his tone didn't change, he exuded anger and frustration.

"That might be a reference to his wife's accident," Kowalczyk noted.

"But now it's time for the third challenge. So, while Nora and Skylar prepare themselves, let's take a look at another entertaining video I prepared for the world to see."

Massey began pacing back and forth behind Skylar's chair while he continued, "If you recall, we've reached 'Speak no Evil' in our homage to the ancient prophets. The original proverb literally translated, says 'speak not what is contrary to propriety'. Propriety by modern definition means the state or quality of conforming to conventionally accepted standards of behaviour or morals."

"So what did they mean by contrary to propriety? Well, our modern term has become 'speak no evil', which most take to mean that we shouldn't speak ill of other people. That's a simplified interpretation, and the statement was more likely intended to cover a broader reach of damage done by words. Such as telling lies.

"Challenge three will be a test of speech. It will require a clear and precise explanation from one human being to another, without error or falsehood. I think you'll find it quite entertaining, and a lesson we could all learn. But now, as promised, is a short video of important people in key positions in business, education and government, speaking 'contrary to propriety'."

The Internet feed switched to the prepared video, starting with the Governor of Florida standing at a podium, addressing a large crowd at an outdoor venue. His tie fluttered in the breeze and the bright sun reflected off his mirrored sunglasses. He stood bold and upright with both hands on the podium.

"My good friend Donovan Briggs has not only made a commitment to the environment ladies and gentlemen, he has made a commitment to you, the great people of Florida."

Cheers rang out. Banners were waved, and the governor did nothing to dissuade the crowd. He patiently waited with a large smile until the noise quietened.

"Briggs Paper & Packaging International is setting new standards for an industry that's come under scrutiny in recent times. Well, I'm here to tell you, scrutinise all you want. This plant behind us in these beautiful grounds employs the latest clean energy and water waste techniques. And you know what else is employed here? Hundreds of Floridians."

The crowd rose to their feet in raucous applause, primed no doubt by the champagne reception and generous gift bags at every seat.

The clip moved on to a woman addressing a crowd at another venue, this time inside, and Whittaker tore himself away. He did notice the viewer counter had reached 1.6 million.

Beth re-joined them. "I see he's back live. Any clues to where?"

"Dark room, cloth hanging to cover the walls, it appears," Whittaker commented. "Seems quite small but nothing to give away the location. Any luck with Miss Shah?"

"She didn't answer her phone, but we left a message and the Tampa branch is trying to track her down," Beth replied. "They'll send someone to her home to see if she's there."

"Massey made a disparaging comment about the Tampa police," Kowalczyk said, adding to the conversation, "and clearly he's targeting Briggs's company, so unless they're aggrieved former employees or contractors, which we have no record of, then maybe there is a tie to his wife. Or at least what he believes is a connection."

"Briggs is a major contributor to the university Olivia Massey worked for, and both Skylar and her brother, Grayson, have been enrolled in classes there. We've discovered that much," Beth offered. "Skylar wasn't there long and transferred to another school about eight months ago. One of her arrests was a few weeks before that, so potentially related. Grayson graduated this year. Neither appears to have taken a class with Olivia Massey."

"Could the link we're looking for be something to do with Skylar leaving?" Whittaker asked. "But the school probably booted her and kept it quiet as the father makes significant donations. Called it a transfer."

Beth shrugged her shoulders. "Skylar left after Olivia's accident. A few days after, I believe. Could have been revenge I suppose, if Olivia had an involvement in the girl's expulsion, but seems risky after the fact."

"What about all this environmental stuff Massey keeps rattling on about?" Kowalczyk asked. "It must have something to do with it. He's just thrown the Florida Governor under the bus, and by the looks of things, a group of politicians and businessmen are next," he added, throwing a thumb towards the monitor. Various dignitaries continued praising Briggs Paper & Packaging International.

"Olivia Massey taught environmental science, and Grayson Briggs took an environmental course, but he was under another professor according to what we've found," Beth confirmed. "Skylar was enrolled in the same course as her brother before she quit, or was asked to leave."

"Her social media feed is full of environmental save-the-whale shit," Kowalczyk added. "Looks like she went on rallies and various fund raisers for manatees."

"Seems like the Briggs family wants us to believe they care about the environment," Whittaker said.

"Skylar may well," Beth replied, "but records indicate Donovan Briggs didn't do squat to help the environment until he was forced to. The company was cited multiple times for waste over the years. His conversion to cleaner production came after big public pressure three years ago."

"Where is Grayson now?" Whittaker asked.

"In Tampa. Our office has spoken with him over the phone," Beth replied. "He works at the paper mill with his father."

"Hey, what's the name of the university in St Pete?" Kowalczyk asked.

"University of St Petersburg," Beth replied. "Oh, here we go," she added, following her partner's gaze to the television.

A man stood on a stage singing the praises of Briggs Paper & Packaging International in a large auditorium. Across the back of the stage was a large banner for the University of St Petersburg.

24

SPEAK NO EVIL

I blinked against the bright lights that weren't very bright, but I'd been in the dark for what felt like hours. The room was small and did not contain any obvious sharp objects or electrified railings. In fact, it held nothing but my chair and a white dry-erase board mounted to the wall beside the only door. Three dry-erase pens lay in the shelf at the base of the board, along with an eraser. The walls of the room were draped with black cloth, and I got up and pulled the material back to reveal bare studs and panels. No windows I could see. The wood was fresh untreated pine but dry, dark green paint had leaked through the seams in the plywood panels, suggesting the exterior had been painted.

I tried to wedge or hook the cloth back in the hope the broadcast may catch the construction on one of the many cameras I noticed blinking red lights from the dark corners of the ceiling. A single sealed light fixture was mounted to a rafter, illuminating the white-board. It was an exterior style fixture, with screws fastening the lens, preventing me from darkening the room or using the glass bulb as a weapon. Even the wiring was tightly pinned to the rafter and disappeared through the ceiling, making it useless to me. I nudged the chair, and it didn't move. It too was screwed to the floor with metal brackets.

Stepping to the board, I took the cap off a blue dry-erase pen and wrote in big letters on the board, 'Small wood building in Barkers'.

I moved back to give the cameras a clear view.

"I'd be disappointed with anything less, Nora," came Massey's voice over speakers I hadn't noticed tucked away in the rafters. "But please erase that and we can begin the third challenge. I have a button in my hand at all times to switch the feed, so attempts at signals, messages and clues are pointless. They will also forfeit the challenge, for which Skylar will suffer, as you know."

Well, at least I was keeping him on his toes. I looked up at the camera aimed down at me from above the board and nodded. I couldn't think of a way to delay any further, so we may as well get on with whatever his next bag of tricks contained.

Detective Whittaker and the two agents turned their attention back to the monitor where the pre-produced video ended and Massey appeared on screen standing behind Skylar.

"Welcome back ladies and gentlemen around the world. Thank you for tuning in and following along with the story I'm unfolding for you. Speak no Evil is the subject of the moment, and the lost art of speaking the truth. Our third challenge today provides an opportunity for our players to demonstrate to us the difficulty involved in providing clear and accurate facts. 'Listen and Draw' has been used for decades. From school rooms to test laboratories, the process of one human describing an image to be drawn by another is a lesson in communication, precision, and attention.

"Our teachers use this as a game to teach young children how to diligently listen to directions, an ever-losing battle with a world that's training our kids to have attention deficit disorder. Intelligence services use the process to train their agents in carefully paying attention to instructions and gathering minute details from conversations and surroundings.

"For our challenge, Skylar Briggs will have five minutes to accurately describe an image I will reveal shortly. In a separate room, Constable Nora Sommer will attempt to recreate that image from Skylar's directions. Skylar must not say what the image is or represents. She may only describe the shapes and forms that make up the picture. Breaking the rules forfeits the challenge, and I think we all know what's on the line by now. Skylar will lose a finger if they fail this, the third challenge. Next, will be the final test, where they'll play for much higher stakes.

"But now it's time for our 'Speak no Evil' challenge, and their five minutes begins now."

A countdown clock started in the corner of the screen, opposite the ever-increasing viewership number. The tape had already been removed from Skylar's mouth, and Massey reached over and hung a large white card on the wall in front of her.

"What the hell is that?" I heard Skylar say over the speakers.

I'd listened to Massey's diatribe and was poised with a pen, ready to start drawing – which wasn't one of my fortes. I was good at stick figures and snowmen. Unless we were drawing sailboats. I could draw the sailboat I'd lived on from memory. But I guessed that wouldn't be today's challenge.

"What do you see?" I asked, trying to kick-start the young woman.

"It's like a science fiction-looking logo thing," she replied, sounding baffled.

"Do not say what it is," Massey reminded her, "I'll let that one slip, but not again."

"How can I say what it is when I don't know what the fuck it is," Skylar whined.

"Hey, Briggs," I snapped. "Focus. It doesn't matter what it is, just describe what I need to draw. Circles, squares, rectangles, lines."

"It's got a bunch of circles and parts of circles," she mumbled back.

I pictured Skylar in the back of a classroom making snapping sounds from the bubblegum in her mouth while she scrolled through social media on her mobile. Her teachers must have loved her.

"Start with what's in the middle of the image, the centre," I persisted.

"A circle, I guess?" she replied.

"Okay, how big? Half the whole image, or one tenth the size?"

"Jeez, I don't know," Skylar mumbled. "Closer to a tenth I suppose."

I drew a circle on the board.

"You said it's a bunch of circles, so what's the next one?"

"There's a bigger circle," she replied, "But it's not really a circle."

"You mean it's an oval?"

"No, no, it's round, but it's got a hole in it," she said, and I was as confused as she sounded.

"A circle with a hole in it?"

"Yeah, you know, like a doughnut."

"A fat ring?"

"I guess you could call it that," she replied.

I seemed to remember the Egyptians were considered the originators of geometry, so I presumed they named it that. But if Skylar Briggs wanted to give me credit for inventing the shape known as a ring, I wasn't going to argue with her. Time was ticking away.

"How much bigger than the first circle is the ring?"

"Um," I heard her deliberating.

Maybe I was wrong. I was starting to doubt she could chew gum and operate her mobile at the same time.

"So, if you drew another circle next to the first one, making it the same size as the first one, it would touch the inside of the doughnut," she declared, "Except there's not another circle there, I'm just saying so you know the distance."

"Are they concentric?" I asked, then realised I'd have to phrase it differently.

"They are," she replied before I could come up with another way of asking, "if that means they have the same centre?"

"It does," I confirmed, and drew a second circle next to the first, using it as a guide to make the inside circle of the ring. She was chewing gum again in my mind, and had graduated a few IQ points.

"How wide is the ring?" I asked. "Use the original circle as a reference."

"Two thirds-ish."

I drew the outer circle of the ring.

"What's next?"

"Now it's the goofy bits," she replied. "There are three of them and they're like circles, but not really. They're more like moons, or you know a moon having an eclipse or something."

I was confused and thought about what she was saying. The moon is a circle, but an eclipse has one planet passing over another, like two non-concentric circles. Off to the side I drew one circle and then another smaller one inside the first with their edges touching.

"Halvmåne," I blurted. "Damn it, what's the name in English? A crescent?!"

"Yes, yes, that's it. A crescent," she replied excitedly. "But most of a full circle so it looks kinda like a pincer."

That threw me for a loop again until I looked at my two circles off to the side. I took my finger and erased the edge where the two circles touched, and it sort of looked like a pincer.

"Okay, where do I draw these relative to the other circles? There's three, right?"

"Yes, three," she said, and I gave her a moment to think. "The first one is upside down on the top. I think the bottom would go through the centre of the first circle you drew, the small one."

"That's good," I encouraged. "And how big are these crescents?"

"Kinda the same size as the doughnut."

I drew a new circle straight above the original circle, passing through its centre.

"How thick is the back of the crescent?" I asked.

"Huh?"

"The pincer shape. On one side the two circles touch, but on the other side they're how far apart?"

"I don't understand," she replied, and I took a deep breath, trying to figure out how to ask in a different way. This was pushing the abilities of my second language.

"On one side the pincers come to sharp points, but on the other side, how far is the inner circle away from the outer circle?"

"Oh, a little thicker than the doughnut," she replied.

I drew the second circle to form a crescent and erased the section where they were tangent. I now had three concentric circles and a crescent resting over them.

"And there's two more crescents, or pincers? Are they all the same size?"

"Yes, same size," she said. "One points towards the lower right corner and the other points towards the lower left corner."

"Do they look evenly spaced," I asked. "Think in degrees."

That brought silence.

"The first crescent is at 12 o'clock – are the second and third at 4 and 8?" I continued.

"Oh, yes, I see what you mean. Yes, they are."

I drew two more pairs of circles and erased the edges to form crescents. The image began to look familiar, but mine was now a mess of lines.

"Is some of this filled in?" I asked. "Is it multiple colours or just one colour?"

"It's black," she replied, "And the doughnut and crescents are black, but the doughnut has bits missing."

"Wait, what?"

"The doughnut has the places next to where it goes through the crescents missing."

"The ring, or doughnut, is black, yes?"

"Yes."

I coloured in the ring.

"Okay, so where the doughnut meets the crescents, the borders are missing?"

"Yes, so the doughnut isn't really a doughnut," she tried to explain. "It's really three pieces inside the crescents. I just said it was a doughnut so you could draw it."

"One minute left," Massey said calmly.

"Shit, we're running out of time," Skylar said, sounding panicked.

"It's okay, stay focused," I urged, not that I felt calm either. "Are the crescents coloured in too?"

"Yes, yes, but not the middle, not the original little circle and some other bits."

Faen, this was the first I was hearing about other bits. We really were running out of time.

"Let's start with the doughnuts. How thick is the gap between the doughnut and the crescents where they meet?"

"Like a third the thickness of the doughnut," she said.

I erased a small path through the ring, leaving three segments, as she'd mentioned. I had to guess that was right.

"If I colour in the crescents, I need to leave the original circle open, right?"

"Yes. But did you do the gaps?" she said, her voice rising, "There has to be gaps between the doughnut and the crescents."

"I've done that, I'm colouring in the crescents now, all except the centre circle."

"Okay, so the doughnut bits and the crescents are black now, you've coloured them in?" she asked me.

I finished colouring and looked at the image. It was now familiar.

"I know what this is!" I whooped.

"You do?" Skylar asked.

"Yeah…" I stopped myself before I said what the icon represented and gave Massey an excuse to forfeit us.

Then I remembered we weren't finished.

"Times up," Massey announced, and something in his voice told me we'd failed.

"I think we did it," Skylar shouted. "I think we got it. Can I see what she drew now?"

I looked at my shaky drawing and tried to picture what we'd missed from the logo commonly displayed as a warning of toxic substances. I wasn't familiar enough to remember what I'd screwed up, but something didn't look right.

"Hey, why are you tying me down again? Let me see her drawing!" Skylar yelled, and I could hear her voice through the wall and the speakers.

"Did we get it right or not, you fucker?" she screamed.

Everything went quiet, and I hoped he was showing her on a monitor. I spun around and wondered which camera was on the whiteboard.

"Fuck," Skylar groaned, "those stupid little bits."

"Hey, let me see. We had to get it pretty close," I shouted and banged on the wall. "Close enough! I know you don't want to do this, *drittsekk*, let's move on to the last challenge."

"No, no, you motherfucker, let go of me!"

Skylar's words echoed around the little building, and the scream she let out next pierced my ears. I felt every ounce of pain in her voice.

25

HE'S NOT A VIOLENT MAN

Whittaker turned away from the screen as the garden shears sliced through the pinkie finger on Skylar's left hand. She screamed in agony. The detective glanced up to see Massey visibly shaking. The kidnapper dropped the bloodied shears with a clatter to the floor.

"Just remember," he said into the camera, his voice cracking. "I take full responsibility for the awful thing I've just done. But all this is happening because of those people who haven't taken responsibility for what they've done. Greedy, evil, deceitful people are getting away with their violence and lies because those in power to stop them are just as corrupt."

Massey took a look at the young woman sobbing in the chair beside him and quickly turned away. He reached for something in his pocket.

"We'll be back shortly to conclude today's broadcast. Meanwhile, here's a reminder of why we're here."

The feed switched to a replay of the video he'd shown before the third challenge. The Florida Governor launched into his speech and one of the IT techs turned the volume down.

The dock area had fallen eerily quiet. The background buzz from reporters and news teams constantly talking, broadcasting and lobbing questions from behind the police barriers had subsided to whispered comments.

"That was awful," AJ commented, standing by Casey at the edge of the tent.

Whittaker took a deep breath. "Okay, what did we learn?" he said, turning to the FBI agents.

"He's not a violent man," Beth started. "This has to have a connection to his wife's death. Something catastrophic has pushed him into what he's doing. He truly believes a serious wrong has to be set right. I don't know if he could bring himself to kill the girl – you just saw how traumatised he was harming her."

"He just mutilated her! Maybe he's getting a taste for it," Kowalczyk retorted. "My partner's comments are not an official Federal Bureau of Investigation analysis, detective, and shouldn't be taken as such."

Beth glared at Kowalczyk, and Whittaker sighed. "That's not helpful. While you two bicker about official FBI lines, we still have a kidnapper to find. I don't care about whatever grievance you two have. What I care about is useful, actionable input." He turned and looked directly at Kowalczyk. "Got any? What's the official party statement?"

"Listen Whittaker," Kowalczyk growled, gritting his teeth, "we're here to advise, and…"

"Then advise," Whittaker snapped. "Or get back on your plane and go home. We'll ship you your citizen's body parts once we collect them all up."

AJ and Casey both looked at each other in shock. They'd both known the detective for years, and had never heard him lose his cool. The two IT techs sank lower in their seats and waited for whatever was coming next.

Kowalczyk's shoulders dropped. "Look, he's laid out his threats, and he just carried out the first one as promised. We have to proceed based on him being willing to go the next step."

"I agree," Beth said, and both men turned to her in surprise. "Before I was interrupted, the point I was trying to make is I don't think he could kill her in the same close proximity he just experienced. Whatever he has arranged for the fourth challenge, he'll have a plan to carry out her death remotely in some way."

"You think he'll run and leave her to die by some means?" Whittaker asked.

"That's my guess," Beth confirmed. "Something clean and tidy, not messy or bloody. Possibly even humane. A lethal sedative in a drink would be the closest I could see him getting to her death. He'll want a layer of separation from the act. He'll put it in motion, but he won't want to see her die, or be there when it happens."

"That's a lot of assumptions about a guy who just cut the finger off an innocent young woman," Kowalczyk commented, with slightly less challenge in his tone.

"It's a psychological profile from the evidence the man's presented and what we know of his history," Beth retorted, looking at Whittaker and ignoring her partner.

"Ricci likes making assumptions," Kowalczyk bit back.

Whittaker held up his hands. "I'll take useful assumptions over pointing out the obvious, agent. Any other observations?"

"Look back at the video of your constable," Kowalczyk said, pointing to the nearest IT tech. "There was one wider view of her, where the back of the room could be seen."

They walked over behind the constable who rewound through their recorded footage of the feed until Kowalczyk said stop.

"There, play this view, it's brief."

They all watched as the camera angle from the corner of the small room showed Nora at the whiteboard. The view looked from her left side across the back of the room.

"The drape is pulled back," Beth noted.

"Yup, can you do anything with that shot?" Kowalczyk asked.

The tech zoomed in and played with contrast and brightness controls. The picture improved slightly, enough for the lighter wood to be clear, and a seam between two boards became evident.

"Looks like a wooden structure," Whittaker said, staring intently at the image.

The tech pointed to the seam with a pen. "See da fine line of lighter colour, right der? I'd say dat's light shining through."

"So that's an outside wall, and he's gone to some trouble to cover it over," Kowalczyk agreed. "He was just sloppy with that one drape."

"He's not been sloppy about anything," Beth remarked. "I'd say Nora did that, so we'd see it."

"Hanging those drapes would be faster than painting, panelling or sealing in any other way," Whittaker said thoughtfully. "He may have constructed this building himself. It would explain why we don't know about another building in Barkers."

He turned to Jacob, who'd just returned to the tent. "Get to work on the building supply store, Jacob, see if Massey purchased anything in the past three weeks."

"You know it's Sunday, sir?" Jacob replied timidly.

"I don't care if it's Easter, Christmas and New Year all in one, Jacob, get hold of Thompson and have him look. I'll text you his number."

Whittaker quickly found the contact on his mobile and texted it to his constable.

"I'll check with our office and see if his credit card records have been received yet," Kowalczyk said. "We may be able to see from his purchases."

Whittaker nodded, and the agent stepped away to make the call.

"This means he could still be in Barkers as you thought, detective," Beth pointed out. "But I guess the bad news is he could have built this anywhere in those woods."

The digital radio sitting on the table crackled to life. "Dis is Unit 2. We've found signs of recent activity by one of da canals. Over."

The detective swooped up the radio. "This is Whittaker, Unit 2, give me a description and exact location."

"West of da building we found, North Sound side of da roadway, sir," came the reply. Whittaker recognised Williams's voice.

"Hard to tell how many people, but several footprints and slide marks. Da bank is steep here."

"Could someone hide a small boat in the canal that would be hidden from the road?" Whittaker asked.

"I think we'd see a boat, sir, especially from da height of a vehicle," the officer replied, "but der's a culvert under da roadway dat keeps the canals either side at da same water level. You could hide a kayak-sized vessel inside der."

"Good work," Whittaker replied. "Follow the canal and look for exit tracks."

"Yes, sir."

The radio went quiet, and the detective went back to the IT tech. "Bring up the FBI's high-definition satellite image of Barkers, please."

He and Beth both leaned in for a closer look.

The tech had highlighted the building, and Whittaker tapped on the screen in the general area the footmarks had been reported. "Here, put an arrow in this spot. Now, let's figure out where that canal leads without having to exit the water."

They traced the canal east, where it led to the tip of the park and ended. The more likely direction was west, where it continued alongside the road, running parallel to the shoreline until it met the edge of the park at the border with The Shores. The road ended, but the canal continued, connecting to the inland-side canal and running along the edge of the park to the south-west corner. Four side roads with similar canals led away from the main waterway. The tech highlighted each one, and the large scope of the area to be searched became clear.

"Send a screenshot of this map with the highlighted areas to the field teams, please," Whittaker asked. "They're looking for any recent signs of activity. Have them focus on the highlighted areas."

"Whittaker," Kowalczyk said, tucking his mobile away in his jacket as he walked over. "Massey spent $4,100 at a place called A. L. Thompson Building Supplies Ltd, ten days ago. Two more purchases from the same store for lesser amounts in the past week."

"That's our main building supplier," the detective confirmed. "Jacob should be able to verify the details of those transactions shortly. But I think we can safely assume they'll contain materials to build a small structure."

Whittaker looked at the highlighted canals on the screen and allowed himself a moment of optimism. "We still have a large area to cover and very little time, but I think we're closing in on Mr Massey."

"Your young constable has done a remarkable job leaving us clues, detective," Beth pointed out. "It's hard to believe she's only been on the force a few weeks."

Whittaker nodded. He thought about his protege and his intention of offering her a distraction from the misery she'd suffered. It wasn't working out in the way he'd hoped.

"She's a tough kid," he remarked, "but right now I wish I hadn't..." He stopped himself. Wishing and wasting time on past events that couldn't be undone were not his style, and he wouldn't allow himself to be dragged down that path. "Yes, remarkable indeed."

26

STAR WITNESS

Agents Brandt and Graham were resigned to their Sunday being spent running around the Tampa/St Pete area, knocking on doors that wouldn't be answered. Brandt knocked again and pushed the doorbell three times. No response.

Mariner South Condominiums were located near Emery Riddle Aeronautical University on the west shoreline of Tampa. They were graced with a superb view of Old Tampa Bay and St Pete across the water, and Faith guessed they were too pricey for the average student. Myra Shah's unit was on the third floor of the eight-storey building.

The two agents walked back to the lift, Brandt hit the button, and the doors opened. They rode the lift down and stepped into the stifling heat of the car park on the ground floor. Her partner walked ahead towards the guest parking and their SUV, but Faith paused a moment.

"Can you get me a licence plate for Shah's vehicle?" she said into the mic on her lapel.

Brandt stopped and, realising what his partner was up to, walked back and joined her in looking at the parking space numbers.

"Here," Beth said, finding the spot corresponding to Myra Shah's condo number.

A Kia Soul filled the spot. The car looked to be a few years old, with a couple of light scratches around the hatchback door. A rainbow-coloured peace sign sticker adorned the lower left corner of the back window. The licence plate surround suggested Myra had attended the University of Texas in Austin. Brandt peeked in the back window of the Kia.

"Dog," he said, pointing to a blanket on the back seat, liberally covered in pale hair.

Faith looked out through the open sides of the car park. "Maybe she's walking the dog."

A voice came over their earpieces and read off the licence plate number associated with Myra Shah. Faith verified they'd found the right vehicle.

"Let's go back up," Brandt said, and Faith followed him to the lift.

The two agents had worked together for the past 18 months, since Faith had been assigned to Tampa. They were good together in her mind, and she was confident he felt the same way. He had more experience than her, but Brandt had always been respectful, and after a year and a half working closely together, they often knew each other's thoughts.

Brandt banged on the condominium door once again, and waited. After the same lack of response, Faith put her ear to the door.

"There's music playing. Check the neighbour," she said, nodding towards the adjacent unit.

Brandt listened at the door of the next unit and shook his head. Faith did the same at the unit in the other direction.

"It's not very loud, but it's coming from her condo," she confirmed.

Brandt gave Shah's door a listen and nodded in agreement.

"Hey, I hear a dog," he said, holding up a finger. "Sounds like it's whining."

Faith keyed her lapel mic. "Permission to force entry. We have music and a possible dog inside, but no response at the door."

She paused and looked at the lock and then at her partner. He nodded.

"We can make a non-destructive entry," she added over the radio.

"Proceed with entry," came the reply from the operations van down the street.

Brandt took a small lock-picking kit from his pocket and crouched down. Selecting the right tool, he fiddled with the key slot for less than 15 seconds before the mechanism released and he turned the handle.

"FBI! We're entering the residence," Faith announced loudly, with the radio keyed.

A door across the hall opened and an older woman stared at the two agents wide eyed. Faith flashed her badge with her free hand, her Glock 19M already drawn.

"FBI. Go back inside ma'am and keep the door closed."

The woman stood still, her face a mixture of shock and panic.

"Everything's fine ma'am, no cause for alarm, go back inside," Faith repeated.

The old lady started to say something without moving.

"Now!" Faith growled, and the woman snapped her door closed.

Brandt pushed the door open and scanned the room, his weapon drawn, pointed at the ground in the low ready position. Soft music played from another part of the condo, and the muffled sound of a dog yipping greeted the two agents as they entered the room. To their right was a kitchen, open to a living space, with a small dining table and two sofas facing a glass door with a view of the bay. A small dog ran back and forth on the balcony, barking behind the double-glazed hurricane-proof glass.

Faith nodded towards a closed door to their right, and Brandt moved that way while she checked around the living room furniture.

"Clear," she said quietly, and joined her partner by the bedroom door.

The music was coming from the room beyond, and Brandt placed his hand on the doorknob. Faith nodded, and Brandt swung the door open. She stepped inside and scanned the room, pausing just inside the doorway, facing the window.

"One victim, no movement," she said methodically, and moved in the opposite direction towards the bathroom.

Brandt followed her into the room and, after scanning the room himself, waited while his partner cleared the bathroom.

Faith holstered her weapon and keyed her mic. "One victim, female, signs of strangulation," she said, observing the red marks around the woman's neck.

Brandt checked for a pulse and shook his head.

"Victim unresponsive. No pulse," Faith added over the radio.

Myra Shah lay slumped in an office chair near the bed, fully clothed in black leggings and a cotton top. Her long, dark hair was pulled back in a ponytail, and her lifeless eyes stared blankly at the ceiling. From her name and smooth, pale brown skin, Faith guessed the woman was of Indian descent. They knew she was 34 years old. Faith noticed a framed photograph on the bedside table. Myra was smiling at the camera with a blonde woman kissing her cheek.

Beyond the victim in the office chair, by the window over-looking the water, was a simple wooden desk. Underneath, on the right side, was a file cabinet with the top drawer partially open. On the desk sat a printer surrounded by various cables connected to nothing. A mouse remained on a pad to the side, but the computer was gone. Brandt used a pen to probe inside a satchel-style computer bag next to the desk. No laptop.

"No sign of forced entry. Victim was killed right here, with the perp strangling her from behind while she was seated at the desk. Sometime today by the body temp. Maybe even this afternoon," Brandt commented. "She's still warm."

"Knew them, or was willing to let them into her home at least," Faith concurred.

"Computer taken," Brandt added, and peeked inside the open file drawer. "Looks like paperwork too."

Faith keyed her mic. "We need to contact the security company. I noticed cameras in the under-building parking, including one facing the elevator."

"Roger that. We have crime scene on their way, and local police to secure the property and help with canvassing. Any evidence this is tied to the case?"

"Computer and paperwork appear to be missing, and we haven't found a phone yet," Faith responded. "Can't say it's connected to the case that brought us here, but initial evidence suggests it has something to do with her work."

Brandt returned to the living area and looked around. The dog had stopped pacing and was now staring forlornly at him. The agent wondered how long it had been out on the balcony in the sweltering Florida heat. He wanted to let it back in the house, but they couldn't risk the contamination of evidence. It would mean using the handle on the sliding door, and the killer was probably the last to do so. By the pictures pinned to the fridge, Myra was a dog lover, and Brandt doubted she would've locked her dog outside. He moved on through the room.

"The nosy neighbour," Faith said, following her partner from the bedroom. "I'll go."

Brandt nodded his agreement, and Faith went out the front door into the hallway. She knocked on the lady's door, on the opposite side, and didn't have long to wait.

"Show me your badge," she heard the old lady demand from inside.

Faith held her badge up to the peephole, and the door opened a crack, stopping against its safety chain.

"Let me see it properly, I can't make out anything through that damn hole in the door," the old lady complained, and squinted at the badge held up to the opening.

She grumbled something and pushed the door to. Faith heard the chain being removed, and the door opened halfway.

"What's going on over there?"

"Ma'am, did you happen to notice anything unusual across the hall earlier today?" Faith asked. "Anyone coming or going?"

"Apart from you two breaking in, you mean?" the old lady replied, giving Faith a hard stare. "She keeps herself to herself, that one," she continued, "But I happened to notice a visitor a few hours ago."

"Could you describe the person you saw, ma'am?" Faith asked. "Had you seen them before?"

The old lady shook her head. "I've never noticed him before," she replied, "but of course, I don't see everyone."

Faith doubted that.

"He wasn't like her, though," the lady added.

"How do you mean?" Faith asked, noting the visitor was male.

"Well, he was younger than her, not like these university types that are all around this part of town. But not much older than that."

"So you think he was younger than Miss Shah?"

"I'd say so, yes, but you know," the old lady replied, "he was different."

"I'm sorry, ma'am, I don't understand," Faith responded. "You keep saying he was different, how so?"

"Well, he was a nice-looking white fellow, and I've only seen another woman come visiting. She stays over. If you know what I mean."

Faith managed a smile and thanked the old lady for her help.

"Anything useful?" Brandt asked as Faith came back into the condo.

"Good-looking Caucasian male in his mid-twenties came by a few hours ago," Faith confirmed. "Hopefully CCTV will give us a good look, so we don't have to chase a better description out of the neighbour. Find anything else here?"

Brandt nodded towards the sliding glass doors, where the dog sat panting and staring up at the two agents.

"Found a notebook on the kitchen counter by the coffee maker. Maybe she set it down there while she made lunch or something. I get the feeling whoever did this wasn't very thorough or systematic, maybe even panicked. I can't believe he didn't find the notebook."

"Maybe it doesn't have anything in it pertinent to his concern," Faith suggested.

"Then this isn't about our case," Brandt replied. "There's a bunch of notes in it, a to-do list, and two phone numbers. Both 345 area code which I'd never heard of. So I looked it up. Cayman Islands prefix."

"Hm," Faith murmured. "Maybe it is unrelated."

"Perhaps. But I think the man was just sloppy," Brandt replied. "We'll have a better look through the notes in a minute and see if there's anything helpful."

Faith looked over at her partner. "So why are we standing by the window looking at a thirsty dog?"

Brandt pointed to the corner of the balcony. "Because I'm pretty certain the dog was shoved out here after the murder took place."

"Did he tell you that?" Faith chuckled. "Is Fluffy the terrier our star witness?"

"Could be," Brandt grinned, "because I think that's a piece of the guy's pant leg Fluffy dropped on the balcony."

27

LOCOMOTIVE

I sat in the chair and held my head in my hands, tired and drained. My body weighed a thousand kilos, and I felt like I'd never stand up again. Everyone has a breaking point, and for months my whole existence had teetered on that edge. Why did this *drittsekk* have to choose me?

The past three years had been marked by a violence I didn't know existed beyond movie screens. One minute I was a 16-year-old schoolgirl infatuated with my handsome teacher, and the next I couldn't remember the innocent girl I once was.

In my last-ditch efforts to resurrect an affair that he never should've pursued, the teacher and I both went missing. He, permanently, in a sailboat accident that I find hard to keep clear in my mind, and me, on the run for 18 months. It all seemed so long ago. After boat and island hopping around the world, I was recruited into a high-class resort on Grand Cayman. What appeared to be my ticket to a new life turned out to be a human trafficking operation preying on lost girls like me. I lived in a luxurious prison, provided company for sleazy old men, and lost myself deeper in a well of insecurity and doubt. My escape came with AJ and Whittaker's help, and instead of money to start over, I was lucky to keep my life.

After 'borrowing' a sailboat, I went back into hiding, and that's when I met Ridley Hernandez. He changed my life. For the first time, I discovered the way a relationship was supposed to be. I could never return to the innocence of my youth back in Norway, but Ridley made me human again. Loved and secure. When he reconnected with his mother in Mexico while she battled cancer, he was also introduced to her husband, Aldo Trujillo, head of the cartel in Acapulco. Trujillo's greed over Ridley's inheritance of diamonds that we searched to reclaim from the bottom of the Caribbean Sea led to a confrontation, and his stepfather's death.

Four months ago, the Mexican cartel sought vengeance for Aldo Trujillo, and murdered Ridley.

Grief, despair, sorrow? These are just words that poorly described the depths of emotions I sank to. Ultimately, apathy would best explain my state of mind. I didn't care what happened to me. Or around me. I would gladly have slipped away into oblivion. A fine, delicate thread kept me from taking my own life. That thread came from the respect I held for my parents, and my friend AJ Bailey. I couldn't put them through the same pain that consumed me.

Whittaker took me by complete surprise when he suggested I join the police service. I was a perfectly poor fit for law enforcement, yet somehow he saw an opportunity to turn my past into a way forward. Through my months of training and first few weeks on the job, I'd revelled in the distraction, and allowed myself to be carried forth with new purpose. But now I felt like I was back where I had started. Another person had been harmed. And it was my fault. I failed to save Ridley, and now Skylar Briggs was in agony because I'd screwed up. People put their faith in me, and I let them down.

I was certain Massey had believed I could pull through and pass his stupid challenges. If I'd done a better job of leading Skylar through the process, we could have completed the drawing. I looked up at the whiteboard, frowning at my rough approximation of the toxic icon. My imperfect circles glared back at me, an embarrassing attempt at preventing the suffering. I wondered again what was wrong or missing. It didn't matter. Time had no rewind button, and her severed finger would remain on the floor in the next room.

My biggest mistake with the man sent to kill Ridley was hesitation. Waiting for the perfect opportunity meant doing nothing until it was too late. There's never a perfect opportunity. The hitman had lured Ridley by holding me captive, and once he had us both, he moved us to a boat intended for Mexico. I'd seen several chances with low percentages of success, but I should have taken them. Even if I'd failed, Ridley may have stood a chance.

My frustration began to boil over, and I refocused on taking whatever control away from our captor that I could. I didn't want to be too late again. Being shot attempting to free us both held more appeal than sitting idly by while Skylar was mutilated. I stood up and booted the door with my foot. The whole partition wall shook, but the door was a lot stouter than I had anticipated.

"Stop that!" Massey shouted over the speakers.

I kicked the door again, aiming right by the lock. The wall rattled and the dry-erase markers flew out of the tray below the whiteboard.

"Nora, sit down or you'll force me to hurt Skylar again!"

"*Faen!*" I screamed and glared at the camera looking down at me. "Skylar? Are you okay?"

I put my hand against the wall between us, hoping I could sense or feel something.

"It fucking hurts," I heard over the speakers, her voice sounding brittle and hopeless.

Massey was letting us talk.

"You need to hold it together a little longer, Skylar," I shouted, lightly tapping against the wall so she'd know I was right there, close by. "We have one more of these bullshit challenges. I'll do my best I promise, but I need you to help me as much as you can."

"He's gonna kill me, so what's the point?" Skylar moaned.

"Not if we pass the fourth challenge," I countered, although I wasn't sure I believed my own words. Massey had done exactly what he'd said so far. I tended to believe he'd let us go if we passed the challenge, but I was more worried we wouldn't.

"You'll both go free if you pass this challenge," Massey said. But of course he'd say that.

"Have you wrapped her hand?" I asked, picturing the poor girl tied to the chair with blood dripping to the floor.

"I've dressed the wound," he replied. "I've numbed it as best I can, but she wouldn't take the pain pill I offered her."

"That's weird," I retorted, "her having trust issues with you."

I heard a faint laugh. "I guess that's true. Anyway, her finger is on ice, so there might be a chance to save it. When this is all over."

"If we pass the damn test," I reminded him.

"Yes," he said hesitantly, "of course."

"Don't you think this has gone far enough?" I said, trying to sound more sympathetic than authoritative. It came out somewhere in the middle and reminded me I suck at this.

"We're almost done, and the final part is the most important," he replied firmly. "I can't stop now."

"Then let me trade places with Skylar," I said, and wondered where that idea had come from.

"I'm sorry, that's not possible. You'll see why shortly."

"Surely she's sacrificed enough? Just let her go and let me do the final test," I persevered. "She still has the chance of a life ahead. Mine's already fucked up."

"She's made a pretty good mess of hers so far," Massey pointed out.

"Enough to deserve this?"

"Neither of you deserve this," he said softly, barely audible through the wall. "But life isn't fair, as you well know."

I wondered how he knew anything about me. Maybe he'd discovered the story about Ridley, but the names of the girls at the resort had been withheld from the press. To my knowledge, the incident with the teacher only made the Norwegian local news. But he was right, life wasn't fair. It was impartial and uncaring. Life was a locomotive made of iron and steel, riding down the railroad tracks of time like a soulless machine in complete disregard of the devastation in its wake. Fair was a myth spawned from human optimism.

"Let's make a deal," I blurted. "Failure in the final challenge is paid with a life, right?"

"Yes," he replied suspiciously.

"Then it shouldn't matter whose. So make it mine. I don't care if I die. I'm pretty sure she does."

All fell quiet, and I noticed the low drone again in the distance. It was coming from behind me, which if I was correct about the trail coming from the water, meant it was deeper into the woods. I wondered if it was civilisation, or maybe a generator to power the building we were in. That started to make sense to me. He had air conditioning and electronics, which all required reliable electricity.

"It matters," Massey finally said, and I forgot about the noise and remembered I'd just offered up my life.

"What has Skylar done to hurt you?" I asked.

"She has done nothing, to my knowledge," he replied.

"Then why hurt her?"

"Because it's the only way I can hurt her family," Massey snapped back. "And they deserve everything that's coming."

28

SPEECHLESS

Whittaker stared into the eyes of the kidnapper. Jensen Massey finally looked away from the camera and left Skylar in view, tied to the chair. Her left hand was wrapped in a bloodied bandage.

The detective was aghast. The exchange between Massey and his two captives had been aired to the world. Hearing Nora offer her life for the stranger in the next room left Roy Whittaker speechless, and desperately anguished. He was responsible for her being there. She'd joined the police on his invitation, and he'd persuaded her to do so.

"They," Beth pointed out. "He said they, not him," she clarified, nodding towards the police car where Donovan Briggs was still being detained.

Whittaker forced himself away from his guilt and turned to the agent. "If there's someone else involved, then maybe he'll throw them under the bus to save himself."

"True," Beth agreed, "but we have no idea what they have even done to aggrieve Massey."

"But Briggs doesn't know that," Kowalczyk added.

"Then let's formally arrest him," Whittaker suggested, looking out from the tent towards the police car. "That should get his attention."

The two agents looked at each other. "As representatives of the US, we would need to remind you of the rights of our citizens, detective. We could not support an arrest without probable cause or evidence of wrongdoing," Kowalczyk said, with little conviction.

"Duly noted," Whittaker replied. "And as representatives of the US, I assume you'd like to be present when your citizen is interviewed?"

Beth glanced at Kowalczyk and grinned. "Yes, sir, that would be appropriate."

Whittaker nodded. "Jacob."

The constable heard his name called and jogged over to the tent.

"Bring in one of the vans and park it over there, away from your car," Whittaker ordered. "Then arrest Mr Briggs, put him in handcuffs and lead him to the van, where I'll question him shortly."

Jacob looked nervously at his boss. "If I put the van behind da car, I could probably sneak da man in without all da cameras seeing, sir? They probably make a big deal if I arrest da victim's father, and all."

"I'm counting on it, Jacob," Whittaker replied. "Now get to it, I want to question the man."

"Yes, sir," Jacob said, and ran from the tent.

Whittaker turned to Kowalczyk. "I have a feeling you're an effective individual in an interview room, agent."

Kowalczyk nodded. "I can probably help the RCIPS out, as I insist on being present while our citizen is being questioned."

Satisfied, Whittaker picked up the digital radio. "This is Whittaker, status update please."

"Unit one here, sir," came the reply from a man with an English accent. "We've made it to the border with The Shores, sir. We've had a team on both sides of the road until now, but here the canal continues on the park side and the only way to follow it is on the water or from the road inside The Shores. We have a small boat being brought over, but we're doing our best until it arrives.

Trouble is, there are trees and shrubs between us and the water, so we have to fight through that to get a look. We then move farther down and repeat. Sorry, it's slower than we hoped, sir."

"Dis is Unit Two," Williams said. "We searching da canals alongside da smaller roads of da interior. Nothing to report so far, sir."

"10-4, thank you," Whittaker replied, and put the radio down.

"Sound's like it's slow going," Beth commented sympathetically.

Whittaker thought for a moment. "It is," he said absent-mindedly, then looked at the two agents. "At some point I'll have to risk putting the helicopter up."

"Do you have a drone?" Kowalczyk asked.

"The RCIPS doesn't, but I know someone who could bring one over and fly it for us," Whittaker replied. "I understand it would stand a better chance of not being seen or heard, but my concern is our response time if we find Massey's location. From the helicopter we can drop a few armed men within minutes. With the drone we get the location, but still have to reach it from land."

"Fair point," Kowalczyk conceded.

"If our ground search fails to turn up a result," Whittaker said, "I think we have to take to the air and risk the consequence."

Beth's mobile rang, and she looked at the caller ID. "It's ops," she said, and answered the call. "Agent Ricci."

Beth's face slowly turned to a frown, and she covered the mobile's microphone with her hand, "They just found Myra Shah dead in her condo. All her files and computer are missing."

For the second time in less than five minutes, Whittaker was left without words. As one of the safest islands in the Caribbean, the Cayman Islands averaged three or four murders a year. Florida regularly logged well over 1,000 homicides in the same time frame. Of course, the populations were vastly different, but as the detective who dealt with most serious crimes on the island, he could recall the name of every victim. They were almost exclusively men who had lost their way and become involved in the small amount of gang and drug-dealing activity that took place. These things almost never happened to law-abiding, hard-working citizens.

He let out a long breath. "I was speaking with the woman just a few hours ago," he said to no one in particular. "She was going to call me back with more details."

He looked up at Beth, who was ending her call. "This whole mess is out of control."

"The perp missed one notebook, which appears to be one she started today," Beth reported. "They're going through it now and will let us know if they find anything of use."

"Do they have any idea who did this?" Whittaker asked.

"Not yet, but they're working on CCTV and they have a rough description from an eyewitness of a male in his mid-twenties who visited the condo earlier today. They're hoping the security cameras will give them something to work with."

They all looked up at the sound of a car horn and saw Jacob waving a police van through the barriers. The press were eagerly filming the activity. Whittaker noticed the crowd had grown considerably. Many more news teams with foreign network insignias were scrambling for front-row positions.

"If he turns out to be innocent, this could turn into a big media problem for you and your island, detective," Kowalczyk pointed out.

"Do you think he's innocent?" Whittaker challenged.

"I didn't say that," Kowalczyk replied with a smirk. "But innocent and unable to prove guilt are the same thing in a court of law. This guy will show up with more lawyers than they'll fit in the courthouse. If this arrest isn't by the book, that's the first thing they'll throw out."

The van parked near the tent, a good 50 feet from Jacob's police car.

"Donovan's crimes are almost certainly on your soil, agent," Whittaker said. "My arrest will have no bearing on the case you'll bring against him back home. Besides, my immediate concern is any information that will help us right here, right now."

Kowalczyk shrugged his shoulders. "True."

"And I certainly don't care what the press have to say," Whittaker added. "That's for poor Pam in communications to deal with." He made a mental note to buy the woman a gift basket and a spa visit when this was over. "All I care is that Briggs sees the cameras of the world on him while he's in handcuffs."

Jacob ducked under the tent, beads of sweat running down his dark skin. "Sir, one last question."

"Yes, Jacob?" Whittaker replied calmly.

"What am I arresting da man for, sir?"

"Obstruction of justice and withholding vital information in a criminal case."

Whittaker looked at the two agents. "Sound good?"

They both nodded. "Great place to start," Beth replied.

Jacob returned to the van and opened the sliding side door. The driver joined him and they walked over to Jacob's car, opening the back door. Briggs was already steaming. He exited the car and started towards the tent, pointing at the detective. Jacob grabbed the man's wrist and had him cuffed before Briggs realised what was happening.

"What the hell are you doing, man?"

"I am placing you under arrest…"

Jacob didn't manage anything more, or at least anything more that could be heard over Donovan Briggs's tirade. The man cursed, screamed and fought the two constables all the way to the van while being live-streamed to multiple countries by the news crews barely constrained by the police barricade. The irony of using Jensen Massey's own method of coercing attention was not lost on Whittaker.

"I'll go play good cop for a bit," Kowalczyk said, and walked towards the van, trying his best to stay out of camera view.

"He's an ass," Beth said, once her partner was out of earshot, "but he's a good agent."

Whittaker was watching the man walk away and wondered if

Beth had read his mind. "I'm hoping so," he said, and turned her way. "How come you two are partnered if you don't get along?"

"There's not many of us in our department and my regular partner was out of town," she replied. "Just luck of the draw he was on call today."

Whittaker had far more pressing matters at hand, but his natural curiosity got the best of him. "You appear to give him a lot more respect than he reciprocates. You're more tolerant than most people would be."

Beth looked at the ground for a moment. "I made a mistake on a case a few months back, so I'm paying my dues."

"You still have your badge, so the law and your boss must have felt you acted appropriately," Whittaker said kindly.

"As I'm sure you do here, detective, we have in-depth procedures and protocols we follow. But in law enforcement, the situations always vary. That's what we're trained to handle. Adjust, adapt and make the right decision. I had to make a call on the Indian Creek case, and I went with a hunch. Someone died."

"If you made your decision based on all the information available in the moment, then it's all you could do," Whittaker pointed out.

Beth took a deep breath before replying, "The decision was whether to wait for back-up, or enter the building. I chose not to wait. A gunman was inside the warehouse with a hostage. An informant of ours, whose cover had been blown. I thought we could save him if we went in right away. I made an assumption."

"But you couldn't save him?"

"He was already dead. We were never going to help him," Beth answered, "and the agent with me was killed by the gunman inside the warehouse. If we'd waited, we could have taken him without a loss."

"Now that's an assumption, Miss Ricci," Whittaker replied. "No one knows what would have happened, as it never took place. There's a million different scenarios that could have happened."

Beth managed a weak smile.

"Our job revolves around data and facts," Whittaker continued. "We gather all we can, but it's rarely enough. If we waited for all the evidence to be in place before we did anything, we'd never solve a crime. At some point in the process, we must make decisions that only humans can make. Often that involves hunches, gut feelings, and sometimes assumptions. It's the nature of our job and we pray we get it right more than wrong." He rested a hand on her shoulder. "Post event, the data and facts are always different. More information is available, as the scenario has already played out. Everyone has the answers and thinks they know best the next day."

Beth slowly nodded and bit her lip. "Thank you. I appreciate the kind words. I have to keep my head down and do a good job. Hopefully, one day everyone will move on."

"You need to be the first," Whittaker said.

She smiled, but he knew that was much easier said than done. His own guilt presently threatened to give him a stomach ulcer. Whittaker went back to the map on the table, then paused, thinking of one more question. "But why is Kowalczyk so uptight over it?"

Beth squinted as she looked at the detective. "It was Dan's partner who was with me that day."

29

TENUOUS LINKS

Faith turned the last page containing Myra Shah's chicken scratch and looked at her own notebook where she'd copied everything relevant. Or at least what she estimated to be relevant. And could read. Miss Shah would not have won any awards for her penmanship.

Brandt returned from the bedroom, where the crime scene team and medical examiner had taken over. "Could you decipher those hieroglyphics?"

"Some," she replied. "A few have me stumped. I'm guessing she started these notes today after speaking to the cop in Cayman. This notebook looks brand new and there's only a handful of pages used. I get the impression she was reminding herself of the story and jotting things down as she recalled or looked them up."

Brandt turned a pocket-sized spiral-bound notebook, similar to the one from the kitchen, around in his hand. "They found a box of these things under the bed," he said, pointing a thumb towards the bedroom. "I had a quick look and they all appear older. She writes a date on the front of each one, the date she starts that book would be my guess. Everything in the box was at least 18 months old."

"I bet the newer pads were in her desk, and he took them," Faith commented.

Brandt nodded. "So, what have we got?"

"Search for the University of St Petersburg and find the staff listing," Faith said, by way of reply. "We know Massey's wife was a professor there, so it's not surprising the university is in her notes, but she mentions another professor by name. I think she wrote down Griffin, but look for anything with seven letters beginning with G. Or maybe C."

Brandt used his mobile to search the internet, finding the university's webpage and then their faculty listing. After a brief hunt through the website, he looked up.

"Davis Griffin, professor of Environmental Studies."

"Bingo," Faith exclaimed. "Same department as Mrs Massey."

Faith keyed her lapel mic. "Grant, let's dig up anything you can find on Davis Griffin. He's a professor at the University of St Pete."

"10-4," came the short reply.

Faith tapped a finger on her own notes she'd made. "What was the father's name?" she asked her partner.

"Briggs."

"Right, but what's his first name?"

"Um, Donovan I believe," Brandt replied.

"So maybe this is a company name," Faith mused. "Does Grayson mean anything to you?"

"That's the son," Brandt recalled. "Someone talked to him this morning."

Faith keyed her mic again. "See what you can find on Grayson Briggs, particularly in connection with Griffin."

"10-4. Griffin is coming up clean as far as any police record. A couple of parking tickets and one speeding violation in the past ten years. Looks like he's tenured at the university. Been there a long time."

"Okay, thanks," Faith replied into her mic. "Let us know if you find anything else."

An EMT wheeled a gurney across the living space towards the

bedroom and a commotion broke out by the front door, where a policeman held someone at bay. The two agents looked around and saw a blonde woman in tears having a heated discussion with the officer.

"I think that's the woman in the picture," Faith said, and nodded towards the bedroom where she'd seen the framed photograph.

They both walked to the door.

"Excuse me, officer," Brandt said politely to the policeman who was blocking the doorway. "Ma'am, please calm down and tell us your name."

Brandt positioned himself so the woman couldn't bolt past the policeman into the condo.

"I'm Erika, Erika Novak," the woman said, wiping tears away. "What's happened to Myra?"

Brandt glanced over his shoulder to his partner, who nodded, confirming the woman was the one in the picture.

"Step inside ma'am, and we'll talk in the living room."

He guided Erika inside and steered her towards the sofa facing away from the bedroom. She allowed herself to be herded and sat down without a fuss.

"Can you tell us your relationship to Miss Shah?" Faith asked softly.

Erika looked back and forth between the two agents. "We've been dating for nearly six months. Please tell me what's going on."

"I'm sorry to tell you we found Miss Shah dead, here in her condo," Brandt said firmly, but with sympathy in his tone.

The partners waited while Erika broke down into sobs and buried her head in her hands. The worst part of law enforcement was delivering a death notice, and they both thanked their lucky stars it was a rare occurrence for an FBI agent. It was usually a uniformed police officer left with the awful task.

After a few minutes, when the first wave of grief began to subside, Brandt continued. "Miss Novak, can you think of anyone who'd want to hurt her? An angry former boyfriend or girlfriend, perhaps?"

Erika looked up, her face red with mascara smeared around her puffy eyes. "Someone murdered Myra?"

"It appears that way," Faith replied.

"Murdered?" Erika repeated, struggling to process the news that undoubtedly would be a defining event in her life. "She was a beautiful soul; I can't imagine anyone wanting to hurt her."

"Had she mentioned any recent difficulties? Work issues? A difficult story? Anything like that?" Brandt asked.

Erika shook her head. "Not that I can think of. I mean, she was with me last night, and this morning we had breakfast out, while we walked the dogs. It was maybe eleven or so when we caught the news coverage of the girl abducted in the Caribbean. Myra said she knew the kidnapper."

"Did she explain anything to you about the story or how she knew the man?" Faith asked.

"Not really. She just said he'd come to her months ago, and she'd worked on a story with him," Erika said, trying hard not to break down again. "Then she began trying to reach the police on the island."

"Did you hear Myra talking to someone over there?" Brandt asked.

"Eventually, yes. But I don't know who it was. Right after that, she said she had to come here to her condo. Her old notes and computer were here. She usually kept her laptop with her at all times, but we went to a movie last night and ended up at my place instead of hers."

"She didn't say anything more to you about Jensen Massey, or mention any other names?" Faith probed. "We believe she met someone here earlier today and obviously we'd like to talk to them."

Erika shook her head but thought for a few moments. "I don't remember her mentioning anyone, and she definitely didn't talk about a meeting. She was busy making notes in one of those little books she always kept with her, so I left her to it. She gets really intense when she's on a story." Erika realised her own use of present tense and the tears flowed in torrents.

"Brandt, Graham, come down as soon as you can," came the voice over the agents' earpieces. "We have CCTV footage. You'll find us in the parking lot out front."

They rustled up a uniformed officer to take care of Erika and made their way down the stairs. The elevator had been put out of service while CSI checked for evidence. Outside in the searing heat, Brandt spotted the FBI van in the guest parking behind the building. Stealth had been thrown out the window once Myra's body had been discovered.

"Hey Grant, what do we have?" Faith asked as they crammed into the tight quarters of the van. Two men in headsets sat before an array of electronic equipment.

"Rich is pulling all the individuals from the CCTV footage right now," said the first man, Grant, who'd been the voice in their ears. "He'll then run facial recognition," he added as he clicked his computer mouse and brought up a web page on his monitor. "Meanwhile, I have a little more background on our university professor."

"Where does Griffin live?" Faith asked.

"We'll get to that interesting part of the story in a minute," Grant replied.

The image on the screen was from the university website and described some of the work the Environmental Studies program handled, which partially funded the department. They all read quietly for a few minutes, learning how the Florida Department of Environmental Protection paid several universities, including the University of St Petersburg, to carry out short- and long-term studies on water quality in their areas. The main focus for St Pete was the Manatee River, whose sprawling estuary fed into Tampa Bay and the Gulf.

"Okay, got the gist of that?"

Both agents nodded and Grant brought up a PDF file which

loaded from a web page. The title read 'Florida Department of Environmental Protection Water Quality Assessment for Tampa Bay and St Petersburg'. It was dated for the year created and credit given to the University of St Petersburg for supplying the report to the Florida DEP in keeping with the Federal Clean Water Act requirements. Named on the report were Professor Griffin, two names neither agent recognised, and Grayson Briggs.

"Wait, so this is last year's report, but Olivia Massey wasn't involved?"

"Not according to the report and I've found it in multiple locations, all credited to these four people," Grant explained. "It appears Briggs and the two other students were studying under Griffin and we don't see Massey's involvement anywhere."

"Seems like a lot of work for four people to handle while taking or teaching classes," Brandt commented. "I wonder if that's normal to involve such a small group."

Grant shrugged his shoulders. "I've no idea. I know professors often hand pick their brightest students for the most important projects."

"Can we see the grades of those students?" Faith asked. "They're not public record, are they?"

"The federal Family Educational Rights and Privacy Act prevents us, or anyone else, from accessing those records without consent," Grant replied. "It would be interesting to know if those three were indeed the stars of the department, or if daddy's generous donations to the school came into play."

"So without all of us reading the gazillion pages of this exciting report, do we know what it says?" Brandt asked.

"Funny you should ask," Grant replied with a grin and clicked to another web page on his screen. "Here's an article that came out about six months ago, discussing the report and its findings."

They all stared at the article from the *Tampa Bay Gazette*. Written by Myra Shah. The title read 'Conflicting Water Quality Results'.

"Well, we're getting a connection between all our players, but still nothing pointing towards any wrongdoing. And certainly no evidence leading us back to Olivia Massey's accident," Faith pointed out.

"Yeah, it's all tenuous links," Brandt added. "And why is Donovan Briggs the focus of Massey's attention? You'd think he'd be after the son if there was something going on at his wife's university."

Grant clicked his mouse one more time and brought up a satellite map. "Here's Briggs Paper & Packaging International, located in Fort Hamer. It's a suburb to the south of Tampa." He zoomed out from the factory to reveal a large body of water flowing past the property.

"Let me guess," Faith said. "That has to be the Manatee River."

"Bingo," Grant confirmed.

"And paper factories are notorious users of water in the manufacturing process," Brandt pointed out. "Millions of gallons of toxic waste that have to be treated before being safely returned to the environment."

"That can't be cheap," Grant noted.

"Maybe it's cheaper to shortcut the treatment and buy off the report," Faith suggested.

"We have a match," Rich blurted from the back of the van. "From the CCTV footage," he explained as everyone turned his way.

"Who?" Grant asked impatiently.

Rich angled his monitor towards the group. "I threw student IDs in the data to search along with the usual police and FBI records." He pointed at the man's face on the screen. "That's Grayson Briggs."

"Oh shit," Faith exclaimed. "I better call the agents on the island. They just arrested his father."

30

THROW HIM A BONE

Detective Whittaker looked at the monitor showing Massey's Internet feed. Skylar Briggs was still tied to the chair in a location he guessed was within a few miles of where he stood. Her chin rested on her chest, and he could see her muscles tensing and twitching as twinges of pain coursed through her body. The counter in the lower corner of the screen read 3.4 million. Whittaker couldn't process the number. It was more than the whole population of some countries. His little island in the Caribbean was currently the centre of the world's focus. For all the wrong reasons.

He'd given Donovan Briggs enough time to stew in the van with Kowalczyk's prickly assistance, so he turned away from the monitor. Beth stopped him before he reached the van, putting her mobile away in her pocket.

"I just spoke with Tampa," she told him. "They're looking for Grayson Briggs. Seems he's the prime suspect in Myra Shah's murder. They have him on CCTV entering the building earlier this afternoon."

"The son?" Whittaker questioned, trying to put the pieces together.

"He works for his father and recently graduated from the

University of St Petersburg. He studied under Griffin, the professor in the same department where Massey's wife used to teach," Beth explained. "They're working on a connection. There's a study on water quality by the university, paid for by the EPA, that could be a link. Briggs's paper manufacturing plant is right on the Manatee River estuary which is part of that report. Griffin headed the study, and Grayson was one of the students on the project."

"Do they have any evidence to suggest wrongdoing?" Whittaker asked.

"Nothing yet," Beth replied, "beyond Grayson's presence in Myra Shah's building. They also have an eyewitness who saw a man fitting his description at Shah's door."

Whittaker nodded. "Okay, thank you. If you hear anything more, please interrupt us."

The detective slid open the side door to the van and faced a very angry Donovan Briggs, seated on a bench inside.

"What the hell is this bullshit, detective?" Briggs bellowed, waving his handcuffed wrists in the air. "Have you any idea how much money I've spent on your little pile of sand in the middle of the ocean? Fucking millions! More than you'll ever make in your lifetime. And this is how I'm treated when my daughter is the victim of a lunatic!"

Whittaker slid the door closed and sat alongside Kowalczyk on the opposite bench.

"I'd like to ask you a few questions that may help us with your daughter's situation, Mr Briggs," he said calmly.

"What would help my daughter's situation is you getting back out there and hunting down this piece of shit whose taken her," Briggs shouted back. "Do your fucking job instead of holding me on trumped-up charges!"

"We believe your daughter's abduction has everything to do with you and your family, Mr Briggs, so your cooperation could greatly aid your daughter."

"I want my goddamned phone call," Briggs retorted, "and I want it now. I have a right to my lawyer being present."

"He does have the right to a phone call. And to representation," Kowalczyk said, playing his good cop role.

"You do indeed have a right to both, within a reasonable time frame," Whittaker pointed out. "And you can certainly choose to provide us with no information that may help us find your daughter. Or you can help us. It is, of course, your choice to make."

"I don't have any damned information to help you, detective. This is a waste of your time and mine."

"No problem," Whittaker said, rising to his feet, staying hunched over so he didn't hit his head on the roof. "I'll arrange for your phone call once we've resolved the emergency situation we're currently facing. We'll process you at the station and go through the formal procedures first, and then you can make your call. I'll leave it up to the FBI in Tampa to see what your son has to say."

Briggs was about to bluster about the delay in his phone call until the last sentence. "What?"

Whittaker put his hand on the door and looked back. "Your son, Grayson. He's being arrested under suspicion of murder as we speak."

"Murder? What the fuck are you talking about?" Briggs barked, but his tone had changed and Whittaker noticed he'd paled from his deep tan.

"The reporter who was about to expose you and your company, Mr Briggs," Whittaker bluffed. "She was murdered earlier today. By your son, it appears. I'm sure he'll tell the FBI everything they need to know in exchange for a lighter sentence." The detective turned to Kowalczyk. "That's how it works in America, isn't it?"

Kowalczyk nodded. "Quite often."

"You're full of shit," Briggs said, glaring at the detective. "And I want my call now!"

Whittaker slid the door open. "All in good time, Mr Briggs. I'm sure you'll agree, I should focus on finding your daughter above all else."

He stepped from the van and turned to close the door. Briggs was up off the bench with Kowalczyk holding him back with a hand to the chest.

"You motherfucker," Briggs shouted. "Wait till the Cayman Islands Governor hears how I've been treated, he's a friend of mine. You'll be handing out parking tickets next week!"

Whittaker slid the door closed with a firm clunk.

"Looks like that went well," Beth said with a smile.

Whittaker grinned. "Now we'll see how good your partner is."

"Hand me your phone," Briggs said, the moment the door closed.

"I don't have it with me," Kowalczyk lied. "He made me leave it out there with my partner."

Briggs awkwardly slapped the cushioned bench with his restrained hands. "Fuck, come on, man. I'm a US citizen, I have rights. Get me out of this fucking van."

Kowalczyk held up his hands. "I'll fight for you, sir, but there's only so much I can do on foreign soil. It's their laws here."

"What's this bullshit about my son?" Briggs said, lowering his voice. "He's lying, right?"

The agent shrugged his shoulders. "I don't think he can lie, but I've been in here, so I'm not fully up to speed." He shuffled to the edge of the bench seat and leaned towards Briggs. "You know, if you throw the guy a bone here, I'm guessing he'll cut you loose. The detective knows you're not involved in kidnapping your own daughter, he's just perceptive and figures you're not telling him everything you do know."

"I don't know shit," Briggs scoffed.

Kowalczyk shook his head. "Come on, Donovan. You know this Massey guy from somewhere. Just tell the detective how you know him and he'll lighten up. It's like you said, we need him laser focused on finding Skylar. Everything else is a distraction. Give him something so he feels like you're being straight with him."

Briggs blew out a long breath. "I want my fucking lawyer,

there's all kinds of ways that island Barney Fife could twist my words."

Kowalczyk waved a hand in the air. "I'm here to witness anything you say, Mr Briggs. He can't twist anything around. In fact, tell me and I'll relay it to Whittaker. That way, we're a hundred per cent covered. How do you know this guy, Massey?"

Briggs sat back and looked around the van, considering his predicament. The agent left him brooding for a few moments.

"I don't know him," Briggs finally said. "But I know who he is."

Kowalczyk nodded slowly. "Okay, that's good. How do you know about him?"

"Grayson, my son, went to the university where Massey's wife used to teach," Briggs admitted. "It's a good school in Tampa. I donate money to the place. Anyway, Massey's wife was killed in a road accident and the nutcase tried to come up with a crazy conspiracy theory involving me and the school. The guy's fucking crazy. I mean, I'm sorry his wife was killed, but these things happen. He couldn't handle it I guess."

"So Massey approached you after his wife's accident?" Kowalczyk asked.

"He left messages with my secretary," Briggs replied. "I never spoke to the man."

"Did the reporter contact you?"

Briggs tightened and looked away. "What reporter?" he asked, pulling his gaze back to the agent.

"Myra Shah," Kowalczyk replied. "Worked for the *Tampa Bay Gazette.*"

"He had some reporter trying to dig up dirt and make a story where there wasn't one," Briggs said dismissively. "Could have been her."

"But you didn't speak with her?"

Briggs shook his head.

"So what is Skylar's connection in all this?" Kowalczyk asked.

Briggs frowned. "Nothing, this nutjob has grabbed her to stir up all these old baseless claims of his. She's just a college kid for fuck's sake."

"Who also went to the University of St Petersburg for a brief time," Kowalczyk pointed out.

Briggs stiffened again. "She didn't like the school, she was only there a semester or two. She transferred."

"You mean she was kicked out and found another school that would take her?"

Briggs sat up and tried to point at the agent, which was cumbersome in handcuffs. "Whose fucking side are you on here? My daughter wasn't kicked out, she decided to leave. Sure, she's made a few mistakes like teenagers do, but she wasn't expelled from the university."

Whittaker put the digital radio back down on the table. They still hadn't found any obvious trace of activity along the narrow roadside waterways. He looked up at the sound of the van door closing and watched Kowalczyk walk towards him.

"Any luck?" he asked the agent.

"Claims Massey and Shah tried to contact him but he never took their calls," Kowalczyk said. "I told him I'd pass on the information and try to get him his phone call."

"At least he's finally admitted he knows the guy," Beth said, "and the reporter."

"I figured I'd give him a few minutes to think things over and I'll give it another run," Kowalczyk said. "I'll push him on his son's involvement, but I'll need to offer up something in return."

"That's your call," Whittaker replied. "Strictly speaking, we've arrested him but not processed him yet, so it's our discretion on the call. If you think he's given up all he's going to say, then let him have his call."

"He'll clam up as soon as he talks to his lawyer," Kowalczyk pointed out. "That's guaranteed."

"Agreed, but I never planned to process him anyway," Whittaker admitted. "So once he gives you all you think he will, let him make his call. We'll keep him tucked away in the van for a while after that while his people scramble around like headless chickens."

Beth couldn't hold back a grin.

"He did say one thing that was interesting," Kowalczyk added. "He claims Skylar wasn't kicked out of the university. He says she decided to leave."

"If he paid a bunch of money to smooth things over with the school, I'm sure he'd claim that to be true," Whittaker replied.

Kowalczyk nodded. "I agree, but he reacted differently when I brought it up. I think I believe him."

"Makes that timing more interesting, doesn't it?" Beth said.

"It would be quite the coincidence," Kowalczyk replied sceptically, "but Skylar has shown no signs of knowing either of the Masseys."

"Correct," Whittaker said. "Or she hasn't recognised Jensen Massey, at least."

31

FISH IN THE BOAT

Don Brandt and Faith Graham pulled up to the driveway of a large home on Culbreath Isles, an affluent bayside community in Tampa. Brandt parked their SUV, and they stepped from the air conditioning to the sweltering heat of the Florida afternoon. The light breeze off the bay filtering through the buildings did little to stave off the beads of sweat instantly forming on their foreheads.

"Grant wasn't kidding," Faith said under her breath and her partner shook his head.

Grant had finally got around to explaining where Professor Griffin lived and had noted the significant upgrade in dwellings just four months prior. The two agents looked at the Spanish villa-styled home on the water and raised their eyebrows.

"My professors weren't living large like this," Brandt commented.

They walked across the perfectly landscaped courtyard to a large wooden double door with black, wrought-iron hardware. Faith slipped a quick look at her cell phone and checked for any new messages. Nothing. Tampa police should have been knocking on Grayson Briggs's door about now, and hopefully arresting him. If the timing worked out as planned, she and her partner would be interviewing their suspect after leaving the professor's house. Brandt knocked on the heavy door and a dog barked from inside. After a few moments the door opened and a woman peered outside, keeping a golden retriever at bay with her leg.

"Can I help you?" she asked, her voice sounding as frazzled as she looked.

She was in her fifties, by Faith's estimation, and would normally be an attractive woman. But her eyes appeared puffy and her cheeks flushed.

"Mrs Griffin?" Brandt asked, and they both produced their badges.

She stared back at them, her lower lip quivering slightly, and Faith wondered if the professor's wife was about to burst into tears, slam the door, or simply pass out.

"Yes," she finally managed.

"Is your husband home, ma'am?" Brandt asked.

The woman glanced over her shoulder as though it was questionable if he was still where she'd last seen him. Or was she buying time, wondering whether or not to lie? She turned back to the visitors and let out a long sigh.

"Come in," she said, taking hold of the dog's collar as she swung the door open.

They stepped inside and took in the expansive living area and view of the bay through floor-to-ceiling windows.

"I don't know what's going on," Mrs Griffin began shakily. "Davis isn't usually like this, but I'm sure it has something to do with why you're here."

"Ma'am?" Faith questioned. "Like what?"

Both agents scanned the interior again, checking for threats. The big screen television was playing loudly in the living area, but they couldn't see anybody else in the house.

The woman shook her head. "He's been glued to the TV and I'm afraid he's been drinking," she said apologetically. "Honestly, I'm a little afraid, I don't know what's going on with him."

Faith reached out and held the woman's arm. "It's okay, ma'am.

Please stay here and keep hold of the dog. Where is your husband?"

"He's in there," she said, nodding towards the living room.

Brandt slid his jacket back, placing his hand on his firearm as he stepped from the foyer towards the living room. Faith followed after making sure the woman was staying put. Brandt circled to the right, and Faith took the left. Brandt nodded towards the sofa and Faith stopped and carefully took out her firearm. She kept it in the Sul position, within the confines of her body so Mrs Griffin didn't see it and freak out.

"Sir, we're with the FBI. We'd like to have a word," Brandt announced, shouting over the news anchor talking about the Cayman Islands kidnapping.

Faith saw a man's head appear as he rolled upright on the sofa.

"Figured you'd show up," the man slurred.

Brandt slid his firearm away and nodded to Faith, indicating he saw no threat.

"Are you Professor Davis Griffin, sir?"

The man laughed. "I hope so or he'll be pissed I drank all his best Scotch."

Faith heard a whimper from the doorway and saw Mrs Griffin was in tears. At least she was keeping the dog in check. The golden retriever didn't appear aggressive, but interviewing someone while being licked to death was always awkward.

"I see you're following the events in Grand Cayman, Mr Griffin," Brandt proceeded.

Griffin threw a hand in the air. "Who knew?"

Faith moved around the far side of the sofa near the windows and made sure no one else was around.

Griffin startled when he saw her. "Are you with him?" he spluttered.

"Yes, sir," Faith replied. "FBI Special Agents Graham and Brandt."

"FBI, huh?"

"Yes, sir. FBI," Faith said sternly. "This is a federal case as it's crossed borders."

"You know," Griffin bumbled, picking up a tumbler of Scotch from the coffee table, "when these things start, they're so harmless, you know?" He held the glass in the air as though it made his point for him, "But then they escapate... I mean escapalate... fuck..."

"Escalate, sir?" Faith threw out, hoping to help the man finish his sentence.

Griffin waved the glass around some more. "That's it."

He took a gulp and set the glass down with a thud on the table, spilling some of the amber liquid. His wife made more sobbing noises. Faith eased over next to Brandt.

"Let me get her and the dog away from here, upstairs maybe," she whispered. "I think this guy is about to spill his guts."

"It's not often the fish leap into the boat before you cast a line," Brandt replied, "but I think you're right."

Faith walked over to the front door. "Mrs Griffin, is there somewhere private you and your lovely dog here could wait while we chat with your husband?"

The woman nodded and led Faith to a room off to the side of the living area. It was a large study with bookcases lining three walls and windows to the bay on the fourth.

"Perfect," Faith said. "Give us a few minutes and I'll come and get you when we're done, ma'am."

Mrs Griffin nodded and sat down heavily on the chair behind an ornate wooden desk. The dog gave up on greeting the agents and flopped down beside her. Faith closed the door and returned to the living room. Brandt was seated in an overstuffed chair and had found the remote for the TV. He turned the volume down, but left the show on. The talking heads were already repeating the same lines they'd been saying five minutes ago, so Faith guessed nothing new had happened lately.

"So tell me how this situation went so wrong, Mr Griffin," Brandt asked casually.

The professor swayed on the sofa and eyed the agent suspiciously. Maybe he'd figured out somewhere in his stupor that he hadn't been slapped in cuffs yet. He swayed a little more and his head dropped as though his neck could no longer take the strain.

"I never should have trusted them," he mumbled, barely coherent. "By the time I knew, it was too late."

He picked his head back up and threw both hands in the air dramatically. "If you lie down with the Devil... you know," he said, rolling a hand in the air as though the rest of the idiom would spin itself onto his tongue, "you'll wake up in the deep blue sea."

Faith kept a straight face, but it took some effort.

"And obviously he paid you through..." Brandt started, but deliberately trailed off.

"Consultancy for the company. That was easy," Griffin gloated, shaking his head like the answer was the most obvious thing in the world.

Faith couldn't believe their luck. The man had obviously decided his ship was sunk before they ever showed up, and now in his drunken state he assumed they knew everything already. They'd need a bigger boat if the fish kept jumping in on their own. Brandt had barely taken the bait out of the bag.

"Of course, we have those records," Brandt lied. "And I assume it was Grayson you dealt with most of the time?"

Griffin made a nodding, head-shaking sort of motion which Faith guessed was intended as an agreement.

"You know what I don't get?" she said, playing the less informed partner, "is how Skylar fits into all this? She was your student, right?"

Griffin looked up at her through dull, unfocused eyes. "She blew the whistle," he mumbled, and the two agents looked at each other.

Faith thought about the timing. Skylar had left the university and was already in trouble several more times elsewhere before Myra Shah became involved. Besides, to Faith's knowledge, the reporter hadn't mentioned the girl.

"And everything crumbled from there, huh?" she tried, seeing if she could lure a little more information.

"Took eight months," the professor scoffed. "Enough time that I thought we were free and clear. And then this," he waved at the TV screen. "Dredged it all up again. Now we're fucked."

If she blew the whistle eight months ago, that was right at the time of Olivia Massey's accident, Faith thought.

"Do you think Jensen Massey knows it was Skylar who told his wife all about your scam?" Faith asked, piecing together the story.

Griffin frowned. "He didn't," he said firmly. "I stood three feet away from the man at his wife's funeral. Don't know how he'd find out since."

"Shit," Faith whispered. "Massey doesn't know he's mutilating and threatening to kill the only Briggs that's done the right thing."

Brandt stood up. "Grayson Briggs is being arrested as we speak for the murder of Myra Shah," he said boldly.

"The reporter?" Griffin said, looking confused.

"Murdered, earlier today," Brandt confirmed. "So if you want to help yourself out on this, you'd better tell us everything you know. That's what Grayson Briggs will start doing when we interview him. Now's your chance to beat him to it. We'll only work with one of you."

Griffin slumped back on the sofa. "Grayson's just a puppet. He won't talk. Sure, he'll tell you all about me, but we're the pawns in this game."

"We want Briggs," Faith announced. "Can you give him to us?"

Griffin looked up at her. "Grayson, no problem."

"Not Grayson," she clarified, hoping she was on the right path, "Donovan."

Griffin sneered, "Grayson won't give you his old man, and probably can't. Donovan Briggs rubs shoulders with governors and Fortune 500 execs, he doesn't get his hands dirty."

"But you have something on Donovan, don't you?" Faith pushed.

"I want my lawyer here," Griffin demanded, and Faith cursed herself for leaning on him too hard.

The professor sighed. "Get my lawyer here, and I'll tell you how to get Donovan Briggs. But I need a deal," he said, and Faith held back a smile.

"And protection. If you can't protect me, I'll end up like Olivia."

32

JOAN OF ARC

I knew I was running out of time. Trying to bash my way out had proven harder than I'd hoped. I wondered if I could break out of the exterior wall, but that wouldn't get me to Massey. I couldn't abandon Skylar at this point. Conversing had got me nowhere. I was scared of pushing him the wrong way and causing more damage. And by damage, I mean pain to Skylar Briggs.

With no other options, I focused on preparing for the final challenge. But how do you prepare for something when you have no idea what it is? He'd said something about 'speak no evil' in his description of the last challenge, but if he was using the saying with the three monkeys, that should have been the last one. See no, hear no, speak no evil, right? I questioned myself and began wondering if I had them in the right order. The first challenge had been about holding my breath and solving a puzzle. I supposed it could be construed as a sight task. In the second one I'd been blinded and relied on hearing, and the last one I was hearing again, but we were both speaking. Apparently I had them in the right order, but none of that gave me a clue to what lay ahead. We were out of monkeys.

I could hear movement from the other room, but it was impossible to tell what was happening. Massey was walking back and forth, his heavy footfalls vibrating the flooring, and I thought I heard water running. Hopefully, he was cleaning Skylar's wound, or at least wiping her face or something pleasant. There were occasional clunks and bumps, but it was all muffled to my ears and hard to identify.

"Hurting me won't get to my dad," I heard Skylar say. "You should take your problem up with him. Maybe he'd meet with you to sort it out."

Massey laughed with no hint of humour. "Meet with me? He wouldn't even take my phone calls. He had his chance. I tried talking with him and he chose to ignore me, which was to be expected from the likes of him. Now it's come to this."

"I don't understand," Skylar whimpered. "I have as little to do with my dad as possible, it's not fair to take your problem out on me."

"Not just your father," Massey pointed out, and I heard him moving with more haste and heavier footsteps. He was getting agitated.

"Whatever. His company too," Skylar said. "I don't work for him, you know, I'm just a student."

"Sometimes you're a student," Massey corrected. "I lost track. Are you currently enrolled somewhere, or did you get kicked out again?"

"Fuck you," she groaned.

Skylar seemed to give up, and all I could hear was Massey moving about, setting up whatever he'd concocted for the next part of his show. I looked around my tiny room again, looking for anything remotely useful. I had no idea what constituted useful, as my situation was unique, at least to me, but I looked regardless. Picking up the helmet, I checked it over for any loose parts that could become a tool or weapon. Unless I resorted to bashing a hole in the wall with my head, I couldn't come up with a use.

Next, I wiggled the whiteboard to see if it was screwed in place or hung there. It moved slightly, but didn't come away from the wall. I heard a tearing sound that was familiar. Velcro. I tugged firmly at the board and it pulled away, accompanied by more tearing sounds. The board was too big to utilise for anything I could think of, but I sat on the floor and studied the aluminium pen tray along the bottom. I couldn't see any screws, so I guessed it was glued to the board. If I ripped it off, maybe the piece of extrusion could be a pry bar or even a bat, although it didn't weigh very much. Being hit with it would be more annoying than damaging.

"Nora, what are you doing?" came Massey's voice over the speakers.

I'd hoped he was too busy to notice what I was up to. "I'm bored," I said, looking up towards the camera above where the whiteboard had been. My eyes never made it to the camera. Two long Velcro strips remained stuck to the wall and between them was a TV screen or monitor of some sort, set into the partition. It had been hidden behind the whiteboard.

"I'm sorry I've failed to adequately entertain you," Massey said, "But I think you'll find that will change shortly."

"Take your time," I replied, shoving the whiteboard aside and standing up.

"We have a few more minutes, but I'd planned to have you take the board down once I was ready, so you could watch the next video," he said.

"One step ahead of you," I said to the wall.

I heard a chuckle from the other room. Glad I could amuse the man. Maybe he didn't realise I was over this shit and would gladly beat him over the head with an aluminium whiteboard pen tray, given the chance. Perhaps I could annoy him into submission. His gun was probably more effective, but he shouldn't underestimate a pissed-off Viking.

"So, Mr Massey," I started, "what does this final challenge have in store?"

"Hey!" I heard Skylar blurt. "Your name is Massey?"

It hadn't occurred to me that Skylar didn't know the man's name, but it made sense when I thought about it. The only reason I knew was from Whittaker. They'd made the ID before I got in the water at the dock. That felt like so long ago already. The video I'd seen hadn't mentioned his name and neither he nor I had used it until now.

"Jensen Massey, yes. I apologise I didn't formally introduce myself."

"Shit," Skylar blurted. "Now I understand."

The movement next door stopped.

"You don't know me," Massey said, sarcastically.

"Not you," Skylar replied hesitantly.

I moved closer to the wall and rested my hands against the plywood, listening carefully.

"I knew your wife."

The room went quiet for a few moments.

"I know you briefly attended her university," Massey said. "You met her there I presume."

"I didn't have her class," Skylar said, still sounding unsure.

"I know that," Massey replied, beginning to sound impatient. "You studied under that bastard, Griffin."

I heard his feet moving again and presumed he'd gone back to his preparations.

"I saw her that night," Skylar said, her voice shaking.

All movement stopped once again.

"What?" Massey snapped. "You saw Olivia the night she was killed?"

"I met with her."

I was riveted to the conversation. His wife had died. Or more accurately, had been killed. This was news to me.

"You met? Where?" Massey asked, his voice changing. "About what?"

It was difficult to pinpoint the emotion in his voice. It was a mixture of surprise, suspicion, and something else.

"In her office," Skylar replied. "It was late, no one else was there."

"Why? What was it about?"

For a moment I wondered if Skylar was talking so softly I couldn't hear her, but then she spoke again.

"Your wife was looking into the study the university had conducted for the Florida Environmental Protection Agency."

"I know that, but why was she talking to you?"

"It was my fault," Skylar replied, her voice breaking, and I guessed she was crying.

"You were in on this with your brother?" Massey boomed, and I began to panic. If he was going to lose it, I had to try again to break down the door.

"No, no," Skylar quickly replied, "I had no idea they'd go that far."

"Then how did you know about the study?" Massey grilled, and I pictured him towering over the girl tied to the chair, gun in hand.

"I heard Grayson and my dad talking about it," she said defensively. "We were out on our boat and they forgot I was there. Or didn't care."

"You helped Olivia look into the study?" Massey asked incredulously.

There was another pause, and I held my breath, pressing an ear to the wall.

"I'm the one who asked her to look into it," she said weakly.

Massey had said that Skylar had nothing to do with the day's events. An innocent victim. She had the misfortune of being Donovan Briggs's daughter as her only sin. Against Massey, at least. But this changed everything. If she was working with his wife, it seemed like they were on the same side. Surely he'd let her go?

"You're the anonymous tip that started it all?" he muttered.

"Except, I wasn't totally anonymous," Skylar corrected. "I met with your wife and asked her to look into the study. What they were doing was wrong. Once I knew about it, I couldn't let it go on. I asked her to keep my name out of it, and she promised."

"What about that night?" Massey urged. "You still haven't told me what happened that night."

"Olivia was stuck," Skylar began. "Everything on the university servers was bogus figures from the water tests. She could see from historical data and a test she conducted herself that the numbers weren't right. She asked me if there was anything else I could provide her."

Skylar paused and took a few breaths. I was glad she hadn't taken the pain pills she was offered, as I doubted she'd be this coherent. This was a different side to the gum-snapping rich kid I hadn't imagined. A side worth saving.

"My brother and two of his buddies conducted all the tests, then provided fake data to Griffin. To make sure the data was realistic, Griffin had created a formula to offset the real results. Grayson applied the formula before uploading the data. But the formula itself was on the server. I snooped in Grayson's university email account and found where Griffin had sent an attachment with a revised formula. That's why I went to see Olivia. I told her about the formula."

"She called me," Massey said, sounding utterly deflated. "On her way home, shortly before the crash. She told me I wouldn't believe what she'd found. I'd been asleep on the couch and the phone woke me up. It was really late. She was going to tell me everything when she got home. But she never made it home." His voice trailed off, and I waited, unsure what was about to happen. He continued, on the verge of breaking down. "She told me she loved me, and we hung up. I said nothing back. I had the chance for my last words to my soulmate to be 'I love you', and I was too tired to say it."

The room fell silent once again, and I tried to process all the new information. Skylar was on his side. She could provide the evidence he needed to prove whatever these reports they were talking about were fake. He had to let her go.

"This changes nothing," Massey barked. "Maybe you're telling the truth, maybe you're lying to save your own skin, but I'm finishing what I started. You've had eight months to come to me and tell me what you told Olivia, but you didn't. You chose to stay quiet and let her death go unpunished. You knew they killed her to shut her up."

"I didn't know for sure!" Skylar screamed. "I was scared to death. I had no idea what to do. My dad moved me to another school and never told me why. I was terrified."

"It's too late now. The world is waiting to hear about your family and how Olivia was murdered for their profit," Massey ranted. "If you're lying, then you deserve the suffering I've caused you. If you're telling the truth and this ends badly, then I'll be the Devil and you'll be Joan of fucking Arc."

I banged on the wall. "No! She's innocent, damn it! She helped your wife!"

Massey ignored me, and I heard Skylar sobbing. I banged harder and yelled.

"It's over! You have the evidence you need!"

More movement echoed from next door, and Skylar yelped. My whole view of the girl had shifted. For all her problems, attitude and mistakes, she had tried to do the right thing. Now she was being punished by one of the people she was trying to help. I hoped his reference to Joan of Arc was figurative, and burning was not involved in the final challenge. There was nothing I dreaded more than being burned alive. I smashed my hand against the wall, but Massey didn't respond.

I stepped back and considered taking a run at the door when the TV came to life. A video began playing and haunting music drowned out anything happening in the next room. I was looking at the crushed remains of a BMW.

33

A BASKET FULL OF EGGS

The wrecked car was hardly recognisable as a BMW, the emblem on the boot the only clue. Whittaker winced at the news footage showing the wrinkled front of the box truck, dragged off to the side by a tow truck. Massey's voice began narrating over the film.

"Olivia Massey was killed in a hit-and-run accident while driving home from work late one evening. The truck which hit her had been stolen, and two men were observed fleeing the scene by two separate eyewitnesses in neighbouring buildings. A car pulled up and stopped moments later, according to the same eyewitnesses. A man in dark clothing walked along the top of the divider wall that Olivia's car was crushed against, and took something from inside the vehicle. He spent an estimated 30 seconds at the crash site before returning to his own car and leaving.

"The witnesses, who observed from the windows of their apartments, both over 100 yards away, could only give vague descriptions of all three people and the vehicle that stopped. Neither the man, nor his car, nor the two men from the truck, were ever identified. Olivia's cell phone, laptop and satchel she always carried with her were all missing and never recovered."

Images of Olivia Massey in running gear scrolled across the screen. They were all from events with competition numbers pinned to her shirt, and in many she stood proudly holding up a medal on a ribbon.

"Olivia ran marathons. She usually placed in the top three for her age group and top thirty overall in the women's division. Yet, according to the autopsy report, she died of a heart attack."

More pictures appeared on the video, all clearly showing a fit, lean woman with a broad smile. Olivia was a pretty lady.

"A marathon runner with no history of heart trouble. A perfect picture of health. The injuries sustained in the impact were extensive, she had multiple broken bones and a punctured lung. None of which were life threatening if treated in a reasonable timeframe. An ambulance was onsite within ten minutes of the two eyewitnesses both making 911 calls. Olivia should have been alive when they arrived. Instead, she was already dead.

"What did the man do when he leaned into the car? Obviously, he stole all the crucial evidence she had gathered, but what else? She was probably conscious, and likely thought help had arrived. But rather than come to her aid, the man was making sure she was silenced."

After a long pause on the wrecked BMW, the video switched to shots of a large building with nicely landscaped grounds.

"Olivia was a professor at the University of St Petersburg in Florida, where she taught Environmental Studies. She enjoyed teaching at the school she described as big enough to make a difference and small enough to know people's names. Like many universities, the school took on outside projects for which they were compensated. These projects provided students with valuable real-world experience and the kudos of having their names attached to the reports.

"The Florida Environmental Protection Agency are required to test drinking water sources and coastal waters annually. They employ several universities throughout the state to conduct these tests. They also provide standards to which the tests must adhere and be reported. Olivia's tenured associate, Professor Griffin, headed up USP's annual study. He had done so since they gained the contract three years ago.

"Hand chosen by Griffin to be part of the project last year were several students. One of those selected was Grayson Briggs, the son of Donovan Briggs and heir to the Briggs Paper & Packaging International company. Brother of Skylar Briggs, who you've all met today. The area of focus in the study was the Manatee River and its sprawling estuary that runs into Tampa Bay and on to the Gulf of Mexico. Situated on the banks of the river, in Fort Hamer, is Briggs Paper & Packaging International, who use massive quantities of river water in their manufacturing process. That water is highly toxic post process and requires extensive treatment and purification before a large percentage is returned to the source. The remaining amount is held in retainment ponds. Managing the water supply, processing and disposal is one of the highest costs in the paper manufacturing business.

"By definition, Grayson Briggs checking water pollution levels near his father's paper mill, was the fox guarding the henhouse. It should never have been allowed, and Professor Davis Griffin was the man responsible for the oversight."

A picture of Griffin with three male students appeared on the screen. One of them was Grayson Briggs.

"Except this wasn't an oversight," Massey continued his narration. "It was planned."

Whittaker found it hard to turn away from the screen, but watching Massey's riveting presentation wouldn't find Skylar and Nora. The most recent report from the FBI in Tampa suggested Griffin was about to roll over on Donovan Briggs, so the detective was happy to keep Skylar's father secured in the police van for now. The hunt was on for Grayson Briggs, and by the counter rolling along like an electricity meter on Christmas Eve, a large portion of the world was watching it all unfold. He needed to find the two women.

"What's the next move, detective?" Beth asked, pulling herself away from the TV feed now showing screenshots of toxicity reports and talking about pH, dissolved oxygen and turbidity.

"Put the helicopter up," Whittaker replied. Her timely question was the final catalyst in his decision. "Once he moves to the final challenge in a few minutes, I think the risk of him interrupting whatever he has planned is lessened. The chopper can cover the park in a few minutes and hopefully spot what we've not been able to find from the ground."

"If he has constructed that building in the past few weeks, there should be signs of activity around it," Beth offered. "He had to get the timber and supplies there somehow, right?"

Whittaker quickly moved to one of the IT techs seated at the table, "Bring up the high-res satellite image again, please."

He tapped his fingers on his leg while the tech opened the large file.

Beth joined the detective. "Come up with something?" she asked.

Once the image appeared on the screen, he pointed to the west end of the park where the border doglegged around The Shores property. "Zoom in here."

The tech made the area larger, and Whittaker stared at the screen. "There," he said, pointing to a cleared area surrounded by trees and shrubs. "It's another maintenance storage area for the development. They stage building supplies rather than have them littered all over the neighbourhood when new construction is going on."

"It backs right onto the woods of the park," Beth noted.

"We've been searching the canal edges, because that's how we think he took the women from the first building," Whittaker explained. "I had it in my mind that he would have used the same entrance to build the shack. I was relying on my guys finding obvious marks on the bank."

"But maybe he only used that entrance once, and came in

another way when he was constructing the place," Beth said, finishing the thought.

"From the maintenance area, there's probably a fence of some description, but then he'd be straight into the woods without a canal to cross if he built on the far side of the last marl road," Whittaker added as he snatched up the digital radio. "Firearms Response Units, report your positions, over."

The radio crackled, and they both listened to the systematic reports.

"This is Unit One, we're on the road to the south of the sea pond. Nothing to report. Over."

"Dis is Unit Two, we're on da road runnin' parallel to Shorewinds Trail. Nothin' to report. Over."

"Unit Three reporting, we've patrolled the roads leading to the park entrance. Nothing to report. Over."

Whittaker thought for a moment before replying, "Units One and Three continue the search. Report when complete. Unit Two exit the park and come around to The Shores. You're looking for the storage area north of Vulgunner's Pond on the east side of the development. It borders the park. Over."

All three teams verified, and Whittaker turned back to the satellite image on the screen, nervously rubbing the light stubble on his chin. Massey's prepared video had moved on to results of his own independent water tests which showed elevated levels of contaminants in the water, downstream of the paper factory. He looked at Beth.

"I'm thinking of putting all my eggs into one basket," he said.

Beth chewed her lip, and their eyes met. "You make your decision based on all the information available in the moment," she said. "That's all you can do."

Whittaker managed a smile.

"A smart fellow told me that," Beth added, "not too long ago."

"What's your gut telling you?" Whittaker asked.

Beth shook her head. "I think you've heard; my gut isn't to be trusted."

Kowalczyk walked under the tent and went to speak until he realised the detective and his partner were in the middle of a discussion. He paused and waited. Beth nervously glanced at Kowalczyk, then back at Whittaker.

"Time is up. Once the fourth challenge is under way, there's nothing stopping him attempting his escape, whatever he says about handing himself in," she said. "I don't believe he'll shoot either one of the women at this point, even if you break his rules. He wants the show to play out and I'm sure he wants distance from any further violence."

"Fuck me," Kowalczyk blurted. "Do you never learn?"

"What would you do?" Whittaker snapped back, turning to Kowalczyk.

"We're not here to tell you what to do," he replied defensively.

"I'm not sure why you're here at all," Whittaker said, glaring at Kowalczyk.

The agent threw his hands up. "If this was back home, I'd have our tactical team covering the whole park. They'd be crawling around the place like ants and we'd find the building and take it. But you don't have enough people, or highly trained teams."

"That's correct," Whittaker replied firmly. "So we can't take a shotgun approach, we have to be a sniper."

He took out his mobile and made a call.

"Sergeant?" he said when the call was answered. "Put the chopper up and make sure they're ready to drop a couple of guys in. I'm sending you the location to focus on. How soon can they be airborne?"

"Dey'll be up in less than tree minutes from when I hang up, sir," the man replied. "Dey waitin' on the command. All aboard and ready."

"I'm texting you a picture of the location as soon as I hang up," Whittaker said, and ended the call.

He leaned over and took a photo of the screen with the satellite map. He quickly marked a circle around the area where he guessed the structure to be, using the phone's drawing tool, and sent the text.

On the Internet feed, the recorded segment ended, and Massey appeared on screen. He was outside with thick woods behind him. He looked up at the camera.

"It's time to bring today's events to a close with the final challenge," he announced, and Whittaker noted how tired the man looked.

"As I've laid out in the series of videos you've seen this afternoon, my beautiful wife, Olivia, was taken from me." His voice broke, and he paused a moment, collecting himself. "Taken from us, not just me. She was murdered to keep a secret hidden. A secret about the corruption and lies created to increase one man's profits. Donovan Briggs, his son Grayson Briggs, along with Davis Griffin, supplied falsified reports to the EPA to allow his paper mill to shortcut safety and water purification measures for their own personal gain. They have caused enormous harm to the environment, along with polluting the waters where thousands of citizens work and play. And they murdered my wife.

"The final challenge is about 'Do no Evil'. In response to the evil these men have done, I have been forced into doing evil today. I take that responsibility because the system failed to provide justice. Skylar Briggs has suffered, and her life is now on the line, because of her family's transgressions. The innocent are paying the price once again.

"For this final challenge, Nora must find the combination for two locks securing Skylar inside a tank that is filling with water. The clues to the combinations are in the room. Good luck to you both."

Massey took a deep breath and stared into the camera. "The challenge begins the moment Nora opens the door."

The feed switched to a shot inside the shack of a closed door. Whittaker didn't wait to see anymore. He marched from the tent towards the van where Donovan Briggs was still being held.

"Where are you going?" Kowalczyk asked.

"To my basket full of eggs," Whittaker replied. "There's no point staying here any longer."

Beth jogged along behind him and took the passenger seat as Whittaker got behind the wheel.

34

DO NO EVIL

As soon as Massey suggested the door was unlocked, I threw it open and immediately regretted my stupidity. In the middle of the room, which was slightly bigger than the one I'd been in, was a thick Perspex tank. Inside the tank, with barely enough room to fit on her hands and knees, was Skylar. Water gushed into the tank from a tube coming up through the floor. Tied to the door I had opened was a line running through a hole in the floorboards. Opening the door had triggered a valve, letting the water in. If I'd paid attention to what he said, I could have left the door closed and we both could have waited to be found.

"Help me, for fuck's sake!" Skylar screamed, and I ran to the tank.

A Perspex lid was hinged on one side with a clasp and a combination padlock on the opposite side. Massey had said there were two locks. I looked inside, where the terrified face I'd only seen on a TV screen until now stared back at me. Her wrists were handcuffed to a U-bolt in the floor of the tank, secured by a second combination padlock. I had to get past the lid and then solve the second lock to free her from the tank before she drowned. At least it wasn't fire.

I stood up and scanned the room. There were pictures on two walls, but I ignored them and ran to the door leading outside. It was locked. I stepped back and gave it a kick. It didn't budge at all but a pain shot up my foot as all I had on my feet were the thin water shoes. I tried one more kick on the hinge side with the same result before hobbling back to the tank. I wasn't sure how getting outside would save Skylar from drowning, but maybe I could shut off the water source.

"Come on!" Skylar yelled, "You have to get me out!"

I looked at the wall. A large number two hung above three white picture cards. I spun around. The opposite wall had a number one, and a single picture card. I went over and looked at the picture. It was a stone monument of some sort overlooking the ocean. It looked familiar. Pale white stone formed a rectangular block with a plaque on the front. I couldn't read the writing on the plaque from the printed picture. I had seen the monument some-where, but I couldn't think where.

"What the fuck are you doing? Get me out!" Skylar screamed again.

"Shut up," I yelled back, "I'm trying to think."

I heard her continue cussing and grumbling, but at least she did it quietly. The monument was somewhere here on the island and I'd stood in front of it. I'd experienced the view depicted in the photograph. If this was being live-streamed, which it undoubtedly was, I imagined all the Caymanians and a shit ton of tourists, shouting the answer at their screens. That wasn't any use to me. Neither the prompts I couldn't hear, nor me wasting time worrying about being watched as I botched this up. AJ would know what the hell this was.

"East End!" I yelped. "AJ took me to this lump of stone at the other end of the island!"

It memorialised the famous wreck that happened there hundreds of years ago. I rushed back to the tank and looked at the combination lock. It had four digits.

"The Wreck of Ten Sail," I said, looking at Skylar through the clear Perspex. "What year did it happen?"

"What?" she said, the water already over her knees.

"The famous wreck at East End," I repeated. "What year did that happen?"

"How the hell do I know?" she replied in a high-pitched panic.

"You don't know about it?" I asked, unsure why I was surprised.

"Sure I do, there's a statue-type thing. I've been there."

"But you don't remember the year?" I persisted.

"Do you?" she said, frowning at me.

"Sure, I just wanted to see if you knew before you drowned."

I know that didn't help, but just when I started thinking she was worth saving, she pissed me off every time.

"17 something," she said, still frowning.

I rolled the first two digits to 1 and 7.

"It was late in the century I think." Half guessing, and partly remembering.

Skylar nodded.

I rolled the third digit to 8 and began at zero on the fourth tumbler, giving the lock a good tug as I paused at each number. No luck, it wasn't 1780 something.

"1770 or 1790?" I asked, already setting the third tumbler to 9.

"90," she replied, which made me feel good, for no reliable reason.

I spun the fourth digit with no luck until I got to 4. The lock pulled open and I flipped the lid over. One down.

"Yes! You did it, you did it!" Skylar yelped.

"We did it," I said and stood to look at the other wall. "But we're only halfway there."

There were three pictures. The first was a box, or a square, I wasn't sure which. The second, a simple illustration of a tree with roots below the ground. And the third was the number 60,516. Below the three white picture cards were the words 'Days since Olivia Massey was murdered'.

"When was Olivia Massey's accident?" I shouted to Skylar.

"Like, eight months ago," she called back.

"But when exactly? Do you remember the date?"

I heard splashing and turned around. The water was up to her chest. The way the handcuffs held her wrists on the floor of the tank, it forced her arms into a bend so she couldn't straighten them. This kept her head lower, so even with the lid gone, she couldn't raise her airways above the top of the tank. I looked back at the wall. I had no idea what these clues meant.

Picking one of the cameras, I began describing all I knew about where we were, pantomiming as best I could in case there was no sound. I could only hope the camera I chose was the one broadcasting and Massey didn't switch it away.

"We're in a small building in the woods about ten metres from the water. We were brought here by a canoe or small boat," I said, paddling as though I was in a boat.

"It was a canoe!" Skylar yelled, "And we came along a series of little rivers or canals. They were next to a gravel road above the water."

I relayed the details as best I could in signals. At the end I tapped on my ear, remembering the droning sound. "Listen for what I think is a generator."

Maybe they could get here to help, because without it, I was sure I couldn't save her. I felt a panic rising as I realised I'd be watching a human being drown before my eyes with nothing I could do about it. The thought was terrifying.

I looked around the room. He'd bolted the chair to the floor one metre from the wall. The tank was dead centre, and a folding table was against the outside wall by the door. I needed something to smash the tank. I could try to break the chair apart, but the pieces would be too light. Much like my aluminium extrusion next door. There was a small hole in the wall down low behind the table and I wondered why? Power cable. It was just big enough for a power plug to pass through. But the table was cleared of any electronics.

On the floor by the table sat a small plastic cooler. I winced at the thought of what was in there.

I went over to the folding table. It had a two-part plastic top, hinged in the middle so it folded in half for carriage and storage. Hollow metal legs supported it, which also folded away. Hollow legs. Plan B.

I flipped the table over and looked at how the legs were mounted to the plastic. Metal clasps wrapped around a lateral tube as its pivot and the leg assembly was welded to the tube. I dragged the table onto its side, held the leg frame of one end, then kicked like hell on the underside of the plastic top.

"What are you doing? I can't see you!" Skylar screamed, but I didn't have time to deal with her. Actually, she didn't have time for me to deal with her. I wasn't the one about to drown.

I kicked as hard as I could and pain shot through my heel and up my leg, but I kept kicking. One clasp began to give way and three kicks later I was holding the metal leg assembly in my hand, separated from the top. The frame was shaped like an 'H', attached to the pivot tube on top. The uprights curved, spreading wider at the top tube and where they met the floor. I needed to break the frame apart. Any one piece of the tube would suit my needs.

Moving across the room, I swung the frame up over my head and brought it crashing down across the back of the chair. A shock wave shuddered through my arms and the frame flew out of my hands, crashing into the wall and landing on the floor.

"What the fuck are you doing?" Skylar screamed.

"Trying to save your arse," I barked back as I picked the frame back up.

"By throwing shit around the room?" she screamed. "You're supposed to be figuring out the clue!"

"Fuck the clue, we'll get to that," I mumbled as I lifted the frame over my head. "First you have to breathe."

I smashed the frame down again, this time making sure I caught the corner of the top tube and the vertical leg right on the top of the chair. The metal snapped and the top tube pulled away from the one leg.

"Hurry, it's up to my face!"

I glanced over and saw the water lapping against Skylar's chin. Even with her head tilted painfully back, she only had another minute at most. I put the legs to the floor and grabbed the top tube, which stuck up at a weird angle, broken away from one leg and bent at the joint of the other. Putting a foot on the crossbar of the 'H', I took the loose end of the top tube and began working it up and down, weakening the second weld. Slowly my wrenches moved the tube farther and farther until it snapped away and I almost fell over.

I now had a tube. Slightly bent, but it was a tube, and I needed it bent more, without it collapsing. I ran back into the room I'd been held in and grabbed the helmet. Sitting it on the chair, I rested the tube over the top of the helmet and pushed down on either side. The thin-walled steel tube began to bend around the curved top of the helmet. I stopped and offset the tube to one side to bend it farther along its length. If I tried to bend it too much in one place, it was going to crush and split. If it split, Skylar was going to drown.

Working the metal tube around the curve of the helmet, I had a long tube that turned roughly 90 degrees. Maybe that would be enough. I leaned over the tank and put the tube into the water, guiding one end towards Skylar's mouth. She looked up at me in confusion.

"It's a snorkel so you can breathe," I pointed out.

She tried to take it in her mouth, but when she held it in her teeth, the other end dragged below the surface and she spluttered and wriggled around in a panic. I took the tube back out, and she gasped for air. A few more seconds and she would only be able to breathe through her nose. I needed more bend.

Back at the chair, I laid the metal over the helmet and began urging a degree or two more from each section of the tube. I was terrified it would yield. I could hear spluttering and choking from the tank behind me.

"Breathe through your nose, not your mouth," I yelled.

From the odd snorting sounds that followed, I guessed she was trying her best. I had almost 120 degrees in the bend now and set it over the helmet for a last round of tweaks. Before I could start, Skylar began thrashing inside the tank, and water sloshed all over the place, spilling over the sides. I guessed her nose had been submerged and she'd freaked out. Understandably. I snatched up the helmet and used it as a scoop, slinging water from around her, although I couldn't get much at a time as her body filled most of the tank.

With the level temporarily reduced, she was breathing through her mouth and coughed violently from the water she'd swallowed.

"Okay, let's try this again," I said and dunked the tube in the tank so both ends remained out of the water.

This time she could just hold the tube in her teeth with the other end still above the surface.

"Perfect. Now gently breathe in long inhales and even longer exhales," I encouraged. "Be calm. If you don't breathe out enough, you'll suck back in the same carbon dioxide."

The water was over her mouth once more, but she was breathing through my homemade snorkel. She was still alive. For now.

35

LOCK UP YOUR SAILBOATS

Fighting through the throngs of media and curious citizens packed behind the barricade at the dock took far longer than Whittaker had hoped. His constables had done their best to keep Batabano Lane clear, but being short handed and overrun by the sheer number of vehicles had left an obstacle course for the detective to manoeuvre. Beth had set her mobile in a holder on the dash so they could all see Massey's live-stream.

"A building, in the woods, ten feet from the canal, next to a road, and they paddled there," Beth said as she watched Nora standing next to the tank, hands on hips, looking at the clues on the wall. "And listen for something."

There was no sound, but they'd both seen Nora perform a series of signals before she'd turned a table leg into a life-saving snorkel.

"Probably metres," Whittaker corrected. "She's from Norway. Nora thinks in metric. She has to convert when making radio calls as we work in imperial on the island."

Whittaker keyed his digital radio and relayed the information to the tactical units and the helicopter swooping overhead, running a search pattern across the park.

"That's one impressive young lady," Beth said after the detective finished his radio call. "Most people would have panicked and not made it past the first lock. She used every resource in the room, including Skylar. Assessing the situation and switching from solving the puzzle to buying time with the tube took poise under pressure. She'll get recruitment offers from all kinds of agencies when this is over."

Whittaker shook his head, and once again cursed himself for getting the girl into this mess. "First of all, it needs to be over. And without anyone else being hurt. Including Nora," he replied. "After which, she may be flattered by offers, but my guess is she'll turn them all down. Although, I admit, Nora is anything but predictable."

"Thousands of applicants are turned down every year for those jobs," Beth added. "They're sought after, and not easy to get."

"Nora doesn't care about money, or position, or how anything looks to someone else. She's more likely to disappear and none of us will know where she went," Whittaker responded, genuinely worried how his protege would react to the attention. "Nora's good at being invisible when she needs to be."

"I hope she doesn't. For your sake," Beth said. "You'd lose a great officer."

"And probably a sailboat," Whittaker muttered under his breath.

"Well, regardless, she did a great job giving us the location, and it proves you were right about that," Beth said as she watched the helicopter through the windscreen, banking for another pass.

"We'll see," Whittaker replied as he sped through The Shores neighbourhood.

"She gave you the type of location, not the actual location," Kowalczyk added from the back of the van through the steel bars and mesh separating them.

He'd scrambled in through the sliding door as they'd pulled away from the dock and had been useful in calming Donovan Briggs down along the way. Whittaker glanced in the rear-view mirror at the agent in the back. The man's glass seemed permanently half empty. But he wasn't wrong. Presumably Nora didn't know exactly where they were. She only knew the details she'd passed on. The building could be ten metres from any canal in the park. But the detective had chosen his basket, and all eggs were present.

In a row of empty, cleared house lots ready for future construction, one plot was surrounded by trees and shrubs, screening its interior from view. Whittaker swung the van through a break in the tree line, the tyres slipping on the loose surface. Skidding to a halt, he looked around. The construction storage area was an open space with a small mobile building in one corner and various stacks of timber and other building materials stacked along the edges. Another police van was already there and the officers from Unit Two were searching the fence line adjoining Barkers.

"Stay with Mr Briggs if you wouldn't mind, agent," Whittaker said to Kowalczyk before jumping out of the van, closely followed by Beth on the passenger side.

"I'm coming along!" Briggs yelled. "It's my daughter, damn it!"

Whittaker leaned back into the van. "You'll remain here Mr Briggs," he said firmly. "I promise we're doing all we can to find Skylar."

"You'd better find her, damn you," Briggs seethed. "Maybe I'll forget about this travesty if you bring my daughter back safe."

"And you might consider being more forthcoming with Agent Kowalczyk. He could be your only hope when this is over," Whittaker added.

He didn't wait for either man's response and closed the van door.

The thumping of the helicopter's blades filled the air as it searched from above. Whittaker looked up and wondered why he hadn't heard from them yet. Surely they would have seen the building by now, they'd made a dozen passes. He ran to the fence line, where the officers were looking for any sign of passage into the woods.

"The fence is intact, sir, all da way along," Williams explained. "Don't see anyway he gone through here."

Whittaker nodded and looked around the area. The helicopter was making a turn out of sight to the west, but as low as it was flying, the noise had the men shouting to be heard. He unclipped the digital radio from his belt and shielded the mic as best as he could.

"Chopper, this is Whittaker. Anything to report?"

"Negative, sir," came the short reply.

Whittaker let out a long groan. Maybe he'd been wrong. He'd focused all their efforts on this area of the park, and Massey could be somewhere else entirely. He'd been sure this had to be an access point, but standing in what appeared to be a dead end was proving him wrong. Too late now, he considered, this was the basket he'd chosen.

"Okay chopper, I need quiet for a minute," Whittaker ordered. "Take a sweep out over the ocean, copy?"

"Roger that, heading to the water. Over."

The engine and pounding of air from the blades receded as the helicopter left the area and all became quiet beyond the crackling of the occasional radio call from the other units. The tactical team all had earpieces, so Whittaker turned the volume off on his radio, the only one making noise.

"Hold up everyone!" he bellowed, and the men stopped their movements. "Listen carefully, tell me if you hear anything unusual."

The men looked slightly confused, but most slipped their earpieces out to listen clearly. Birds chirped and insects buzzed. In the distance, cars could be heard on a road, and the sound of the helicopter was steadily fading. A low hum was barely audible. Like a background bass note to the chorus of critters. Whittaker turned to Beth. She was walking away towards the left side of the lot. He walked softly behind her, following.

Several officers gravitated the same way, but Whittaker held up a hand for them to stop. Their gentle footsteps on the loose gravel and dirt were enough to lose the sound. Beth reached a large stack of plywood sheets wrapped in plastic. The light breeze across the low treetops from the north made the plastic ripple and snap, drowning out the hum they were tracking.

Beth moved behind the stack, down a four-foot gap between the supplies and the fence defining the side of the storage area. Metal poles driven into the ironshore base supported the chest-high chain link. Whittaker looked at the ground and noted the well-worn path behind the plywood stacks. Beth nodded at the fence, and Whittaker joined her. The rattle of the plastic still overpowered the hum they'd been moving towards. Attached to the chain link wire was a strip of metal which in turn was resting on two hooks screwed into the original metal pole. Beth lifted the strip off the hooks and swung the fence section out of the way, revealing access into the woods.

Whittaker stood in the newly opened gap and faced a screen of small trees and shrubs, all over head height, running the length of the lot. The makeshift gate in the fence appeared to lead nowhere accessible. He reached out and shook the first branch he grabbed. The whole section before him shook in unison. He delved deeper into the foliage and, with both hands holding branches, he shoved at the brush. A four-foot-wide clump moved away from him as he pushed. He stepped forward and pushed again, shoving the foliage farther into the surrounding woods.

"Over here," he called out loudly and heard the shuffle of feet from the lot as the tactical team joined them.

With one more good shove, the clump of brush moved easily out of the way and revealed a cleared path. Whittaker set the doorway of foliage aside and passed through. Beth paused to examine the cleverly disguised door made of small trees and sections of shrub, wired together. Once into the woods and clear of the plywood stacks, they left the flapping plastic wrap behind, and the hum became louder.

"Sir," Williams called out, and Whittaker stopped to look behind.

"Let me take lead, sir," the man said and pushed past Beth.

Whittaker nodded. He was unarmed and unprotected. The officer wore a bulletproof vest and carried an automatic weapon, as well as a sidearm. Williams went ahead, and they pressed on through the woods.

A trail had been diligently cleared through the thick growth, carefully cut four feet wide and barely six feet high. Whittaker ducked to stay under the overhead cover. Leaving the foliage overhead made a tunnel undetectable from above. No wonder the helicopter hadn't picked up anything, the detective thought. The hut Massey had constructed was likely covered in the same manner.

The drone grew much louder and Williams entered a slightly widened section with a wooden crate set into the brush on the left. A generator was encased in the crate with sound deadening foam on the inside. A large exhaust tube, aimed into the woods behind, blew hot air away from the generator, driven by a large cooling fan inside the crate.

"Want me to shut this down?" the officer asked.

Whittaker looked at the crate and traced two heavy black electrical cables running from the crate down the trail, which turned hard right ahead of them. The cables would lead them to the hut and the two women, he was sure of it.

"No, leave it on," he said. "They'll be in the dark if we cut the power."

Whittaker hadn't been watching Massey's feed on his phone since they'd left the van, and could only assume Nora was still working on saving Skylar. Priority one was getting to them. Massey had already fled. Priority two would be finding the kidnapper.

"Let's go," Whittaker urged, and waved two more of the tactical team to the front. "The hostages are ahead."

36

UPSIDE DOWN

The sound of the helicopter had been comforting, but when it left, I could think more clearly. I stared at the wall of clues. The answer was the number of days since Massey's wife died. If we knew the date, I could calculate the days, but Skylar couldn't remember. Besides, she was currently in no position to talk. The end of my bent tube had slipped under the water a few times and she'd spluttered and panicked, but fortunately regained enough composure to blow the water through the snorkel to breathe again. It seemed to be stable now, so I'd returned to the clues.

The second picture had me confused. A tree. Family tree? Wood? Forest? I wondered why it showed the roots underground. As soon as I said the word in my head, it fell into place. I couldn't believe how stupid I'd been. The first picture was a square. Square root of 60,516.

"I've got it!" I shouted and gave Skylar the okay sign.

Her eyes were closed inside the tank, with water now spilling over the sides and washing the wooden floor of the room. No matter, I was making progress. What's the square root of 60,516? Shit, I had no idea, and it had been years since I'd needed to figure out a square root. In school. Where I did the problem and wondered why they didn't just teach you to use a calculator. Apparently, this was why.

I started by breaking it down. 200 x 200 was 40,000, which was too low. 300 x 300 was 90,000. Too high. It was between them, so the first digit had to be 2. The next part was more difficult. I ran into the other room and grabbed the whiteboard and a dry-erase pen. I needed to write stuff down. As I started back, I made the mistake of glancing up at the TV monitor in the wall. There I was on screen. Either Massey had set up some kind of motion detection which switched the cameras, or he was still watching and controlling the feed. Whatever electronics he'd set up in the main room were all gone. Presumably so I couldn't shut them down or use them as tools. But he must have taken some with him, and stayed within range of whatever wireless network he was using.

The counter read 5.3 million viewers. That was the population of Norway. The equivalent of a whole country was watching me. 5.3 million people were probably yelling at their TVs, computers and phones, telling me the answer to the simple math problem. That's because they had calculators. A nervous panic began to rise from deep within me. All those people watching, judging, deciding my worthiness. When did I start caring about what anyone else thinks? I guess every human does on some level.

"Fy faen," I shouted out loud. What mattered right now was solving this stupid math problem. And then finding Massey. He wasn't getting away with this bullshit.

I brought the board back into the main room and tossed it on the floor, kneeling down next to it. I took the pen and wrote 2.5 x 2.5, then 5 for 2 x 2.5 plus half of 2.5 which is 1.25. The total was 6.25. Shift the decimal point over and 250 x 250 was 62,500. Just over the target number of 60,516. The second digit was 4. The code was 24-something. I looked over at the tank. I could try rolling through each digit for the last number like I did before, but the first lock was easy to reach. Now I'd have to stretch around Skylar to access this lock at the bottom of the tank. I'd be working blind and might even have my head in the water.

Turning back to the board, I ran through the math for 240 squared. Using 2.4, I applied the same method and came up with 4.8, plus .4, plus .4, plus .16 which equalled 5.76. Shifting the decimal, I came up with 57,600. Taking that number away from 60,516 left 2,916. Now I was baffled. I couldn't remember the proper way to figure it out. It had something to do with breaking the numbers down into pairs, but I had no idea exactly. Water ran around my knees to remind me time was ticking.

On the board I wrote 245 x 245 and started the multiplication. I could remember how to do that. I figured I'd start in the middle. The result was 60,025. Too low. I ran 246 x 246.

"Ha!" I yelled, "I did it!"

The number 60,516 was the result. 246 was the combination. I jumped up and shoved my hands into the tank, one on either side of Skylar's head, which was mostly submerged. When she jolted, I realised she hadn't expected my presence. I pulled my arms out and crouched beside the tank, knocking on the thick Perspex. Her eyes were wide open, and I gave her a thumbs-up and okay sign. She looked terrified and I couldn't tell if she could see me or not. I guessed not without a mask to focus underwater. There was no time to wait, and I dipped my hands in the tank again.

To reach the lock, I pressed my chest against the back of her head, pushing her down a few inches. Spluttering echoed from the end of the tube that was now bobbing slightly under the surface.

"Hold your breath!" I shouted into the back of her head and I heard a long, careful sucking sound from the tube. And then quiet.

That was my cue. I grabbed the lock in my fingertips and found the three small tumblers. I realised I didn't know what number they were starting from. *Faen!* The first lock had been set to all zeroes, so I gambled this one was the same. I used my thumb and rolled the first digit two times. Moving to the second, I rolled it four times and hoped I hadn't inadvertently dragged the other tumblers along with it. I had slim fingers, so I hoped for the best and moved to the third digit. After six gentle rolls of the tumbler, I tried the lock. It didn't open.

I stood up and grabbed the snorkel. Water sloshed and ran over the sides. I was soaked, the floor was soaked, and Skylar was shaking below me. She needed some air. I held the end of the tube clear of the water and knocked on the Perspex. She blew the remaining air from her lungs and water shot from the tube. Then I heard a deep sucking sound as she drew in a precious breath. Her inhales were urgent and fast, like she was panting, so I gave her a few moments to settle down.

Once her breathing eased to a soft rhythm, I made sure the tube was wedged in the corner and clear of the water. I crouched down to see the lock. A fine red mist floated around in the water, stemming from her bandaged hand. I winced in sympathy.

The tumblers read 864. What the hell? I couldn't have been at zero to start. I went back to the whiteboard on the floor and wrote 000. A theory came to me. I counted backwards from 0-0-0 using 2-4-6, which came to 8-6-4. I'd moved them the right amount, but the lock was upside down. Now, I not only had to put in the right combination, I had to reset the lock to zero before I could start. Or, I could orientate myself as I had done, and figure out the movements to reach 2-4-6.

On the board I wrote out 0-0-0 again, with 8-6-4 above and then 2-4-6. From my position in the tank I would be rolling the tumblers in reverse, so from 8 to reach 2 was 6 clicks. The others were 2 and 8 clicks. 6-2-8. This was all too many numbers to keep straight in my head. I repeated 6-2-8 over and over.

Knocking on the side of the tank, I waited while Skylar drew in a long inhale and held her breath. I dived both hands down and found the lock, once more pushing down on the back of Skylar's head. 6-2-8. I carefully rolled the correct number of digits and pulled on the lock. It didn't budge. *Fy faen!* I felt each tumbler with my fingertip and rocked them lightly back and forth, making sure they were perfectly seated on the digit. The third one moved an almost imperceptible amount, but then fell firmly in place. I tugged on the lock. Finally, it opened.

I stood up just in time as Skylar sprang upright in the tank and gasped for breath, sucking in air. "What took… so long? Fuck!" she panted.

"Are you good at square roots?" I asked, frowning at her.

"What?" she spluttered back.

"Exactly," I muttered and ran to the other room.

The camera switched a few moments after I arrived, cutting from Skylar standing in the tank to Massey sitting in the woods. He was looking into the camera.

"Well done, Nora," he said, attempting a smile. "That didn't quite go as the challenge was designed, but the result was perfect. I hope everybody watching realises that I wished no harm to Skylar or Nora. Hurting them was painful for me, but necessary to accomplish the bigger goal. Maybe justice will finally be served to Donovan Briggs, Grayson Briggs, and Davis Griffin. Or maybe it won't, and once again powerful friends will sweep it under the rug and allow my wife's death to go unpunished. She was murdered to keep her silent, and make no mistake, the Briggs family was behind her senseless death.

"I want to thank each and every one of you for tuning in and following along…"

Massey continued his speech, but I stopped listening. He was sitting in a small clearing with several pieces of computer and electronic gear around him. He held the gun in his right hand, resting on his lap. I instinctively knew what he was leading up to. I ran back into the main room where Skylar had climbed from the tank and held her bandaged hand, the sodden wrap stained red. Speeding past her, I lowered my shoulder and barrelled into the wall near the corner of the room.

My whole body shuddered from the impact, and nails creaked as they pulled from splintering wood. I stepped back and rubbed my shoulder. Ripping the black curtain down, I checked out the result. A few planks had broken away from the corner studs, and daylight leaked into the room. I took three steps back and charged again. This time I felt more wood giving way and the soft springy sensation of partially broken planks held only by one end. The door was solid, but based on what I'd seen in the back room, the single layer of 1 x 8-inch pine planks covering the exterior looked vulnerable. Especially at the corners, being the end of the planks. I hoped he'd been frugal with the nails.

"Stay here," I said over my shoulder. "The police will be here shortly."

"What if he comes back?" Skylar screamed, her voice full of fear and panic.

"He's not coming back," I assured her.

I kicked at the loosened planks, which splintered and one broke away. Lowering my shoulder, I crashed into the boards one more time and plunged through the wall into the shrubs outside. I kept my footing and stayed upright, but the splintered wood and sharp nails scraped and scratched through my thin shirt. The heavy foliage outside contributed to more blood-letting, but I was finally free of the building.

Now to find Massey. Before he ended the show.

37

BODY PARTS ON ICE

The RCIPS Firearms Response Unit 2 pushed on through the pathway in the woods. The ground was uneven and rough, but most of the protruding roots had been cut away. Despite the shade from foliage overhead, it was stiflingly hot with the ocean breeze blocked by the woods. Whittaker closely followed the three armed men, and recognised the magnitude of work Massey had undertaken in the past three weeks. Cutting the trails alone would have taken an enormous amount of time, and by the nature of the cuts, it was all done manually with a machete and saw. A chainsaw would have aroused too much interest. As would hired help.

Fifty yards from the generator, the building appeared as a dark shadow amongst the trees. The trail ran down the side of the simple structure to a small clearing in front. Whittaker noted that this section of the woods had the tallest trees. Most were 10 to 12 feet high. Enough to cover the structure after the lower branches were cleared. The roof was flat, covered by tin panels painted dark green.

Ahead, the trail continued to where an opening revealed the narrow canal bathed in sunlight. Whittaker pointed to the building as Beth joined him. The officers moved into the clearing with practised stealth, using hand signals to position the team on either side of the jagged opening in the wooden building. The door was bolted from the outside, with several pieces of electronic gear stacked on the ground. A pair of shears lay nearby.

Skylar screamed as the first man entered the room with his automatic weapon aimed, searching the space for potential threats. They quickly cleared both rooms, and Whittaker followed them in. The main room was a mess with water overflowing the tank and washing across the floor before draining through the seams in the boards. The decimated table lay against one wall and the whiteboard was on the floor. Skylar stood by the tank, soaking wet, her fear slowly shifting to relief.

"Are you okay, Miss Briggs?"

The young woman broke down in tears and threw her arms around the detective, "I thought I was going to die," she sobbed into his chest.

"You're safe now, but we need to get you medical assistance," he said, guiding her from the room, through the door the officers had unlocked from the outside.

"My finger," she moaned. "There's a cooler in there, my finger is in the cooler."

Saying the words and the thought of her severed body part on ice were too much for the young woman. Her knees buckled. Whittaker caught her from falling to the ground, and Beth stepped in to support Skylar from the other side.

"We've got you," Beth assured her. "It's all over."

"Thank you," Skylar sobbed. "You saved me. I thought this was it."

"Constable Sommer saved you," Whittaker corrected. "But we'll make sure you're safe now."

The detective looked around, "Can two of your men take Miss Briggs and this cooler back to the vans, please," Whittaker said to Williams. "I'll call for the helicopter. They can pick her up in The Shores and take her to the hospital."

"Where did he go?" Beth asked Skylar.

The young woman shook her head. "I have no idea. Once he'd

locked me in the tank, I couldn't see much. I think he carried stuff outside and then left. I heard him lock the door."

"Okay, don't worry," Beth said, "We'll find him."

"She's a policewoman?" Skylar asked, as Whittaker and Beth handed her over to the two officers.

"I'm with the FBI," Beth replied.

"No, the blonde girl who was here with me. She's a cop?"

"Nora? Yes," Beth said. "She's a constable with the Royal Cayman Islands Police Service."

Skylar had recovered enough to support herself, but the officers kept a hand on each arm. "She didn't look Caymanian," she said. "She had a foreign accent."

Whittaker decided to skip the point about the American being the foreigner in her current geographical situation. "She's originally from Norway," he explained instead.

"She's kinda crazy," Skylar remarked as the men began to guide her out the door.

Beth shook her head. "Well, I'm sure there'll be an opportunity to thank her later."

Whittaker had turned away. "Leave two men here at the building, and you come with us," he instructed Williams.

"Yes, sir," the man replied and organised the remaining men with quick, precise orders.

Whittaker walked outside. "Skylar, where did Nora go?" he called out to the woman being helped along the trail.

"I don't know," she replied, "she broke through the wall and left."

"Did she say anything at all?"

"She told me to stay here, and you'd find me."

"That was it, nothing more?" he asked.

"She said he wouldn't come back," Skylar added. "The guy, Massey. She seemed sure he wouldn't come back here."

Whittaker nodded and the two policemen hurried her, and the cooler, away. He then radioed for the helicopter to pick up Skylar and asked dispatch to prepare the hospital for an emergency patient.

"See if you can shut off the water," Whittaker said to the two men remaining at the building. "Touch as little as possible. This is a crime scene, but this water may be destroying evidence."

"The valve is under the floor," Beth added. "The door triggered a line that turned it on. You could see on the video when Nora came in. You'll have to pull up a floorboard or two."

Whittaker nodded in agreement. "Do what you need to, men. Stop the water." He hurried down the trail towards the canal. "This way," he continued to Williams.

"He's still armed, correct," Williams asked.

"He is," Whittaker replied as they ran down the path.

"And I presume Miss Sommer has gone after him?"

"She has," Whittaker said as he pushed the foliage screen farther aside.

"She won't try to take da man alone, will she? Him wit a gun and all?"

"She will," Whittaker said, looking both ways down the bank of the canal.

"We better get dere first den," the officer finished.

"That would be preferable," Whittaker replied, and looked at Beth.

The agent held her mobile out and showed the detective, "He's in the woods somewhere, giving his wrap-up speech by the sound of it. He still has the gun, I can see it."

"Which way?" Whittaker asked.

Beth looked at the ground, searching for obvious prints. The bank was mainly limestone and loose stone and surrendered no clues.

"Gut feeling," Whittaker added.

Beth looked up at the man, who stared confidently back at her. She nodded to the left.

"Agreed," he said, and moved down the edge of the canal to their left.

38

SUPPRESSED EMOTIONS

I'd heard the commotion of people approaching from behind the building and knew it must be the police. They were coming from the direction of what I supposed was the drone of a generator. Massey hadn't gone that way. If he had, he'd have been caught instead of still broadcasting his Internet feed. I'd headed towards the canal.

The trail was cleared until a few feet from the water's bank, where a screen of brush blocked my way. I'd tried pushing through the thick mass of branches and leaves, and it fell aside like a gate. I'd looked both ways along the bank and chosen left. Why? I don't know. Away from the first building, perhaps. Odds were 50-50 and time was against me, so I'd picked a direction.

Now, I studied the woods intently as I hurried along the narrow bank, stepping over mangrove roots and loose branches on the ground. I was looking for another screen, hiding a trail, but all I could see were trees, shrubs, and mangroves. They all blended into a sea of greenery. One section looked denser than the rest, so I rushed past, ruling it out. I was looking for some kind of opening behind the first row of brush.

I stopped. Denser was the only thing I'd seen that was different in any way from the rest the of woods. I'd rounded the corner in the canal and was at least 100 metres from the building. It doesn't take long for the mind to start questioning every decision, and I was already wondering if I'd passed the hidden trail. Hell, I didn't even know if another trail existed. I stepped back to the dense section and shoved at the branches. An area the size of a small door moved as one.

Pushing the camouflaged gate aside as quietly as possible, I entered the trail. This one was both narrower and lower. I was stooping to keep my head from brushing the overhead foliage, and the branches on either side scratched and clawed at my battered arms. The rash guard I'd worn over my bathing suit had taken a beating, and the thin fabric offered little protection.

The trail was short and after less than 10 metres, which curved to the right, I could see a clearing ahead. I could also hear Jensen Massey talking.

"An athletic woman in remarkable physical condition for her age does not have a heart attack out of the blue," I heard him say. "Olivia ran marathons for God's sake."

His voice was breaking, and he paused. I risked a glimpse around the last few pieces of cover and saw he was facing to the right, slightly away from me. If I moved carefully, I thought I could sneak up behind him. Massey was seated on a large Pelican case with a laptop propped on a second case before him. I realised the laptop's camera would pick me up if I tried approaching from behind. He'd see me coming.

I judged it to be four or five metres from where I stood to where he sat. How fast could I cover that ground? Faster than he could realise what was happening, turn, and shoot? The realisation and turning parts were the critical elements. I knew how fast bullets travelled. My life had been ruined and Ridley's ended in the milliseconds it took for a bullet to travel about this same distance. A bullet that was meant for me. My boyfriend had thrown himself across the path of the gunshot aimed at me.

The memory pumped adrenaline through my veins, and a

flaming ball of anger in my brain. I took one step back before launching forward.

Massey had composed himself, and begun talking again, "I hope throughout today I've shown the world a series of evidence and truths, that…"

His words abruptly halted as he heard me charging across the clearing. He turned, bringing his right hand around with the gun. I locked my eyes on his right wrist and lunged the last metre, crashing into the man and bowling him from his seat. Latching my hand to his wrist, I pushed the gun up and away as we tumbled to the rough stone and dirt. He hit the ground hard, and I landed on top of him, rolling over and beyond, but refusing to let go. He screamed in pain as my fall twisted his wrist and he finally dropped the gun.

I scrambled to my feet, swooping up the gun, and for the second time in my life, I held a firearm in my hand. Both times I'd aimed the firearm at another human being. The first time I knew with all my heart that I wanted to pull the trigger and would forever wish I'd shot the man a second time. I was less sure about Massey.

"I'm done," he panted, holding his wrist, which I guessed I'd broken. "Please, shoot me so I can join Olivia."

His eyes stared up at me, defeated. I knew it wasn't the battle or the day he'd lost, it was his life. His heart was still beating, but it was empty. Everything he held most dear had been taken away. His life came to an end 246 days ago, the day his wife was murdered. I knew that look. I lived with the same pain.

My wave of anger began to shift. Fuelled by thoughts of Ridley, rage had sent me sprinting across the clearing. Now, the man wanted me to complete the final task for him.

"I'm begging you, shoot me, Nora," Massey whispered, his eyes pleading even more than his words.

"*Fy faen*," I muttered. "You've used me all day for what you wanted. I'm done with your games."

I'd charged Massey and risked him getting off a shot. I knew I couldn't take my own life, but I was willing to put it on the line.

Deep down, it was clear some part of me hoped Massey would do the job for me. Now he was turning the tables. Somewhere, buried in my plethora of suppressed emotions, was a tiny sense of relief. It sparked like the final ember of last night's fire. A warm glow in a hearth of grey ashes. I couldn't say that I was glad to be alive, but for the first time since Ridley's death, I was willing to live.

The police force had given me a distraction, a purpose, and perhaps the crazy events of today had shown me I had something to give. I didn't feel like I'd succeeded, but I hadn't completely failed. Skylar was alive, and the culprit was caught. Of course, the real culprit was Donovan Briggs, but that was above my pay grade, as they say in American movies.

"Pull the trigger, Nora. Please," Massey tried again.

"It's not you I want to shoot. It's Briggs," I replied.

"I want him to live a long life in a jail cell," Massey groaned. "A bullet would let him off easy. Just shoot me and let me be with Olivia."

I knew too well the pain he was in. But I had to live through it, and so would he. My conscience was already overloaded.

"Fuck no," I replied. "You're under arrest. Get up."

39

PAPER MOON

FBI agents Don Brandt and Faith Graham parked by the office of the Harborage Marina in St Pete. Access to the slips passed solely through the office, or via the water from Tampa Bay. Two officers exited a police car parked nearby, having assumed the black SUV belonged to the federal government agents they'd been waiting for.

"Hi guys," Brandt greeted them. "Any movement?"

"Not since we arrived, sir," the first officer replied, a large-framed man with a square jaw. "There's been some folks coming and going, but no one fitting the perp's description."

Brandt nodded, a bead of sweat already forming on his brow in the late afternoon heat. "Okay, thanks. This is a long shot. I doubt he's here, but we'll check out the boat. Stay here and watch the office in case he bolts on foot."

The brawny officer looked disappointed, but didn't question the order. The two agents entered through the front door and enjoyed the blast of cool air. They both flashed their badges to the old man behind the reception desk.

"Oh my," he mumbled, his eyes wide. "What can I help you with?"

"Can you tell us where the Paper Moon is docked?" Faith asked.

The old man shuffled from behind the counter and ambled towards the door leading to the slips. He swung the door open and pointed down a long, narrow pier forming the backbone of the marina. Endless jetties protruded from the east side, extending towards Tampa Bay and dotted with slips on both sides. The view was a mass of mainly white fibreglass, sailboat masts, and various towers.

"All the way to the end on the left," the old man explained. "Big boats are down there. Paper Moon is the last one, tied on the outside of the slip."

"Thank you," Faith replied. "Have you seen any of the family arrive this afternoon, sir?"

"No," he replied, scratching his mostly bald head. "But I only started my evening shift at five. Can't say if anyone showed up before then."

Faith gave the man a smile as she and her partner set off down the long pier. They left the old man with his mouth open, a series of unasked questions rolling through his mind. Apparently, he wasn't one of the millions of people following the news from Grand Cayman.

The pier angled away from the sea wall of the shoreline, allowing room for increasingly larger boats on the west side the farther they walked. On the east side, the jetties and slips were also spaced farther apart, housing large sailboats and luxury yachts. They were in the high-dollar neighbourhood.

The Paper Moon was a 65-foot Ferretti, tied to the end of the final and only jetty extending towards the shore, just as the old man had described. No one was in sight. The lines were still secured to the dock, but the big diesels were idling.

"Somebody's home," Brandt said quietly as they both slowed their approach, assessing the situation.

The operations van had accompanied the team to Grayson Briggs's condo across town, so the agents weren't wired for comms.

Reluctant to raise the alarm over cell service in case they were heard, Faith signalled for her partner to remain on the dock while she boarded the boat. Brandt nodded his understanding and drew his service weapon.

The Ferretti was a beautiful yacht with a spacious cockpit leading to the salon and lower helm through sliding glass doors. External stairs on the starboard side, moulded into the cabin structure, led up to the fly-bridge. Seeing the salon was clear, Faith carefully took the steps, anticipating someone up top, warming the engines. With her weapon drawn, she took a peek over the top stair and saw no one. The fly-bridge was empty.

Standing at the fly-bridge helm, she signalled down to Brandt on the dock that all was clear before hitting the kill buttons and shutting down the diesels. The big engines shuddered to a stop, and the console lit up and beeped. Faith turned the two ignition keys off and all fell silent.

She was about to descend and search the lower deck when she heard movement off the port side. Faith leaned over the fly-bridge and watched several pieces of clothing sail from a porthole into the water. If her guess was correct, the blue jeans she saw floating in the bay would have a piece torn from them that would match the scrap retrieved from Myra Shah's condo.

Faith softly stepped to the starboard side and conveyed the suspect's presence to her partner via hand signals. She descended the stairs and took a careful look into the salon. It was still clear. The sliding door was unlocked and smoothly glided open with the efficiency of well-engineered hardware. Faith stepped inside and felt the cool air conditioning of the interior. To her right was a well-appointed galley and ahead, two comfortable couches lined the sides of the room, one with a dining table.

"FBI. We have a warrant to search the boat," she announced loudly. "Show yourself."

She heard footsteps from the narrow steps at the front of the room beside the helm. A figure appeared.

"Hello there?" came a man's voice. "How can I help you?"

Faith aimed her gun at the floor near the stairs in the low ready position, and the young man stopped.

"Woah! What the hell?" he exclaimed. "What's with the gun?"

"Grayson Briggs?" Faith asked, holding her gun steady as the man raised his arms.

"Yes, yes," he exclaimed. "Put the damn gun down. I'm one of the good guys! Have you recovered my sister yet?"

"Move slowly to the couch, put your hands on your head, and sit down," Faith ordered, tracking him carefully.

"I'm unarmed," Grayson said. "I'm the only one aboard. I figured you were here with an update on my family."

He sat on the couch and placed his hands on his head as ordered. Faith stepped back to the sliding door and called out to her partner. "Brandt, come on in."

She turned back to the suspect. "Where were you going?"

"Nowhere," he replied confidently. "We routinely run the engines when the boat hasn't been out in a while."

Brandt entered, and Faith looked over with a grin. "Mind frisking him before you go for a swim?"

"Swim?" Brandt replied with a frown as he walked across the salon, and after having Grayson stand up, checked him for weapons. The man was wearing board shorts and a T-shirt, so he wasn't concealing anything.

"He tossed his clothes off the side," Faith explained. "Our evidence is floating away."

Brandt rolled his eyes. "Great."

He left the salon, and after spotting the garments in the water, stripped down to his boxer shorts. Faith heard a splash as her partner dived in the bay.

"Why did you throw your clothes away?"

Grayson slumped back down on the couch.

"Hands on your head," she reminded him, her gun still aimed at the floor in front of the man. He complied.

"Not my clothes," he replied. "I didn't throw anything overboard."

"So you lied," she countered.

Grayson shook his head. "I didn't lie, they're not my clothes."

"You told me you were the only one aboard," she said calmly. "You either lied about that, or you threw the clothes off the boat."

His eyes narrowed, and he went to reply, but stopped himself.

"Exactly," Faith continued. "So we've established you're lying to me. That's a bad start, Mr Briggs."

"I don't know anything about any clothes," Grayson said after thinking a moment, although his smug confidence was fading.

"If you don't know anything about them, how do you know they're not your clothes?" Faith asked, finally holstering her weapon.

"I was in my cabin," he mumbled back, his brow furrowed. "I'd know if someone took my clothes."

"So you're settling on some stranger was on the boat, threw some clothes off the boat, but you don't know whose clothes, or who this stealthy person was?" Faith continued, enjoying herself and glad she wasn't the one in the bay.

The boat rocked slightly as Brandt clambered back aboard the large swim step at the stern.

"Where's your cabin, Mr Briggs?" she asked.

"Port side, below here," Grayson said and closed his eyes. He knew he'd screwed up.

"That'll be right below where I was standing on the fly-bridge," she said, grinning at him. "Where I saw the clothes come from. The clothes that will undoubtedly be your exact size, Mr Briggs."

The glass door slid open and Brandt stood there, dripping wet, holding a soaking bundle of garments in his hands.

"Am I under arrest?" Grayson demanded, his voice losing all trace of civility.

Brandt dropped everything with a soggy splash to the floor. Except a pair of blue jeans. He unravelled them and held them by one leg. A small section of cotton was missing.

"You are most certainly under arrest, Grayson Briggs," Faith took pleasure in saying, "for the murder of Myra Shah."

"For starters," Brandt added. "I'm confident we'll be adding charges surrounding the death of Olivia Massey to the list shortly."

"Lawyer," was all Grayson Briggs replied as he stared dejectedly at the floor of the luxury yacht.

40

WORDED OUT

I made Massey keep his hands on his head, although I doubted he would try anything. It was over and we both knew it. He seemed exhausted, and looking at all the physical and mental work he'd put into his production, I could see why. If what he'd said was all true, I couldn't blame him. But he'd still ruined my Sunday.

With the gun at his back, he stepped from the woods to various shouts and commands. Once I followed and they saw the gun in my hand, everyone calmed down. Williams handcuffed Massey, and I gave him the gun for safe keeping. The Firearms Response Unit man was all smiles and congratulations.

"Good job, kid," Williams said, and offered me a fist bump.

I wasn't keen on being called a kid, and I certainly wasn't the fist-bumping kind of person, but I obliged.

"We have your back," he added, with a nod. "You're one of us now."

As Williams marched Jensen Massey away, I wondered why they wouldn't have had my back for the past three months. It was their job, after all. Still, it felt better to have their respect than the bullshit attitude they'd been giving me.

Whittaker looked like he wanted to hug me. He resisted and

settled for a hand on my shoulder. I hugged more than I fist-bumped, but not by much. Part of me would have been okay with Whittaker hugging me. I'd run away from a wonderful family at sixteen, and sometimes I missed my father's embrace.

"You should have waited for us, Nora," he said, attempting to be stern. His relieved smile took all the sting from his reprimand.

"I know," I replied.

I thought about explaining how I knew they'd get Skylar to safety, and I didn't want to lose Massey. But it was too many words that would just require more words, and I was worded out. I was worn out.

"Are you okay?" Whittaker asked.

I nodded and managed a brief smile. The look in his eyes made me want to hug him. I didn't, but the concern and care emanating from the man was comforting, and as the adrenaline ebbed from my system, my own exhaustion continued to grow.

"I'm done with my shift. I'd like to go home if that's okay?"

Whittaker laughed. "I think that's fair. We can debrief tomorrow when you've had some rest." He gently squeezed my shoulder. "You did the right thing."

"Which bit?" I wondered aloud, as though he'd just told me I'd done the wrong thing.

"All of it, really," he replied with a grin before his expression turned serious again. "But at the end there. This wouldn't have been suicide by police. You'd already disarmed him."

"You saw all that?" I said, surprised we'd been on camera. I hadn't thought about it, but I realised the camera had been running when I charged him and bowled him over. Apparently, we were still in view.

"We were watching the entire time," Whittaker confirmed. "It was on the edge of the screen, but we could see and hear you both."

A smartly dressed woman who'd arrived with Whittaker offered her hand, and I shook. She had a firm grip.

"Special Agent Ricci, FBI," she said. "Good work, officer."

"I'm sorry," Whittaker apologised. "Beth and her partner have been helping us this afternoon. Her experience has been invaluable."

My mentor's previous statement still rang through my head. I hadn't shot Massey for selfish reasons. The idea I'd be executing the man had never entered my mind. He was still alive because I was angry. He'd put me through hell and cut off a girl's finger. Living with the pain of his own loss was a far worse punishment than a bullet in the brain.

"I was telling the detective," Beth said keenly, "you're a resourceful and tough young woman. You'd make a fine FBI agent if you were interested."

I pushed my other thoughts away. The FBI lady seemed nice. She had a bold and confident manner, without being overbearing. I wondered if FBI agents got to play with cool gadgets and spy stuff. Somehow I doubted it. I bet they sat around most of the time staring at computer screens and filling out paperwork, occasionally getting to knock on a door and question people. Maybe there was some cool stuff thrown in every once in a while.

"Do the FBI have an office in Grand Cayman?" I asked.

"I'm afraid not," she answered. "But we have a unit specialising in the Caribbean. It's based in Miami and we have offices in the Dominican Republic and Barbados."

"This is home," I heard myself replying.

Since leaving Norway three years ago, I'd been a nomad. Grand Cayman had been where I'd spent the most time, but it was also where I'd experienced several traumatic events. I had no idea why I didn't want to be as far away from the place as possible. People, I guessed. Home can be about familiarity, where you were born, or where you spent the most time, but ultimately it came down to people. Norway would always be home because of my family and wonderful childhood memories. Cayman had become my new home despite the trauma because of people like AJ and Detective Whittaker. Leaving the island also felt like I'd be leaving Ridley.

"Let's get you out of here and see if we can sneak you home,"

Whittaker said, his hand again on my shoulder, urging me along the bank of the canal. "We'll have to dodge the press."

I picked my way along the rough and rocky bank, noticing my feet were sore in the flimsy water shoes.

"My dive gear!" I blurted, remembering I'd left it on the shore of the North Sound.

Whittaker laughed. "Don't worry, we found it," he assured me. "Your directions left a perfect trail for us to follow."

"That was quick thinking," Beth added. "So were the hand signals."

"I'm sorry we didn't reach you sooner, Nora," Whittaker said as we turned into the woods and followed the trail past the wooden building Massey had built. "You did your part. I was slow putting it all together."

I shrugged my shoulders. "It's okay."

Skylar might not agree with me as she'd be short of some notes if she played guitar, but none of us knew what Massey would have done if the police had burst through the door.

"Do you think he would have shot either of you?" Beth asked as we approached the source of the droning sound.

I thought about the question for a moment as Whittaker instructed a constable to shut down the generator. We stood in the small clearing and I faced the FBI agent.

"Maybe, but it didn't fit his objective. Or his character," I replied. "From what I saw," I added, realising I was profiling the man in front of someone who was undoubtedly trained to do that properly.

"What did you understand his objective to be?" Beth asked.

"Show the world that Briggs was guilty of his wife's murder. He needed the whole day to play out, so killing either of us didn't accomplish that."

Beth and Whittaker shared a slight smile.

"If I failed at the tests, the show continued," I added. "Skylar paid the price, but killing or wounding me to the point I couldn't perform his circus tricks brought everything to a halt."

"I think that's a good assessment," Beth said.

"But I realised it too late," I replied. "My best chance was when we were being moved from the first building. I should have taken the stupid helmet off and tried jumping him then."

We continued along the path and came out of the woods behind a tall stack of building supplies. As we walked around the side, the space opened up, with several police vans and cars parked. Massey was being shoved into the back of one of the cars.

"You played it perfectly," Whittaker said. "We'll never know what would have happened if any of us had done anything differently. We all made the best calls we could with the information we had at the time."

I caught the detective giving Beth a slight nod, and she smiled back. I was too tired to worry about what they had going on.

Jacob stepped from one of the police cars, followed by AJ. They both jogged towards me.

"You okay, partner?" Jacob asked, looking me over. "Dis turned out to be a mad day, no?"

Before I could answer, AJ grabbed me in a bear hug. It's okay for AJ to hug me.

"Bloody hell, you crazy Viking, you scared me to death."

I held her tightly. Her love and concern pushed much of the day's anguish away. I closed my eyes and wished I could go to sleep at that very moment.

She finally released me and looked at the scratches and grazes down my arms, "Just a flesh wound," she said and giggled at herself. I didn't know why. Some English thing I guessed.

"Did you find your weights?" I asked.

"Yeah, brilliant," she enthused. "I found the two near the dock and then the others by the first challenge thing."

"In one dive?"

"No, no, you should have seen me, I did a hot deployment from the back of the Marine Unit boat," she gushed. "Then a moving pick-up where they dragged a line past me and I grabbed on and they reeled me in. Ninja stuff, like a Navy bloody Seal!"

"Really? And you call me crazy?" I said, grinning at her excitement.

"Well, the pick-up was more like a Navy sack of potatoes, but only me and two Marine Unit guys know that."

I hugged her again.

41

WHEN LIFE SUCKS TOO BAD

I wanted to stay home, hidden away from the throngs of reporters roaming the island in search of Constable Sommer. Archie's shack — my shack, if I could ever get used to saying that — was perfectly secluded, with no direct access from the road. Hiding the Jeep at the neighbours' left me almost impossible to track down. I'd gone freediving in the morning, shortly after sunrise. The tranquillity of the reef had been cathartic as always, and I'd finally felt relaxed after a restless night.

But after lunch I found myself on the way to the hospital.

When AJ was done with her morning dive trip, she picked me up on her Ducati motorcycle. We were well disguised under crash helmets and jackets. A helmet I could see out of. She dropped me around the back of the hospital in George Town, where Whittaker met me and herded me through an employee entrance. He'd asked me to come. Well, Skylar had asked him to ask me to come.

I'd heard that trauma brings people of all cultures and interests together, forming a common bond. I didn't feel any bond. My preference would be for everyone with anything to do with the Briggs family and the Massey case to leave the island so things could go back to normal.

We managed to dodge the press who'd accumulated in the main waiting area and outside the front entrance, and started down a long hallway with patient's rooms on either side. Halfway down, Whittaker came to a stop and looked at me.

"How are you holding up?" he asked, that same look of care and worry in his eyes.

"I'm fine," I replied.

"I hope the events of yesterday haven't scared you away from police work."

"I'd prefer it wasn't like that every day," I countered.

He smiled and laughed softly. "No, as you've seen, it's not like that every day. Thank God."

I thought about telling him I didn't want to be dead as much as before, but I guessed he'd have a hard time unwrapping the statement. I would have to see myself. It was one thing feeling that way, with adrenaline in my veins and drama unfolding, but time would tell if the desire stuck.

"I'll be at work tomorrow," I said, happy to close the conversation.

He nodded. "Massey and Donovan Briggs will be extradited to America," he explained, moving on to the case.

I realised a lot had probably happened since I'd left Barkers yesterday. I'd been trying not to think about it, but I was curious if justice would be served.

"I'm told Grayson Briggs and the professor, Davis Griffin, are in custody in Tampa," Whittaker continued. "They'll all be prosecuted in Florida."

"Yesterday, when Jacob took me to my Jeep, he told me the son had murdered a reporter," I said. "That's awful."

"Myra Shah," he replied, his brow furrowing. "I spoke with her yesterday about Massey. She had worked with him, trying to expose Briggs's involvement in Olivia Massey's accident. It appears she knew too much. Or at least Grayson Briggs thought so. They haven't recovered her computer or the files he took, but they have him tied to the murder." The detective paused and looked at the floor. "Very sad."

We stood there without speaking for a few moments; the background sounds of the hospital amplified in our thoughtful silence. Footsteps made me look up, and I saw the FBI lady I'd met yesterday walking towards us. With her was a tall, stern-looking man in a suit, who I supposed was another agent.

"Good afternoon," Whittaker greeted them and extended his hand. "Beth, you've met Constable Sommer, and Nora, this is Beth's partner, Agent Kowalczyk. They'll be escorting Massey and Briggs home tomorrow."

We all shook hands.

"That will be a fun flight," I grinned, thinking of the two detainees who'd like to strangle each other.

Beth laughed. "We're taking separate flights to avoid them crossing paths – we've had enough theatrics for one trip."

I noticed Kowalczyk's expression never changed. Fun-loving guy.

"So, was Briggs involved in Olivia's accident?" I asked. It was the one question that had returned to my mind all night and kept me awake. Along with the usual demons.

Beth looked at her partner, who made a subtle shrug of his shoulders, apparently indicating his consent for her to answer.

"It appears so," she said quietly, although the hallway was empty. "We're still piecing it all together, but the professor who was in on the fake reports scam has provided crucial evidence. A few weeks before the accident, Briggs's paper company announced a sponsored scholarship to the university for an underprivileged student in the area. People were invited to apply but according to Griffin, the candidate was already chosen. The daughter of a single mother who showed good, but not exceptional grades in high school. Hispanic girl. The estranged father of the girl is a man with a rap sheet who still lives in the area. According to Griffin, he's the guy who drove the truck which hit Olivia Massey. Police picked

252 | NICHOLAS HARVEY

him up this morning, and he's talking. This would be his third strike and he's facing a potential homicide charge."

She took a breath and checked around the hallway again. I wondered if FBI people were always this wary out of habit. Did they lean in close to their spouse before asking them to pass the ketchup? It confirmed my choice to remain a constable.

"He claims Olivia was alive after the impact. It was Grayson Briggs who drove up and injected her, causing her heart attack."

"Really?" Whittaker uttered under his breath. "But that gives you plenty against the son. What about the father? Seems like hearsay from Griffin, tough to make that stick. Surely, Donovan's lawyer will claim it's one man's word against another."

"Seems like blood isn't as thick as polluted water," Kowalczyk interjected, looking pleased with himself for the pun. "Now he's on the hook for two murders, Grayson is throwing his old man under the bus. Claims he masterminded the whole thing and made Grayson commit both crimes."

"That sucks for the girl," I said, and they all looked at me.

"Skylar will be fine," Kowalczyk replied. "I think she'll still come away with a cushy lifestyle. She wasn't involved in any wrongdoing."

"Not Skylar," I corrected. "The Hispanic girl with the scholarship. Probably the only break she's ever got, and now she'll lose it."

They all nodded and didn't know what to say.

I was glad they would put the bad guys away, but the victims remained the victims. Olivia and the reporter lady were still dead, and a kid who'd just got the chance to make something of her life would have it taken away. For what? A rich guy making a bigger profit at the expense of the planet, and other people. Whittaker broke the silence and pulled me from my angst-filled thoughts.

"Thank you again for your help," he said to the two agents. "Your insight and experience were valuable assets yesterday."

"Glad we could be of assistance," Beth replied.

Kowalczyk went to say something, then stopped himself. Whittaker started to walk away.

"Detective," Kowalczyk finally spoke, and Whittaker halted, looking back at the man. "You handled it well. With the limited resources at your disposal, you handled it well."

"Thank you, sir," Whittaker replied, and glanced back and forth between the two agents. "Neither of you probably want to hear this, but you make a good team. Balanced I'd say."

Kowalczyk stared at the detective, and I couldn't tell if he was about to swear at him or just leave. He did neither.

"I agree," he said. And then walked away down the hall.

Beth's eyes widened in surprise, and Whittaker grinned at her. "I'm sure I'll see you again before you leave."

She smiled. "I hope so," she replied, and followed after her partner.

———

Skylar was in a private room. She was sitting up in bed, and apart from a heavily bandaged hand, looked perfectly fine. She smiled when we appeared at her doorway.

"I'll wait outside," Whittaker said, and closed the door.

"Hello again," Skylar greeted me.

"Hey," I replied, "How's the finger?"

She held up the wad of bandage attached to the end of her arm. "It's back on there, at least for now," she said. "We have to see if it'll take. Apparently there's a 70 per cent success rate."

"Let's hope some have not worked out lately then," I said.

She laughed, but I guessed most other people losing fingers had more important things to do with theirs. Skylar's pinkie wasn't about to cure cancer, or build a house for the homeless.

"They say I'll only have about half the normal movement, but I just wanted it on there so I didn't look like a freak."

There was still a 30 per cent chance that someone more deserving would have better odds of their reattachment being successful. I kept the thought to myself.

"When can you go home?" I asked.

"If my finger looks okay, they say I can fly in a few days," she replied. "Then the hospital in Tampa will take over from there."

We looked at each other. I was out of polite questions, and she had asked to see me, so I waited for her to speak.

"I wanted to thank you in person," she said. "You saved my life. I'm very grateful."

"Just doing my job," I replied. I'd decided that would be my standard line when faced with the myriad of questions that undoubtedly would be thrown at me about the day. "I'm sorry I couldn't stop that from happening," I added, pointing to her hand.

"That was my fault," she said, holding up the thickly wrapped appendage. "I missed the stupid little cut-out bits. I'm going to get a tattoo of that damn icon so I never forget what it looks like."

"Where?" I asked, hiding my amusement.

"I was thinking at the base of my neck so my hair hides it most of the time," she said, tapping the back of her neck with her good hand.

"That won't be very easy to see if you ever need it again," I pointed out.

Skylar thought about it for a second. "Shit, you're right. My second choice was the inside of my wrist. I'll get it there."

I decided pointing out she'd be labelling herself as toxic could be left to someone finding it less hilarious than me. I nodded appreciatively, as though it were a great idea.

"So, what now?" I asked. "You know, once you're home and recuperated."

I didn't usually cave into making conversation, but she'd just tried to be nice so I felt bad saying thanks, see ya, after only two minutes.

"I don't really know," she said sullenly. "Everything will be different now. My dad and brother are going to jail, I guess, so I've no idea what will happen to the company. My stepmother will run off with everything she can take from my dad. I have a trust, so money won't be an issue, but I have to figure out what to do with myself."

I wished I hadn't asked. Sure, it would be tough seeing your family crumble, as it wasn't her fault and even if they were scumbags, they were still her family. But she would have money to do as she pleased, which probably meant snorting it up her nose and playing the victim for the rest of her life. I was ready to leave.

"I've been looking up environmental agencies and organisations," she said, surprising me. "I've supported several for years and do beach clean-ups and mangrove restorations, things like that. School hasn't worked out well for me. I get too easily distracted with the wrong crowd, so I think I'd rather volunteer for something good. Maybe I can help repair some of the damage my family has done."

I looked at the young woman before me in the hospital bed. Her life was at a crossroads. Chances were, she'd succumb to the parties, drink and drugs, especially with the money making it all so easily accessible, but maybe not. An idea occurred to me.

"You know, there's a kid in Tampa who could do with some help," I thought aloud. "She's been innocently caught up in this mess."

"What can I do?" Skylar asked.

I knew the information I'd just been privy to in the hallway was highly confidential, and I could jeopardise the case if I wasn't careful.

"I'll let you know," I said carefully. "Let me see if I can get more details. Might involve a scholarship to the University of St Petersburg. Perhaps something in Olivia Massey's honour?"

"I'd like to do that," Skylar replied, her tone genuine. "Let me know."

For Skylar to have a shot at keeping her life on the rails, she needed some positive influence and guidance. If I hadn't met AJ and Whittaker, I had no idea where I'd be. My life had come off the rails in spectacular fashion. I sat down on the chair beside the bed.

"I'll give you my number," I said. "You can call if you need someone to talk to."

Her eyes lit up and she smiled. "Are you on social? Do you use Messenger or Snapchat?"

I sighed. "No, I don't do that shit. Just call me if life sucks too bad."

ACKNOWLEDGMENTS

My sincere thanks to:

My amazing wife Cheryl and wonderful friend James for their unwavering support, advice and encouragement.

My tireless editor Andrew Chapman at Prepare to Publish.

Lily at Orkidedatter for her Norwegian advice.

Casey Keller, my go-to advisor for all things Cayman Islands related.

Craig Robinson and Alain Belanger for their Royal Cayman Islands Police Service advice.

The Tropical Authors group for their advice, support, humour and, most importantly, rum. Visit and subscribe at www.TropicalAu thors.com for deals and info on a plethora of books by talented authors in the Sea Adventure genre.

My beta reader group has grown to include an amazing cross section of folks from different walks of life. Their suggestions, feedback and keen eyes are invaluable, for which I am eternally grateful.

Above all, I thank you, the readers: none of this happens without the choice you make to spend your precious time with my stories. I am truly in your debt.

LET'S STAY IN TOUCH!

To buy merchandise, find more info or join my newsletter, visit my website at
www.HarveyBooks.com

If you enjoyed this novel I'd be incredibly grateful if you'd consider leaving a review on Amazon.com
Find eBook deals and follow me on BookBub.com

Find more great authors in the genre at TropicalAuthors.com

Visit Amazon.com for more books in the
Nora Sommer Caribbean Suspense Series,
AJ Bailey Adventure Series,
and collaborative works;
The Greene Wolfe Thriller Series
Tropical Authors Adventure Series

ABOUT THE AUTHOR

A *USA Today* Bestselling author, Nicholas Harvey's life has been anything but ordinary. Race car driver, adventurer, divemaster, and since 2020, a full-time novelist. Raised in England, Nick has dual US and British citizenship and now lives wherever he and his amazing wife, Cheryl, park their motorhome, or an aeroplane takes them. Warm oceans and tall mountains are their favourite places.

For more information, visit his website at HarveyBooks.com.

Printed in the USA
CPSIA information can be obtained
at www.ICGtesting.com
LVHW021046140224
771723LV00012B/408